RECLAIMED
Hearts

M.M.
+
R.B.

HIDDEN HEARTS SERIES
RECLAIMED
Hearts
DANIELLE KEIL

ALSO BY DANIELLE KEIL

The Parkdale Series

The Pact Series

The Ainsworth Royals: Next Gen Series

Love Notes Series

The Tangled Web Series

The Hidden Hearts Series

*Sometimes the right one comes at the wrong time.
Don't give up. But remember... keep those that
love you unconditionally close to your heart.
It's okay to let the rest go.*

WELCOME TO
Covington Cove
EST 1879

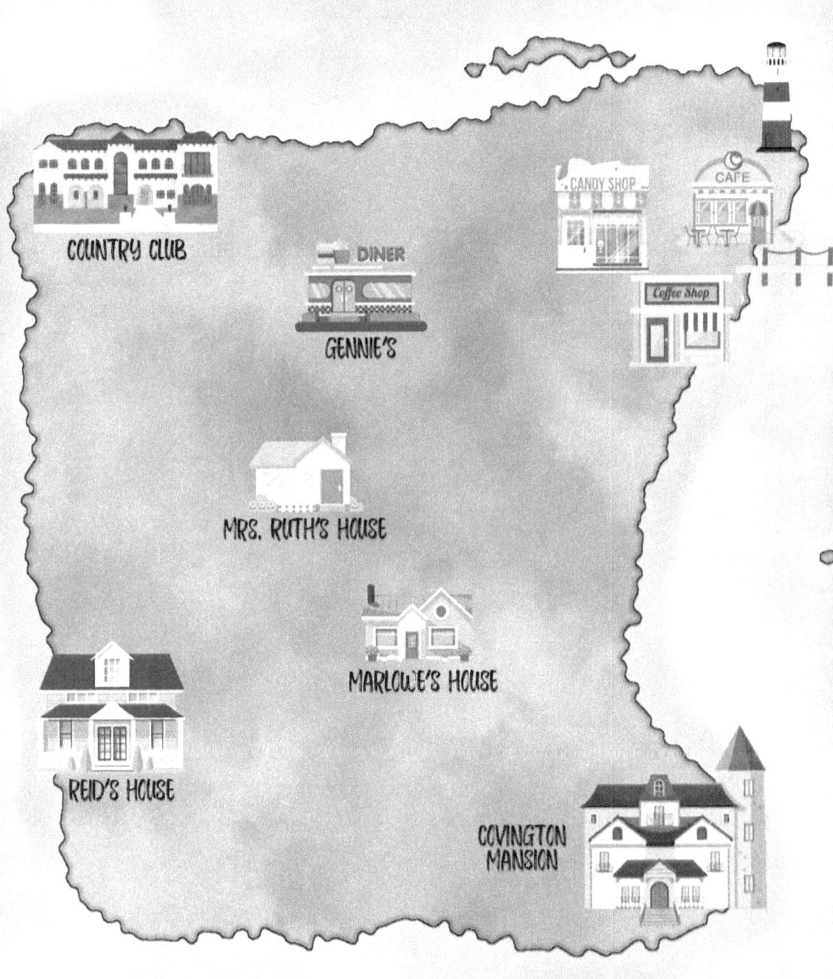

COUNTRY CLUB
DINER
GENNIE'S
CANDY SHOP
CAFE
Coffee Shop
MRS. RUTH'S HOUSE
MARLOWE'S HOUSE
REID'S HOUSE
COVINGTON MANSION

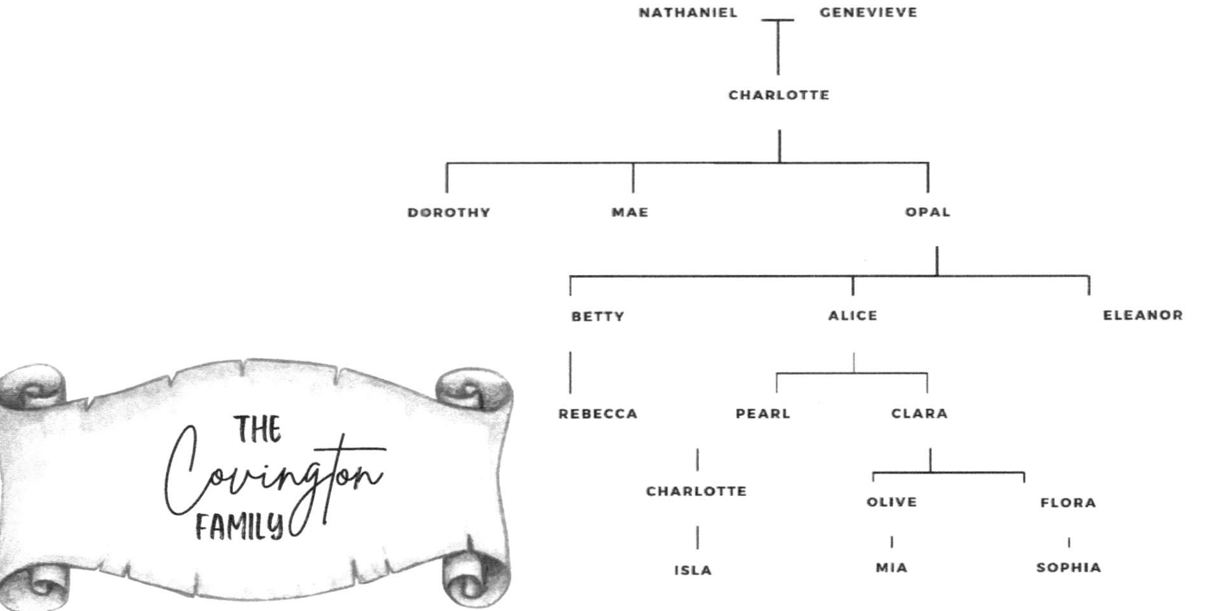

NATHANIEL
GENEVIEVE
CHARLOTTE
DOROTHY
MAE
OPAL
BETTY
ALICE
ELEANOR
REBECCA
PEARL
CLARA
CHARLOTTE
OLIVE
FLORA
ISLA
MIA
SOPHIA
THE Covington FAMILY

Crashing into Fate

CRASHING MY BIKE into the most popular guy in Covington Cove wasn't on my bucket list this summer.

To be honest, I didn't actually *have* a bucket list for the summer. But if I did, it would include things like beach days, a road trip to the mainland amusement park, and to learn how to skateboard-luge down the massive hill outside the Covington Cove Country Club.

It definitely wouldn't include laying flat on my back with rocks digging into my hip, surrounded by Baysiders.

That was just my luck, though. Multitasking was not my strong suit and attempting to look at my phone while dodging curbs, cars, and crowds wasn't the smartest idea. The only reason I had was because of the name that flashed on the screen—Mrs. Bennett. My ex-boyfriend's mother.

I shielded my eyes with my hand and found an excessive number of people gazing down at me. Why had they all been in the bike lane, anyway? The bike lane was for *bikers,* not for standers.

"Are you okay?" A guy with bright, emerald green eyes and perfectly styled wavy blonde hair stood over me, a concerned look on his otherwise perfect face.

I closed my eyes and groaned, covering my face with my hands. This was just what I needed—crashing into Baysider teens. I took a second to assess my body, and found nothing broken or even sprained. My knees and wrists stung, though, and a quick glance showed some gnarly scrapes and spots that would eventually become gross bruises.

"Is she, like, hurt?"

"You realize *she* crashed into *me*, right?" There was exasperation in the tone, making me cringe once again. The exasperated guy with the amazing hair and dazzling eyes?

Declan Storms.

The most popular guy at Covington Cove High. The one all the girls batted their eyelashes at, gave the little fake giggles to, and wanted to be asked out by.

I wasn't immune to his charm, and definitely not to his looks. Standing at an inch over six feet, as he liked to remind everyone, with sandy blonde hair that always looked like it was messy on purpose, and all the right muscles in all the right places, Declan Storms was hot and he knew it.

He was a walking cliche; all the guys wanted to be him and all the girls wanted to get with him. He was also a literal model for the island's tourism brochures.

There was only one issue with this whole situation: Baysiders didn't hang out with Gennies like me.

Covington Cove Island was split into three distinct groups:

The nouveau-riche kids that lived on Bayside Boulevard were the Baysiders.

The old, generational wealthy families lived on Covington Crescent Boulevard, aka the Crescent kids.

Working class families were the locals, like me and my friends. We grew up in the middle of the island, where the first street had been named after the founder of the island's wife, Genevieve Covington. Hence, Gennies.

Someone way back when wasn't all that creative in naming cliquey groups.

The three groups didn't mix all that often, which was why I was hesitant right now.

As Declan extended a hand and lifted me to my feet, I made a mental list of all the people I would have rather crashed into other than Declan Storms. The list included my ex-best friend, Grace; Holland St. Smither, who I vomited on two years ago, on accident, but still never forgotten; Isla Covington, the snobbiest of the Crescent Kids; and preferably even Zane Hunter, the world's biggest teen movie actor heartthrob.

"Thanks," I whispered, brushing gravel off of my legs and shorts, wincing as I ran over the scrapes on both knees, already pooling with tiny beads of blood. It would definitely start dripping before I got to work to clean it up and put a bandage on it. Gross.

I caught Declan's eye just as he finished giving me a once over. Whether it was to check me out or see if I had any actual injuries, I wasn't sure. Maybe a mixture of both.

He turned and took a step away, nodding toward his friend. "This one?"

His friend glanced over at me with a cool, casual look on his face. His name was Bryan Smith, but everyone called him Smitty.

"That one, huh? Sure."

I had *no* idea what they were going on about, but I didn't have time to dissect what that meant. A second later, someone else's hands were running through my hair, shaking out my curls and getting caught in a few knots.

I flinched and jumped to the side.

A giggle came from a girl behind me, followed by, "Sorry. There was some junk in your hair. It's gorgeous, by the way. Where do you get your highlights done?"

Words escaped me. I had never had so many Baysiders speak to me so nicely. Granted, I never had a lot of experience mingling with them, period.

Except for Reid. But as my ex-boyfriend, he didn't count.

"Um, I... I... I don't?" I spat out. My dirty blonde bordering light brown curls had a ton of natural highlights, usually made brighter by the summer sun. But seeing as it was barely the middle of June, they hadn't gotten bleached yet.

Right after I answered her, a pair of hands tightened on my waist. I spun, finding myself chest to chest with Declan Storms.

Somehow, while jumping away from the girl, I launched myself straight into his arms.

He stared at me, his emerald green eyes practically glowing in the mid-morning sun.

"Hey there," he whispered. "It's Marlowe, right?"

Declan wasn't just a breath of fresh air; he was an entire ocean breeze on a cool, crisp, early morning sunrise.

And he knew my name.

"Hi," I whispered back, unable to break eye contact with him. Neither of us blinked, and I was sure my lungs forgot how to function.

He held up his hand, producing my phone. "Your phone

fell. I didn't mean to pry, but a message came through and I saw it. It's your birthday?"

My face flushed. The jingles of notifications were why I had reached for my phone in the first place. Then, the call from Mrs. Bennett threw me for a loop. Instead of pulling over and safely extracting the phone, I had stupidly decided I could ride with no hands for a second.

Which was the same second Declan Storms stepped off the curb right in front of me and we collided. His friends had already been in the street, though, so it was sort of on me for not avoiding them all.

I made a mental note to myself: If you can't text and drive, you shouldn't text and bike. It seemed like a no-brainer, but honestly, sometimes it was the simplest things that I needed to learn the hard way.

"A birthday girl, huh?" Declan said again in a low voice, as if only talking to me. Which, really, he was.

I bit my bottom lip as my neck and face deepened into a crimson color. Everything I could think to say sounded dumb, so I didn't say anything at all.

He reached up and pulled on one of my curls that must have escaped my half-up bun when I fell. He released it, letting it bounce back and settle over my face. That curl was one of my favorites—the sun bleached it the brightest and I loved it.

What I didn't love? This situation I had somehow gotten myself into. I was completely frozen in place. Declan was still holding my waist with one hand, and the other brushed my cheek as he let go of the curl.

In short—Declan Storms was flirting. And I was letting him.

"Well, happy birthday," he said, his voice as smooth as silk. "Doing anything special?"

Words. I needed words. Birthday. Special. Plans. *What*?

Reality came slamming back as my heart sank. My birthday was the reason for all the notifications. Though I knew they were only about the freebies I could get at various retailers today, I had hoped it was something from Grandmum. Or maybe Mom and Dad, even though that would have been a stretch.

Grandmum had already left for work when I had gotten up this morning. She left no note, no present, nothing that signified she remembered it was my birthday at all. The little box for June tenth on the calendar in the kitchen was empty. It was as if it were any other normal Monday.

It shouldn't have surprised me that Grandmum forgot. She hadn't acknowledged the last few birthdays either. Ever since Mom and Dad stopped calling, she stopped remembering.

I was grateful for the amazing people in this town, but it didn't do much to repair a heart shattered by forgetful family and friends.

I stole a quick glance at my phone screen before answering Declan. I needed to say something soon, or else I would look like a complete doofus.

But part of me held onto a sliver of hope that *someone* in my life remembered what today was. Unfortunately, the phone showed nothing but a text for a small coffee from Muggsy's and a plate of fries from Gennie's Diner. And a voicemail from Mrs. Bennett.

Curiosity got the best of me—what would my ex-boyfriend's mother be calling me for? Did she remember it was my birthday? That seemed rather odd, but not entirely out of the realm of possibility.

"Um, no. Nothing special," I finally answered Declan. Not only was today my birthday, and I had absolutely no plans, but it was also a Monday, which meant I had work. It should be illegal to work on your birthday.

At least it wasn't a milestone birthday. Sixteen had been a hard pill to swallow, with Mom, Dad, and Grandmum all forgetting. I had waited until midnight, hoping that day would have been different. That they would come barging in and singing Happy Birthday at the strike of twelve.

They hadn't. In fact, Mom and Dad hadn't called for another three months after. It was the last time they had called, too.

The only bright spot had been my now ex-boyfriend, Reid, and my friends. They had gone all out, surprises and everything. It was the best.

So far, I hadn't heard from any of them, either. I would see Emma shortly at work, but I didn't get my hopes up for anything like last year. Especially with Reid no longer in the picture.

Next year, when I turned eighteen, I vowed to make my birthday special. I would do it for myself, though. It was a lesson I had learned long ago—if I wanted something to be special, I had to do it myself. And so far today, I had done nothing except crash my bike and tear up the skin on my knees.

Declan's grip tightened on my waist, reminding me of our close proximity. I shuddered and took a step back, letting his hand drift away slowly.

"Nothing fun, huh? That doesn't sound exciting. Where are you headed now?" Declan cocked his head to the side, a lock of perfectly messy sandy blonde hair falling over his face. Once he plastered his award-winning smile on, he looked exactly like he did on the cover of the tourism brochure.

"Work." Fear shot through me as I looked at my phone again to see the time. I had left home with plenty to spare, but this little interaction had now made me late.

"Where do you work?" Declan asked, crossing his arms over his chest, and staring at me as I righted my bike and looked it over to make sure it was still rideable.

I glanced down at the teal work tank I had on, with the logo and all, and frowned. "Seaside Cafe. I'm on beach table duty today." I answered like he asked a normal question, but coming from Declan Storms? A Baysider? It was anything but.

A sly smile crossed his lips. He glanced at Smitty and nodded. "Seaside Cafe. Got it. See you later..." he called after me.

I jumped on my bike and brushed my knotted curls off my shoulder before taking off down the road. My knee stung from the scrapes and my elbow ached, but it was nothing I couldn't handle.

Declan Storms, however?

He just made it to the top of my list of things to worry about this summer.

Forgotten Wishes

"DECLAN STORMS? THE DECLAN STORMS?" Emma screeched while she grabbed plates and I expertly picked up four water glasses with one hand.

She dumped the plates into her plastic bucket while I did the same with the glasses in mine. The lunch rush had just ended and we were exhausted, but still had a few more hours to go. Thankfully, it died down enough where I could tell her what happened on the way over.

"Yup. I literally crashed right into him and flew off my bike." The two giant bandages on my knees were proof of my encounter. That, plus the ache in my wrists from smashing them into the pavement and now hoisting tray after tray through the restaurant.

"Ouch," she sympathized, grimacing. She tucked her short, dark hair behind her ears, even though it would fall out a second later like it always did. Especially after she lowered her red heart-shaped sunglasses over her eyes. They were her signature, and she went nowhere without them. It also made it easy to spot her from a distance, considering her size of five-foot one inch did its best to hide her.

She could stand behind me, someone six inches taller, and basically disappear.

"I'll feel it tomorrow, I'm sure. But back to the craziness. Declan Storms. I managed to not only run him over, but basically jump straight into his arms."

Emma came to a dead stop, her jaw dropped. "Excuse-*moi*?"

I shook my head, reaching back to rub at my aching shoulder. From work, not from the crash. "I know. Or, actually, I don't know. But yeah, I landed with his hands on my hips. And get this—he knows my name."

Emma giggled, the same one that most girls did when it came to Declan. I rolled my eyes and chucked my table rag at her. "Stop that! It's so embarrassing! I crashed into the hottest guy on the Cove. I don't think I actually apologized either, I just stood there, blood dripping down my knees. It wasn't cute. It wasn't hot. And then guess what happened?"

All I got was a stare in response, so I continued. "He asked where I worked and said 'see you later.' Like, what does that even mean? Also, why do I care?"

"Girl, if I know you, you've already made a pro-con list in your head about why you care. Or on your phone. Is it on your phone? Can I see it?" A squeal left Emma's lips, eliciting side eyes from a few patrons still at the beachside tables. She bounced on her toes and clapped the pads of her fingertips together softly, as not to make a huge commotion.

"Shh!" I chastised, bumping her hip with mine. But the grin on my face also matched hers. Even though I had no idea what Declan wanted with me, it still set off a few butterflies in my stomach. "I don't have a list. Yet. But even if I did, the first thing on it would be, why me?"

"Why not you? You're a catch. But...," Emma said, this time in a softer voice. I shot her a look, but found only seriousness in her features.

My brows slammed down. "But what?"

She shook her head. "Sorry. I'm still on Team Reid. I have this whole elaborate vision drawn up in my head on the reunion between the two of you. He'll be coming back for the summer, and you'll see each other from across the room." She paused, lifting her hands into the air like she was conducting an orchestra. "Cue the romantic music. You lock eyes, then you both start running across—"

"Alright, alright, I get the point. I highly doubt that is going to happen, but whatever. More like, he comes back, hangs out with us on the beach, and we pretend last summer never happened." A sharp pain hit my gut at that statement. I hated saying it, as I desperately didn't want it to be true.

Emma shrugged. "Well, if you're so dead set on being over Reid, then sure. Go for Declan Storms. If you're worried about Norah, but don't worry, she's totally over him. He's all yours."

The mention of our friend brought back a memory I didn't even consider until now—Norah had a massive crush on Declan Storms our freshman year of high school. But if Emma said Norah was over it, then I was sure she was telling the truth. Emma had never spoken a lie in her life, and she wouldn't start now.

It was the flip-flopping in my heart that confused me. I had never been interested in Declan Storms before. Sure, he was hot. And charming. And not the worst Baysider out there.

But he was still... *Declan*.

The highest of the Covington Cove High hierarchy. The very top. Someone who could get any girl he wanted with a snap of his fingers. Why on earth would he have been looking at *me*?

According to the CCHS hierarchy, I was low on the totem pole. There wasn't anything special about me. I wasn't into sports. My grades were average at best. And while my hair was pretty fantastic with the natural highlights and ringlet curls—it was probably my best feature—it wasn't really enough to make me stand out.

In short, there was nothing about me that set me apart from the other dozens of girls in my grade. Nothing particular that would have caught the eye of someone like Declan Storms.

I sighed and plopped onto the bench in front of me. "Are you going to tell Norah?"

Emma shook her head. That was another great thing about having her as a friend—she kept secrets, locked away in a vault until you brought it back up, no matter how long that was. She said her record was almost ten years, and her brother confirmed it, saying Emma kept a secret on who broke a window with a ball when they were, like, six or so.

"What's wrong?" Emma asked. "Half the girls at school would die to be in your place right now."

I could name a full laundry list of things that were wrong, starting with the attention from Declan, and ending with a myriad of other things.

"Grace? Or Reid?" Emma offered, naming my ex-best friend and ex-boyfriend. I just shrugged. Both of them were issues, sure. Separate issues that caused separate mental strain when I tried to pinpoint exactly where things went wrong with both of them.

I didn't have a chance to answer, though, because a swarm of rings hit just then, from our phones and all the ones around us.

At the same time, our manager, Mason, poked his head out and informed us that a party of fifteen was headed our way.

Emma and I gawked at each other and groaned. We had just finished cleaning up from the lunch rush and now it looked like we would be kept busy until the end of our shift.

In a flash, we dug our feet into the sand and muscled our way to the server station to grab menus and silverware.

Two hours later, we were done, and the group was gone. Emma and I cleared the tables as fast as we could.

Sand stuck to my sweaty leg, which meant I would find a ton in my shoes later. We had gone back and forth between the kitchens and the tables a zillion times. Every muscle ached, both from work and my stupidity earlier.

"I can't believe it," Zach muttered as he came to help us clean up the remaining dishes. "I just can't believe it. How many people on this island have lived their entire life with her just... here? And now she's not?"

I paused and frowned, staring at him like he was speaking another language. He appeared out of nowhere, most likely Mason telling him to come out, and now he was talking to himself?

"Zach? Did someone, um, did someone you know pass away?" I laid a hand gently on his shoulder.

He gave me the same insane look I had given him. "You didn't hear?"

Glancing up over his head, I caught Emma's eye, finding her just as confused as I was.

"Guess not. That party kept us busy. Is everything okay?" I asked.

Zach cleared his throat and wiped at his eyes. "I don't even know why it's making me emotional. It just feels like the Queen died or something. I didn't even know her, but I also didn't know a life *without* her, you know?"

Shifting the bus bucket over to my other hip, I asked, "Zach? Can you maybe tell us who it was?"

His eyes lit up. "Oh, yeah. Eleanor Covington."

The world came to a screeching halt.

He was right—it *was* like when the Queen died. Except, unlike Zach who was trying to justify his feelings because he never really knew her...

I had. Personally.

Emma gasped, her hand flying over her mouth, her eyes wide in shock.

My legs gave out from under me and I dropped to the bench, my bucket ending up in my lap. Emma took it and put it on the table before sitting next to me. "Oh."

Zach's eyes narrowed, his head cocked. "Did you, like, actually know her?"

"I did." I couldn't even muster a nod or more words than that. "She died *today*?"

I needed clarification. Having her die on my birthday felt like a double whammy to my heart.

Zach nodded, then took off back toward the restaurant.

Eleanor Covington had been one of the most genuine, nicest people I had ever met. She never looked down on me, never treated me like the girl whose parents just up and abandoned her when she was five.

I had known her my entire life. Grandmum worked at the Covington Mansion, and after my parents left me with her, she had to un-retire and go back to work.

Mom had worked in housekeeping with Grandmum. She and Dad were only eighteen when I arrived, so Mom would bring me to work with her.

Grandmum had done the same once I became her responsibility. I ran around the mansion like it was my own playground while she worked. And every time Eleanor found me, instead of chastising me, she would bring me to a new spot in the mansion and tell me stories of her youth there.

She was the one who let me play in Charlotte's playroom, a room usually off limits to guests except to look through the door on tours.

Charlotte had been the daughter of the founders, Nathaniel and Genevieve. She had also been Eleanor's grandmother.

I was in a state of shock. I practically grew up in the mansion, and to this day, when there were big events or they were short staffed, Grandmum brought me in to help with the housekeeping.

Eleanor had watched me grow up. We would have conversations about life on the Cove, how it differed from her generation to mine, and all sorts of things. There wasn't a time when I went to the mansion that one of us didn't find the other.

I had seen her just a few short weeks ago.

"Marlowe..." Emma whispered. "Don't do it."

I blinked, looking up at her with so much sadness around my heart, it physically hurt.

"Don't add her to your list. Eleanor didn't leave you. By what you've told me over the years, she loved you. But she *died*, Marlowe. She didn't leave you on purpose. I mean, she was in her mid-nineties. It's not that unexpected, right?" Emma laid a hand on my shoulder, trying to console me, but it didn't work.

She knew I had a list of people in my dresser drawer at home. A list of people that said they loved me, then vanished from my life.

My parents being the first two on the list.

"It's... a surprise, that's all. She was so nice to me. I... I'm going to miss her," I muttered, staring down at the sand now. "Just a surprise."

Emma cleared her throat. "Speaking of surprises..."

I glanced up, looking at her, but she jutted her chin toward the restaurant's back door.

Where Declan Storms stood, a small bouquet of flowers in his hands and a bright, megawatt smile on his face.

Passing Storms

NORMALLY, I HAD no issue talking to guys. Or to anyone, for that matter. Creating conversation was an art form I excelled in, which worked to my advantage as a waitress.

However, Declan Storms had rendered me speechless for the second—or was it third—time.

"Declan! Nice to see you. Did you have a reservation? Are you waiting for someone?" Emma asked, jogging up to meet him and bring him down to the tables in the sand.

His eyes never left mine, and when he approached, he handed the bouquet to me and said, "I'm here for the birthday girl."

Emma's jaw dropped. She stumbled over a few words before clearing her throat. "Birthday? Who's birthday?" By the tremble in her voice, and the way her eyes sliced over to mine, she knew exactly whose birthday she forgot. She cringed, and I could almost see the expletives rolling through her mind.

I gasped, air finally filling my lungs again. I didn't know what it was about Declan Storms that made me incapable of breathing, thinking, talking, or moving, but I stood there frozen, unable to stop what was happening.

I hadn't mentioned my birthday to Emma. By now, I wanted the entire day to just be over and forgotten about. Even before we learned about Eleanor, the crash itself was enough to make me want a do-over.

Besides, I couldn't handle the pity. The inevitable looks of sorrow and sadness that came when a friend forgot something as important as their friend's birthday. The endless apologies that followed. I didn't want it. Nor did I want to embarrass her for forgetting.

It was only seventeen. It wasn't a huge deal.

But now, here was Declan, making it sound like the *hugest* deal of all time. His bronzed, chiseled face twisted into a look of annoyance as he stared at Emma.

"Marlowe's birthday," he stated confidently, shoving his hands in the pockets of his well-worn jeans. He stood a foot taller than her, his shoulders straight, his chest puffed out slightly, like he was challenging Emma to come back at him and say something.

I grimaced, feeling the temperature rise in my cheeks. So far, he was the only one that really acknowledged my birthday. And he hadn't even known it was today until a few hours ago.

"So...," he said, turning his attention back to me. "I took a shot in the dark. Are you done working, by chance?"

I nodded, my grip on the flowers so tight, the tiny, prickly hairs on the stems tickled my fingers. A bead of sweat slid down the back of my neck, pooling on the hem of my teal Seaside Cafe tank top.

That's when I realized what a mess I looked like. Running back and forth between the restaurant and the beach tables made me sweaty and gross. My hair stuck to my skin, getting caught more than once under my armpits, and there was sand in places I *really* didn't want there to be.

With Declan randomly showing up like this, I didn't even have a chance to run to the bathroom to fix things.

"She is. And we were just about to celebrate! You're right on time. Why don't you two take a seat, and I'll be right back!" Emma exclaimed, like she didn't just make that up on the spot. She gave both of us the fakest smile I had ever seen.

I scrunched my face, in an attempt to silently grab her attention, but she bolted away and ran into the restaurant.

Declan gestured to the closest table. "After you. I mean, I thought about taking you somewhere nice for your birthday, but I don't want to interrupt whatever you had planned already."

His words struck me. Somewhere nice? Did he think that the Seaside Cafe wasn't good enough? It was such a Baysider comment, and it definitely rubbed me the wrong way.

All the sudden, his mention of 'see you later' had context. Was he planning this the whole time we stood in the street, his hands on my waist, blood dripping down my legs? Or was this a random, spur-of-the-moment idea?

I didn't get answers to any of it, though, because before I could ask, Emma reappeared, her tray full of lemonade and an appetizer.

"Start with these. The treat is still to come," she stated before rushing back off. I wasn't sure I wanted to know what she was planning. When Emma got an idea in her head, it was better to let her run with it.

"So... working on your birthday sucks, huh?" Declan said, picking up an onion ring and examining it like he had never seen one before in his life.

Which I knew to be false, because the cafeteria served them almost every day.

I wasn't hungry, though, so I pushed the plate closer to him and rested my elbows on the table instead, setting my chin on my fists. "Yeah, kinda does."

"You having a party or something? Beach bonfire? Isn't that what most Gennies do?" The wicked little smile that accompanied his statement made me tilt my head.

I wouldn't have classified beach bonfires as something 'Gennie's did' often, but it was an option. We didn't have private beach access like the Crescent kids or a good number of Baysiders, but we knew how to party with what we had.

"Um, no. Nothing planned besides work."

He reached across the table and grabbed my hand. "It's a good thing I showed up, then, huh? Looks like your coworkers were planning something, but what's a birthday without a celebration?"

He winked at me as if he was the most thoughtful person in the world.

Truthfully, it *did* mean a lot to me that he made an effort. Even though his path and mine hadn't really crossed over the years, he had still known my name and went out of his way to do something nice for me.

It was more than anyone else had today. I needed to be grateful and get my attitude in check. I couldn't let the day get me down, and right now, it was looking up anyway. It was time to roll with it.

I plastered on a smile, trying to muster up some of the sunshine I usually had.

"There it is! That's more like it. You can't be sad on your birthday. It's, like, against the law or something," Declan declared with a grin.

"Did you hear about Eleanor Covington?" I blurted out, knowing that was what was still upsetting me.

Declan shrugged and took a sip of his soda. "Yeah, a little bit ago. My mom was all upset about it, but Eleanor was like, what, a hundred right?"

I wanted to correct him. I wanted to say she was only ninety-five, that she was the last granddaughter of Charlotte Covington, and one of the last remaining Covington's on the entire island.

The Covington family tree was enormous, but only a handful still lived here. A few branches of the tree had stayed on the island, including Mia and Isla Covington. They were cousins, the same age as Declan and I, and Crescent kids.

With Eleanor being the oldest Covington, she lived in the Covington Mansion, where she had her entire life. I wondered who would move into the mansion now. A Covington had always occupied it. Other family members lived in property on the estate, or along the Crescent.

Maybe Eleanor's will would leave it to the town. Maybe it would only be kept open for tours and events.

Eleanor had never married, and she had no kids. She treated all the kids on the island as her own, though, always opening her doors and providing what was needed whenever she could. She thought of herself as the entire island's grandmother, and there was no better description for her, especially to those of us that knew her personally, like I did.

But I didn't correct Declan. I let it slide, not wanting to bring the vibe of this afternoon down.

If Declan came all the way out here to celebrate with me, then that's what we would do. I would look on the bright side, and celebrate not only my birthday, but Eleanor's amazing life as well.

"Thanks for coming," I said with another genuine smile. "Really, I appreciate it. Today was... not the best," I admitted. "But definitely better now."

Declan flashed me one of his signature megawatt grins, and my flip-flopping heart went into overdrive.

Emma showed up a minute later, with two slices of our famous cheesecake in her hands, one with a sparkler on top.

"Couldn't find a candle," she admitted as she put the plates on the table. "But happy birthday, Marlowe!"

I gave her my thanks, and we waited for the sparkler to die down before I removed it. Declan lifted a piece up on his fork, waiting to cheers with mine.

"To Marlowe on her birthday. May it be a fantastic year," he said, his whole face lit up with excitement.

I grinned right back, feeling happy for the first time today.

When we finished, Emma shooed us away, saying the food was on the house in honor of my birthday. I thanked her, grabbed my belongings and an extra bag of food from the kitchen, and headed toward the door with Declan.

"I don't understand you. I practically ran you over this morning and you still came to do such a nice thing for me. It means a lot," I said, placing my stuff in the basket of my bike. It was a bit dented from this morning's crash, but it worked fine.

Declan shrugged. "Everyone deserves a second chance, right? Have a great night, Marlowe. I'll see you around..."

And with that, he took off, and left me with a million more questions, just like earlier today.

Unexpected Offers

AFTER I LEFT work yesterday, Emma must have spread the word, and messages from our group of friends had finally popped up. The twins, Livvy and Liam, were out of town, so I forgave them for forgetting. Caleb and Norah swung by my house after dinner, hanging out until just before midnight when Grandmum told them it was time to leave.

But to not hear from Reid... that one stung. Even though things didn't work out between us, I had still sent him a message on his birthday.

Last summer, he went out of his way to get to the Cove early for my birthday, surprising me with an entire day planned. Which, for someone who lived on the opposite side of the country, was a big deal. He flew in early, set up an elaborate beach surprise, and, best of all, told me he loved me.

It had been the start of the most amazing summer, one I never knew I even deserved. Silly me thought that maybe, even after all that had happened, that he would have still remembered...

I hadn't been the only one who thought about him recently. Norah had asked about Reid last night, if he was coming back this summer.

Truthfully, I didn't know. Besides saying happy birthday earlier this year, I hadn't spoken to him at all. And it seemed like no one in the group had either. It was as if he cut off all communication with everyone.

Part of me wondered if he did that because we broke up. Like he felt as if the crew were my friends, and he assumed they took sides in the breakup. They hadn't, and I knew the guys especially felt hurt by being cut off.

The most recent list in my phone, the one about all things Reid, had one giant question at the top: *Could I handle being around Reid, the guy who broke my heart, for the sake of our friend group?*

Ever since school got out last week, Reid had been on the forefront of my mind. Typically, as this would be his fourth summer with us, we would count down the days until his flight came in and summer *really* began once we were all together again.

Now, though, I had no idea what to expect and that threw me into an entirely different anxious spiral that I couldn't deal with right now. I had other things on my mind, like Declan showing up to work yesterday and what all that meant.

Was Declan worth more of my time and energy than Reid right now? Probably. Especially since he was here and, for some unknown reason still, showing me attention.

I rolled over and checked the time on my phone. That's when I saw it—the voicemail from Mrs. Bennett from yesterday.

I bolted upright with a loud gasp. With all the crazy Declan-related things yesterday, I had completely forgotten that she had even called.

My heart began to pound as I opened up the voicemail and pressed play. I held my breath, listening to her lithe but stern voice coming through my speakers.

"Hola, Marlowe. I hope you are well. We have a bit of a situación and are hoping you can help out. Por favor, call me back. Adiós."

A warmth spread throughout me listening to her accented speech. She had the motherly kindness I hadn't really experienced in my life. It was yet another reason I had loved going to Reid's house every summer.

In a flash, I clicked the call back button and put the phone on speaker.

"Hola," Mrs. Bennett said after only two rings.

"Hi! Mrs. Bennett, hi. I'm so sorry I didn't get back to you yesterday. Oh," I paused, realizing I didn't even tell her who I was yet, "it's Marlowe, by the way."

"Of course, dear, I know it's you. Thank you for calling. Listen, Mr. Bennett and I are in a... Well, we have a problem."

I froze. "Is everything okay? Is Reid—" I couldn't even finish that sentence. My heart came to a screeching halt and my stomach plummeted toward the floor just thinking of anything happening to him.

"What? Oh, no. Oh dear me, no. He's fine. We have... una situación and we're not sure what to do. I was about out of options when Jonathan mentioned you."

Mr. Bennett mentioned me? Now that I knew Reid was fine, she piqued my curiosity.

"Okay... what can I do for you?"

"Marlowe, please tell me you're on the island for the summer," was the first statement I got.

"Well, considering I live here year-round, I am."

That received a laugh from the frantic Mrs. Bennett. "Sí, sí. I seem to forget who is year-round and who isn't sometimes."

Easy to say for a summer-only Baysider, but I let it slide.

"Fantástica. Listen, Jonathan and I have gotten ourselves into a little pickle. We just got here on Sunday with the dogs and everything, basically moved in for the summer. And late that night, we discovered an issue with a client over in Spain. An issue that will require us being at the airport in, oh, three hours." The last part was rushed, the sound of her heels click-clacking on the floors in the background adding to the effect.

I could immediately picture her. Her long dark hair swooshing across her back in a perfect blow out that took away from her natural curls. The same ones Reid inherited. Mrs. Bennett was always in heels no less than four inches, since she was barely over five feet tall. Her husband was over six, like Reid.

He was the perfect mix of both of them. He had his father's height and deep voice, but his looks leaned toward his mother's Spanish genes. His dark, almost black ringlets were perpetually messed up, and his dark onyx eyes never failed to draw me in.

"I'm sorry to hear that. I'm not quite sure how I can help, though?"

"Right, right, that part. Look, Marlowe, I wouldn't be asking if we weren't desperate. I know you have your job at the cafe and are probably super busy with your friends and all, but I need a favor."

I frowned. It was sweet that she remembered my job, but other than that... I really didn't have any plans this summer. Especially with my now ex-best friend Grace nowhere to be found and without Reid...

My heart twisted into a knot at the thought of him and what we had last summer.

"Do you think you could house and dog sit for us? We'll be gone for almost a month, and I have no idea what else to do. Both pups are here with us and the house is completely opened for the summer, and I just..."

"Housesit? For you? What about..." I didn't have to finish the sentence. She seemed to pick up on my hesitation quickly. I swung my leg over the side of the bed, but didn't stand yet. I wasn't sure my jelly legs would support me.

"Reid? Oh dear, sí. Listen, I am so sorry it didn't work out between you two. You were absolutely adorable together. But no, mija, he's not coming to the Cove this summer."

Island Intrigues

R EID WOULDN'T BE here for the summer.

He wasn't coming back.

I didn't know if that made me feel happy or sad. It threw me into a tailspin of confusion, that was for sure.

Did I want him here? Debatable. Our friends were looking forward to seeing him, and eventually I would have to deal with it at some point. But until that happened, I sat in a state of limbo. There was no telling how I would feel until I saw him.

And now Mrs. Bennett confirmed that he wouldn't be coming. I had to get my emotions in check.

So far, sadness won. There must have been a part of me that hoped to see him again. It was expected, after all, being the beginning of summer. I must have been clinging to that bit of knowledge in order to push back my feelings until later.

But later wasn't coming. Later was now. And knowing Reid wouldn't be here this summer broke my heart all over again.

Had I been expecting to fix things with him if he came back? Maybe. We ended last summer on such uncertain terms. At least, for me, that was. Reid had been pretty clear when he said, "I think we should break up." Though I understood the words, the meaning behind it still didn't make sense to me. And without talking to him for the past ten months, I had no concrete conclusion to jump to.

"Marlowe? Are you still there? Did I lose conn—"

"I'm here! I'm sorry. Did you say... did you say Reid wasn't coming?"

Mrs. Bennett must have covered the phone with her hand for a moment while whispering to someone next to her. "What was that, dear? Oh, Reid. No, he stayed at home with some friends for the summer instead. I wanted to call and ask him to fly out, but Jonathan said it was better to let him be with friends. Ever since... Well, let's just say it's been a hard year for him. A hard few years, actually."

My heart sank. Mrs. Bennett and I were excellent at not saying what we really meant. But we understood just the same.

"So, can you?" she asked, and I could tell her patience was waning.

"Of course," I replied quickly. "Do you need me to swing by before you leave?"

"No need. I'll put the key in the planter. You know the dogs and your way around. We leave in three hours, and will let them potty before we go, so anytime this afternoon is fine. Ainsley already made up the guest room on the first floor, so it's yours while you're here. I'll drop a credit card on the kitchen island for you to use for groceries, food, or whatever. We should be back by the end of the month!

Muchas gracias, Marlowe, you're a lifesaver. Call us if you need anything and make yourself at home, alright?"

I opened my mouth to reply, but she had already hung up. Mrs. Bennett was super sweet and the perfect mothering type, but she and her husband also ran a multi-million-dollar company, so her time was limited.

With a groan, I rolled out of bed and threw on a pair of jean shorts I found on the floor and a clean purple tank from the drawer. After getting ready in the bathroom, I headed to the kitchen to grab a water bottle. It was time to cash in the freebies I had from yesterday, starting with a coffee from Muggsy's in town.

Everything seemed normal in the kitchen at first. Then I saw it—a cupcake. With a candle stuck in it. A chocolate with chocolate frosting cupcake sat on one of Grandmum's old blue ceramic plates on the dining table, all alone except for one thing next to it.

A bag of Sea Salt Caramel Pearls. My favorite candy from Cove Candy.

I couldn't help the smile that spread across my face, or the tear that somchow escaped and rolled down my cheek.

Grandmum hadn't forgotten after all. Well, maybe she forgot on the actual day, but it was fine. This made up for it.

I didn't want to wake her just yet, so I wolfed down the cupcake, tossed the Pearls into my bag, and left a thank you sticky note for her.

Then, I climbed onto my bike and took off down the street. The sun peeked over the horizon, filling the sky with cotton candy hues. I hated wasting such a gorgeous morning, so I headed out early to enjoy the quiet before Covington Cove woke up.

The first stop I made was to Mrs. Ruths' house on the next street over, Genevieve Street. She was an OG—an original Gennie. She also owned Cove Candy, the local candy shop that got swamped every summer during tourist season.

I let myself in with the key under the mat. Everyone knew it was there—I wasn't the only one who stopped by as often as possible to check on her, make sure her fridge was stocked, and she had everything she needed, even if that just included company. She refused to move out of her home and in with her son, Sam, who ran the candy shop.

After quietly opening the door, I returned to my bike basket and took out the food I swiped from the cafe before I left yesterday. Now she would wake up to a wonderful breakfast of blueberry muffins and croissants, and lunch for the next few days.

"If you're a robber, there's nothing to steal here. Check Saul's next door," her voice floated from down the hall.

A laugh escaped me before I could contain it. "It's just me, Mrs. Ruth. Marlowe."

"M and M? What on god's green earth are you doing here so early?" she shouted back.

"Just dropping off some food! I'm on my way to grab some coffee from Muggsy's, though. Do you need anything else?"

The sound of the water running clued me in to her location. "Did you bring the blueberry muffins?"

"Of course! I wouldn't dare show my face here without them."

"Good girl. You can go now. Remind your gran that book club is this week, would you? She won't return my calls."

I laughed again, knowing very well Gran's hatred of cell phones. I called out to her as I opened the front door. "Will do! See you later, Mrs. Ruth!"

She reminded me a lot of Eleanor. Between the two of them, I knew so much history about Covington Cove. They were completely different women, one born into wealth and one self-made, but their experiences on the island weren't all that different.

After locking the front door and returning the key under the mat, I waved to Saul, the neighbor to the right, and hopped back onto my bike, heading downtown.

Coastal Charades

THE BELL OVER the front door at Muggsy's jingled as I walked in. I shook my shoulders in a little dance to the beat, eliciting a chuckle from Benji, the barista.

"There she is! One blueberry scone and a dry cappuccino coming right up!" he said with another laugh. "The capp on the house, of course, for the birthday girl." We exchanged some small talk as he gathered my items. I handed him a ten and told him to keep the change.

Once back on my bike, I stored the scone in my basket, moved the water bottle to join the scone, and dropped the cappuccino into the cup holder.

Before leaving, I opened my notes app to start a quick list of all the things I would need to bring with me to the Bennett's house for an extended stay. Everything from my toothbrush to my phone charger made the list.

I tried to ignore the glaring list of all things Reid right underneath it.

It looked like I wouldn't need to worry about that one anymore.

Finally satisfied with my list, I kicked off the ground and rode off down the street. If I didn't have to be there until this afternoon, I had the whole day ahead of me. I wasn't working at the cafe or the mansion, and I had already checked in on Mrs. Ruth. It was a perfect time to just ride around the island.

My mind drifted to Declan as I rode toward Charlotte's Haven Beach, and how he showed up at work yesterday. Though my birthday had gotten off to a horrendous start, he really put a bright spot in it. Part of me still didn't understand why, but I wasn't mad about it. For a moment yesterday, I thought I should have been. Baysiders didn't usually hang out with Gennies, and I let the negative thoughts overwhelm my mind.

But then again, I had never known Declan Storms to be a part of the bullying crowd. The ones that had run Reid off a few years ago. The ones who pulled mean pranks on unsuspecting people, finding entertainment in their victim's humiliation.

From everything I heard from Norah a few years ago when she had her crush on him, he seemed like a nice guy. If he wasn't, why would he have shown up and with flowers?

My stomach rumbled, reminding me I hadn't eaten lunch yet. With the sun directly overhead, it was time to head home.

Grandmum wasn't there when I got back, so I shot her a text. If she was at work, she would check it on her break. She hated cell phones, and only really used it to communicate with me.

ME: Hi! Just got back and you're not here. Mrs.
Bennett asked me to house and dog sit for a
few weeks. I told them yes. Is that okay?

To my surprise, my phone dinged only a minute later.
Grandmum must have been on her break already.

GRANDMUM: It's fine.

ME: Thanks! And thanks for the cupcake and
candy. I loved them. <3

GRANDMUM: You're welcome. The Mansion
Masquerade is Friday. I'll send you a message
on what time to be there.

ME: It's on my list!

She wasn't a woman of many words, but approval was approval. With that, I went directly to my bedroom in the back of the house. Grandmum had lived in this house since the day she and Pops got married and moved to the island. They never really planned on having kids, so a modest two-bedroom house was all they needed.

Mom came two years later, and me eighteen years after that. Mom, Dad, and I all shared the second bedroom for five years.

Then one day, they left. It wasn't unusual; they would disappear for a weekend here or there. They were young and full of spontaneity and adventure. But when I was five, they left and didn't come back for a while. Eventually,

Grandmum moved their stuff out of the room and told me it was all mine now. Which, back then, seemed amazing. It wasn't until I realized it also meant Mom and Dad weren't coming back that I started to despise it.

I stood in the middle of my room, looking around at how plain it was. A pale blue comforter laid on the twin bed, a dresser pushed against the far wall, and a small table to act as a desk against the other, next to the door. The walls were bare, the carpet worn in and original to the house itself.

With a sigh, I headed to the closet and pulled out my duffel bag. Thirty minutes later, I had everything packed and ready to go. I twisted the large strap so I could slip it over my shoulders like a makeshift backpack. It would be the only way I could carry it and ride my bike.

I sucked in a deep breath and took one last glance around the living room as I stood in the doorway. A nostalgic feeling washed over me, like I was leaving forever.

But I wasn't. It was only for a month, tops. It would be the longest I had ever been away before, though, even if I was only going to the other side of the island.

The ride to the Bennett's was uneventful, and I found the key easily. The only issue was the fact that my stomach was still rumbling. I had been so preoccupied packing and leaving home that I forgot to grab a snack before going.

I unlocked the door, waiting for the sound of scratching nails on the wood floors to greet me before I dared move further inside.

A second later, they appeared. Noodle, a large goldendoodle, came charging first, followed closely by Marshmallow, a Corgi. Noodle leaped into the air when he saw me, placing his front legs on my shoulders and pushing me back into the door behind me.

"Hi! Oh gosh, oh gosh, hi! Okay, okay, down! Down, Noodle!" I laughed as I pushed him away from my face that he was currently cleaning with his tongue.

Marshmallow, who was more affectionately called Fluff, jumped and spun in circles until I crouched down to pet her as well. Noodle didn't like that, and barreled between us, knocking me to the ground.

My laughter only seemed to encourage them, and they both pounced on me, wrestling with me for a few minutes.

Once they settled down, I placed them in the backyard, stopping to smell the water wafting from the beach beyond the fence.

I had just gotten to the guest room Mrs. Bennett told me to use when my phone beeped. After sliding the toggle over, I checked the text message.

UNKNOWN: Please see the attached video, a message from Eleanor Covington.

Unraveling Secrets

My finger hovered over the little video attachment icon. I swallowed, a lump already growing in my throat.

Was I ready to see a video from Eleanor? Granted, I had seen her a few weeks ago, but now that she was... gone, it seemed odd. Morbid, maybe.

When did she record it? Why? And why for me?

Maybe it wasn't specifically for me. Maybe it was some sort of generic message to the residents of Covington Cove. Maybe it was—

Enough. I could keep guessing for hours, but the answer was right in front of me. All I had to do was click on the attachment.

But for some reason, it took some sort of superhuman strength to do just that. My finger shook as I forced it to press down.

I gasped when her face filled my screen, her soft smile adorned with the same lipstick she always had on, her white hair perfectly styled.

I could almost smell the sweet, floral perfume she wore, the one that smelled like the Indian Hawthorn bushes that grew outside of the mansion, even though I had never seen any perfume actually contain that particular bloom.

"Marlowe. My sweet Marlowe. The first thing I want to tell you is how incredibly *proud* I am of you. You've grown into an extraordinary woman, and I have no doubt you're going to go off and do amazing things in your life."

My hand flew to my mouth, stifling the sob trying to escape my throat. Hearing her words, in her regal and elegant voice, brought me to tears. They streamed down my cheeks instantly, dripping onto my arm and the plush beige carpet under my feet.

"If you're watching this, it means I have finally reached the end of my time on the island. Please know that I have lived a very long and fulfilling life, and I left wanting for nothing. It was people like you that brought me much happiness throughout my years."

I held my breath, my heart shattering into a thousand pieces. I was extremely proud to have known such an extraordinary woman such as Eleanor, and to have a video such as this helped with the closure, even if just a little.

"Upon my death, I have instructed my estate to withhold the will reading for a short time. During that time, I have something special for you, Marlowe. Soon, you will be receiving more information, but I want you to know that I chose you personally for this quest. You are a special girl, and I loved all of our time together. What you do with this quest is up to you. The only request I have is that you only tell those people in your life that you trust explicitly. I'm sure by the end, it'll be all over the island, but to start... trust your gut. I know you'll succeed. I chose you for a reason. Goodbye, sweet Marlowe. Thank you for being the sunshine in my life every time we crossed paths."

The video ended. I quickly clicked the button again and watched it three more times, sinking to the floor and crossing my legs underneath me. Tears puddled in my lap.

Eleanor left me with more questions than answers, and a deep hole in my heart.

SILENCE WAS ALL I heard for the next few days. Liam and Livvy were due back next week, Emma picked up every extra shift she could, and Caleb started working at the Richards' boat company as a tour guide. Even Norah had been busy.

I went to work, to the Bennett's, and repeated. Life seemed to settle into a normal routine, just in a different house.

A house with two dogs who enjoyed nothing more than endless rounds of fetch and keep away with their squeaky balls. If I didn't hear another squeak for a month, it would be too soon. But they were adorable and had fun, so I dealt with it, over and over and over.

Tonight was the Mansion Masquerade, the one Grandmum asked me to work.

I hadn't spoken to her since then, either. Seeing her tonight would feel weird, but then again, I also didn't think it would be much different than normal. I completely understood where she came from, because if I had lived most of my life already and planned on relaxing in my retirement, only to be saddled with a rambunctious five-year-old and then had to go back to work? I would be permanently grumpy, too. So I did my best to keep to myself and not bother her much.

I checked my to-do list on my phone. I still needed to take a shower before getting ready for the event. The Bennett house had the best showers I had ever used, so I planned on staying in it for quite a while. They even had those shower stereos that hooked up to my phone via Bluetooth, so I could blast some music, too.

"Noodle! Fluff! Time to go in!" I called, whistling for them even though I had no idea if they knew what I meant. They had been trained, but I wasn't exactly sure of all of their commands. They could sit, stay, and paw, but come seemed to be fifty-fifty for them.

Noodle came running back first, a grin on his face with a ball in his mouth. It took a little while before Marshmallow showed up. Thankfully, neither of them had muddy paws this time, so we all went straight inside. They curled up at the end of the bed while I hopped into the shower.

I put on my own personal concert while washing and conditioning my hair. The encore was during body wash, and the final bows while I rinsed.

Another great part of the Bennett house was the attention to detail. The towel warmers in each bathroom provided an amazing touch, and I used it not only for my towels, but also for my pajamas on some of the chillier nights.

After wrapping a warm, soft towel around my body, I stepped out of the shower and wiped some of the fog off the mirror. My hair hung in damp ringlets over my shoulders, dripping onto the counter beneath me.

I would have to wear it back in a full bun for work tonight, even though I hated doing that. It also meant I would have to blow dry my hair and just thinking about that made my arms hurt. My hair was so thick and curly, it took forever to dry.

Knowing I wasn't going to keep it curly, I threw it up in another towel and padded my way out to the bedroom to lay out the two sets of clothes I needed. The first for the bike ride to the mansion, and the second being my actual work uniform.

The Mansion Masquerade was one of the most elite black-tie events of the year. Even the wait staff were in tuxes and gowns. But housekeeping continued to wear our normal uniform of a white button down and black straight legged pants.

The dogs had disappeared, but that didn't surprise me. The concert I put on wasn't really popstar quality. Plus, neither of them stayed in one place for long, especially if they weren't getting any attention.

What did surprise me was the weird noise currently coming from down the hall. Somewhere around the kitchen.

The noises didn't stop, but my heart sure did.

It didn't sound like the dogs. There were no scratches of nails on the floors, no barks, no happy panting.

I froze, not moving or breathing as I strained to listen. The noise stopped, but then started up again. It sounded like... footsteps? Was someone in the house? As far as I remembered, I had locked all the doors after I came inside, not wanting to leave anything to chance, even though crime on the island was low.

My first instinct was to grab my phone and lock myself in the bathroom while calling the police. My second was to man up and see what was going on. More than likely, the dogs would have been going nuts if it were a person, so the logical part of my brain ruled that out. Sort of.

I tucked my lips in and sucked in a quiet, but deep breath, before leaving the bedroom. I braced my back against the wall as I tip-toed my way down the hall. My palms were clammy as my heart pounded behind my rib cage. My moves were slow and deliberate as I kept my eyes open wide.

My breaths came in staggered increments, shorter and shorter with each step I took down the hall.

Trying as hard as I could not to make any noise, I stole a quick glance around the corner toward the kitchen, trying to see what was causing the ruckus.

My heart leaped into my throat when I caught a glimpse of a *person* a few feet away.

A tall person, holding a baseball bat.

"Ahh!" I screamed, jumping out from behind the wall and clutching at the towel around my torso.

"Who are you and what are you doing in my—*Marlowe*?"

8

Scavenger's Surprise

"Reid?"

Reid lowered the bat, and I gathered my wits enough to look at his face, finding the same look of utter exasperation as I had.

He set the bat on the counter and sunk into one of the barstools next to him, his hands rummaging through his head full of dark curls and tugging on the ends.

"Holy crap, Marlowe, you gave me a heart attack. I thought you were an intruder, but then I heard music, and got confused. The last person I expected to come around that corner was you."

I blinked a few times, not sure I wasn't hallucinating. Reid wasn't supposed to be here this summer. His parents all but promised he was staying at home. Which was hundreds of miles away.

Yet... there he was, in the flesh. Sitting on a stool, wearing jeans and a tighter gray t-shirt than I remembered him liking. As I glanced down, I found comfort in seeing the same, old, scruffy black tennis shoes on his feet.

That was the only bit of comfort I took, though. Pure adrenaline had gotten me out of the guest room and to this point, but now anxiety took over, causing everything to crash. My head spun, my vision going slightly blurry on the edges.

Reid wasn't supposed to be here. I wasn't supposed to be seeing him like this. This wasn't how this was supposed to happen.

Emma's comment from the other day hit me—her "vision" of Reid and I seeing each other from across the room. Cue the music, and we ran into each other's arms.

If she could only be here to see how *not* right she was. Me, standing in the middle of the kitchen in a set of towels, and Reid, collapsed onto a stool looking like he wanted to puke.

The expression on his face made me want to match it, too. Nothing was going right. Everything was wrong. This was all wrong. Not just the way we were meeting again, seeing each other for the first time since we stood on the driveway right outside of this house, him holding my hands and telling me that while he loved me, he had to let me go. For my own good. Or something like that. But it was all wrong because this wasn't how *I* imagined things would go.

A few months ago, I had started a mental list of all the ways Reid and I would reunite when he came back to the island for the summer. Most of them had me looking like a snack, so he would be instantly jealous. That's what Livvy said, anyway.

But then Mrs. Bennett said he wasn't going to be here and I mentally erased that entire list. He had been pushed out of my mind, assuming I wouldn't see him again.

I was aware of myself enough to realize I was on the edge of a panic attack. Aware enough to know that the person sitting in front of me used to be the best one to help me through one.

Which, in turn, made me even more anxious, knowing that he wasn't that person anymore.

I took a few deep breaths, trying to center myself by feeling the cold tile under my feet and focusing on that.

"What are you doing here?" I whispered, my heart still pounding in my chest. Except, I wasn't entirely sure it was due to fear...

His brows crinkled, a frown pulling his full lips down. "Me? Shouldn't I be asking that about you?"

I stared at him, just as confused as he was. Did his parents not tell him I was staying here? That they hired me so they could leave on business? What did and didn't he know?

"Where are the dogs?" I asked, my brain turning the conversation completely around. I swung my head toward the back door, finding two extremely happy puppies waiting to be let in.

As I did, the towel on my head fell off, reminding me I was currently standing in Reid's kitchen, with only a towel covering me.

Every inch of exposed skin flushed. I stared at Reid, not bothering to pick up the fallen towel. All I could do was stand there with my arms wrapped around my body.

"I put them outside. Marlowe, what are you doing in my house? In the shower, no less? What is going on?" He stood and took a step toward me, almost like he wanted to hug me. I matched his step with one of my own, backwards, slightly away from him.

The smile on his face fell briefly before he grimaced and sat back down.

He was taller now, and seemed larger somehow. Before, the top of my head came to about his lips, making it easy for him to plant a quick kiss here or there. Now, it was almost as if he could rest his chin on top of my head.

His voice had softened, no longer sounding upset or scared. It sent a direct hit to my heart, but I didn't have time to process.

"I'm house sitting. Dog sitting. Your parents… you do know your parents went overseas for the rest of the month, don't you?" I tilted my head, my hair falling over my shoulder. While it was no longer dripping, it was still wet, and I probably looked like a complete mess.

Reid nodded, a smile turning up on his face. "They told me. But they didn't tell me you were staying here. Not that I'm mad about it. I'm really happy to see you, Marlowe."

I kept my eyes on him, not sure what to say to that. "They said you were staying home this summer. They hired me as a last resort, since they had the dogs and it was a last-minute trip."

Reid pursed his lips, and it took all my self-restraint to not think about having kissed them before.

He and I were done. Over. Moved on.

But it seemed like my heart had forgotten that right now.

His smile fell. "So you only agreed because you thought I wouldn't be here?"

Reading between the lines was a specialty of mine, but it wasn't hard to do in this situation. "They hired me. They're paying me to stay here and take care of the house and dogs for the month." I shifted, pulling the towel around my chest tighter and clutching to it for dear life.

His eyes drifted away from my face and down my body. "I, uh, didn't realize..."

His cheeks went pink against his light tawny skin. "Why don't you go get dressed and we can figure this all out?"

He didn't have to say that twice.

Unlikely Allies

EGARDLESS OF WHERE I needed to be later and what my makeup and hair needed to look like, I rushed through getting dressed. I yanked the tank top over my head, and slipped my legs into my favorite black comfy shorts, the outfit I had picked out to ride to the mansion in. Then, I raced back to the main part of the house.

But all that greeted me was Marshmallow, laid on the couch, rolling over for me to scratch her belly as I passed by.

Reid and Noodle were nowhere to be found. A small squeak of a floorboard from upstairs alerted me to where they could be.

Reid's room. The second floor held all the main bedrooms, except the guest room I was staying in. Though it was only a summer house for the Bennetts, it was still a Bayside house. It had four bedrooms, four and a half bathrooms, a library, a movie room, an outdoor pool, an indoor sauna, a large living room, and one heck of a kitchen.

The pantry alone was almost the size of my bedroom back at home.

I made my way up the stairs, careful to announce my presence with some heavy footsteps this time. Even though Reid obviously knew I was here, I didn't feel the need to create another heart attack situation. For either of us.

My heart rate was still elevated, but I had calmed down enough to come up and have a real conversation. The part of my brain that wanted to make this entire situation logical had shut down, but at least Reid and I could discuss him being home and what it meant for my job.

Noodle bolted out of Reid's room before I reached the door, almost knocking me over. He doubled back to sniff the scented lotion on my legs. I had also taken the time to put on some deodorant and the tiniest hint of lip gloss.

Livvy always said to make yourself look good, so they know what they lost. It must have stuck.

"Hey," Reid called from his room. "Come on in."

I stayed in the doorway, though, still hesitant. I chewed on my bottom lip for a moment, the watermelon lip gloss all but disappearing in an instant. Words escaped me. For the first time ever, I had no idea what to say to Reid.

We used to talk for hours on end, whether in person here on the island, or over the phone. While we had only seriously dated last summer, we had been friends for a few years prior. During the school year before last summer, we spoke almost every day. Sometimes, I talked with him more than my friends here on the Cove.

But after our breakup, all communication ceased. The text I sent him on his birthday had been the only message until right now. And he had never even answered it.

Whatever I had thought our reunion would be like, this

was not it. At all. The last thing I expected to be wearing was a towel, while standing soaking wet from the shower. And my first words to him in almost a year were not supposed to start with a scream, either.

"What are you doing here, Reid?" I started, wanting to get the hard part over with. "Your mom said you weren't coming back this summer." Truth and facts were the easiest to stick to right now. The more I spoke, the more I expected myself to ramble on and on, which, in the end, could make me say something I didn't want to say.

Or something I did.

I was mad at Reid. Hurt. Confused. Broken-hearted. The way he ended things still pained me. I hadn't forgiven him for breaking up with me, especially for such a stupid reason as being long distance. It had been a copout, and we both knew it. I just didn't know what the excuse was for.

Seeing him now was like sticking a knife into my heart. A tiny, itty bitty one that stabbed over and over again, like a tattoo gun. I hated it.

Reid took a t-shirt out of his suitcase and shook it out before slipping it on a hanger. He laid it on the bed and repeated the action with another shirt.

"That's true."

I blinked. Was he not understanding my sub-context here? Did I need to spell it out? I watched as he unpacked four more shirts and added them to the pile, the hangers all facing the same way, before he transferred the lot to the closet and hung them up, separating them by exactly three fingers width.

He was acting like I hadn't said anything worth expanding on at all. Pretending like everything between us was completely normal, that this whole situation was normal.

He was acting like we were still friends. Or, at least, friendly.

I didn't know what to do about that. All I wanted was an answer. He wasn't supposed to be here. Mrs. Bennett said he was staying home with his friends.

My mind spiraled with all the what if's and but's and excuses I could come up with. Every fake answer fell into an imaginary list in my imagination.

"So..."

He paused as he exited the closet. "My plans changed. But, like I said, I'm happy to see you. I thought maybe—" He cut himself off and lifted a hand to scratch at the back of his neck, then tugged at his right ear a few times.

"Are you... are you staying?" I glanced between him and the almost empty suitcase on the bed. Obviously, he was planning on sticking around for a while with all the clothes and stuff he brought. What a dumb question.

Reid chuckled and took out the two pairs of jeans, re-folding them before putting them in the dresser drawer. He was only a few feet away from me now. Something inside me wanted to turn, run down the stairs, and hide.

Being so close to him, the smell of his cologne bringing back every memory of last summer... It was too much. He overwhelmed me, and I didn't know how to process it. It was one thing to break up with someone and then be gone from their lives physically. Being back, in person, and right in front of me was another.

"I am," he said softly, leaning against the dresser and staring directly at me. Was he not having the same reaction I was? Did he not feel the same inside? Was being this close not affecting him at all?

Then again, he was the one who broke up with me.

"Okay...," I drew out. I guess I needed to state the obvious then. "Well, I have to work the Mansion Masquerade tonight." Why I mentioned that, I didn't know. Maybe to tell him that even though he was here, my life still went on as normal? That him being here didn't change the plans I already had?

I desperately needed something to cling on to. So far, Reid was great at pretending nothing was different between the two of us. Like he hadn't spent the last ten months shutting me out and leaving me behind.

It couldn't be that easy, though. I had struggled. Mrs. Bennett mentioned Reid struggling too. But maybe... maybe it wasn't because of me. Maybe he really let me go and forgot everything about last summer that easily.

I gulped down my growing emotions. If he was going to act like he moved on, then I could, too.

Reid pushed away from the dresser, zipped the empty suitcase shut, and brought it to the closet, hoisting it onto one of the top shelves and out of the way.

His t-shirt bunched on his arms as he did, and seeing the muscles ripple didn't escape me. I didn't remember him having such defined biceps and triceps last summer.

I ripped my eyes away before he turned and looked at me again, shoving his hands in his pockets and swaying on his heels. "Have you had lunch?"

Did I... did I what? Lunch? He really was in a world of his own, wasn't he?

"Um, no?" I replied truthfully. I didn't even realize it was lunch time. The digital clock on the nightstand proved him right. It was almost two, which meant I had to get ready for the event and leave soon. Set up wouldn't take long, but neither Grandmum nor the organizers would tolerate tardiness.

"Great. I ordered a little something. The plane didn't offer much either, so I was starving. Want to have lunch with me?"

I stared at him, completely bewildered.

"Gennie's. Delivery. I got you a turkey and Swiss sandwich and those chips that you like," he continued, looking at me with expectation. His warm onyx eyes had a sparkle in them, almost mischievous like.

My favorite. He ordered my favorite sandwich and chips, without even consulting me. Just like he would have done last summer.

Before I could answer, chaos erupted downstairs. Both dogs started barking and, from the sound of it, were either chasing each other around or wrestling. Reid and I both glanced toward the noise.

I jerked my thumb over my shoulder. "I'll go take care of them," I suggested, giving myself an out. He had already taken a step in my direction, and I couldn't let him get much closer.

The closer he got, the more I wanted to wrap my arms around him and nuzzle my face into his neck. I wanted to feel his arms wind around my back, holding me and blocking out the world. With him, I was safe. With him, I was loved.

But now? Now I didn't know what to do. What to think. The best option was to keep my distance. Besides, now that he was here, my job would be over and I wouldn't have to see him. At least, not much. I hoped. We still shared a group of friends here, which is how we became close to begin with.

I pounded down the stairs, finding the dogs tearing up the living room while fighting over a toy rope.

"Out! Both of you, outside!" I ordered, still not sure if they understood what I said. But as soon as I opened the sliding door, they bolted, and so did I. The fresh air and the smell of the salt water coming from beyond the beach filled my lungs, providing me with the calmness I desperately needed. I closed my eyes and tilted my chin toward the early afternoon sun, drinking in the warmth, allowing it to spread through me and wash away any worries building up.

Whatever was about to happen this summer would be fine. I could be a big girl and manage having Reid around. We had been friends before; we could do it again.

Even if I knew what he looked like when he told me he loved me. Even though I knew what his lips tasted like when he kissed me. Even if...

I shook my head, stopping myself from going any further down this Reid rabbit hole. It wasn't healthy for me to keep thinking about him this way when he so obviously wanted to move on.

I let the dogs work out their energy, only turning back toward the house when the doorbell rang. The Bennetts had a special system that also made the chime ring out in the backyard, so they didn't miss anyone at the door while outside.

Thinking the lunch Reid ordered had arrived, I whistled for the dogs, but they paid me no attention. I left them outside, knowing they would be fine in the fenced-in yard.

But just before I made it to the kitchen, I stopped dead in my tracks.

Reid was unpacking a large bag with the Gennie's logo on the side over on the kitchen island. The front door was still open, as if he didn't have the hands to close it while dealing with the food.

Which also meant he didn't notice the guy standing in the doorway with a mischievous, sly grin on his face.

Tides of Change

"**H**EY THERE, CRASH," Declan said, his grin growing. He jerked his head over his shoulder a tiny bit in a 'come here' motion. I caught on, but didn't move. "Looks like you have some company."

Reid's head whipped toward Declan at the first sound of his voice. He dropped the food onto the counter and, in three large strides, crossed the room to me. He positioned himself slightly in front of me, his shoulder blocking me from full access to Declan.

My gaze shifted from Declan to Reid, who was now chewing on the inside of his cheek, his nostrils flaring and a twitch developing by his eye.

Reid was *not* a fan of Bayside kids. Their treatment of him when he first arrived at Covington Cove was not the greatest. It was how he ended up with me and my friends.

As far as I knew, Declan had never been a part of the group that bullied Reid. But he never stopped them, either. No Bayside kid had. And considering Reid was a new Baysider and a summer only kid… no one really cared too much about including him. Except for us, because we knew what it was like to be an outsider to the Bayside and Crescent groups.

"What are you doing here, Storms?" Reid said through gritted teeth. His fists balled at his sides.

"I wanted to see if you were free tonight," Declan continued, talking to me, as if Reid wasn't there at all.

Reid took a step away from me, toward Declan. The veins in his forearms popped out with the strain he put on them. "She's not."

Declan laughed. He had the audacity to *laugh* in Reid's face. "I wasn't talking to you, Bennett."

"How did you know I was staying here?" I asked, remembering that I never told Declan I was housesitting. I leaned to the side to stare at him, needing to interrupt the power struggle he was having with Reid right now.

If Declan knew what was good for him, he would back away. Reid looked ready to tear him to shreds.

But he just shrugged and threw me another charming grin, dimple and all. "Power of elimination? I asked around. And your bike is out front. That was a pretty big giveaway."

I blinked a few times, stopping myself before my jaw dropped. "You… you asked around? About me?"

A low growl came from Reid's throat just then, only loud enough for me to hear. I shivered, but didn't look at him.

"So, are you? Free tonight?" Declan asked again, pulling my attention back to the original question.

"She has to work," Reid answered for me in a clipped tone.

"I wasn't asking you, but thanks for the schedule update." Declan pointed at Reid. "Why are you even here? Word was that you wouldn't be coming back."

I gasped, shocked at the rudeness from Declan. He was one of the most charming and polite kids; all the adults always said so. Was it just an act? Had I not been around him enough yet to see his true self?

Or... or was he *jealous*?

Also, where did he hear that? I hadn't even known if Reid was coming back this summer or not. It wasn't until Mrs. Bennett confirmed that I knew he wasn't. How could Declan possibly have known? Or was he making it all up?

I cleared my throat, needing to diffuse the tension before everyone in this kitchen exploded. "He's right, though. I do have to work. It's the Mansion Masquerade tonight. I'll be there late."

Declan shook his head like it made no difference what time I got off. "The Mansion Masquerade is always a good time. And definitely goes late into the night. But whatever time you get off, just text me. I'll wait up for my girl."

My jaw dropped at the same time Reid lunged for Declan. I grabbed his arm and pulled him back, which seemed to shake him out of his stupor.

He stared at me, his long lashes sweeping over his cheek as he blinked a few times. Then, he glanced between me and Declan once more, his jaw tensing with every passing second.

Reid huffed, getting both of our attention. "Lunch is ready," he forced out in a voice barely above a whisper. He went to plate my sandwich and chips, throwing a can of soda next to it on the kitchen island.

I wanted to grab his hand and apologize for Declan. I wanted to say that what he said wasn't true.

But I couldn't. Because I was still in a state of shock. Did Declan really think that hanging out once meant I was 'his girl?' I didn't even know if I *wanted* to be his girlfriend.

The only time we got together, he surprised me. I didn't have a choice. While it was nice, it was also a surprise and I couldn't say no. Besides, it had been my birthday and he had been the only person to do anything about it.

But *boyfriend*? Girlfriend? What was *that* about?

Then again, I was single and there was no one stopping me from going on dates. No one stopping me from being labeled 'my girl.'

Even if I wasn't sure I wanted it.

Reid rubbed at his chin, his breathing labored, but didn't look at us again. Though I didn't owe him anything, I also didn't want to torture him.

"Right. It'll be pretty late. I'll text you tomorrow, okay?"

"There's also a party on Monday. 372 Bayside. Bring your suit."

"Great. Talk to you tomorrow." Right now, I just wanted him *out*.

I went to take Declan's hand to guide him back to the front door when he wrapped an arm around my waist, pulled me close to him, and leaned down, planting a soft kiss on my cheek. "Okay, Crash. Tomorrow."

He added a wink while I stood there, stunned, before he showed himself out, not looking back once. *Crash?* Did he just give me a nickname? And it had to be one like Crash?

I lifted a hand to my cheek, wondering what in the world had just happened. What made Declan decide that kissing me was a good move? Couldn't he read the same tension I did?

Or... or I was right. And this entire thing was just to stab Reid in the side, to make him jealous.

After a moment, I lowered myself onto the stool next to

Reid, in front of the plate of food waiting for me. Reid was already halfway through his sandwich.

He didn't even glance my way when he lifted his soda to his lips and took a large gulp, slamming it onto the counter with a thud. A splash of soda flew out of the can, but he didn't pay attention. Instead, he yanked his phone out of his pocket and swiped it open. His fingers flew over the screen like he was sending a text.

I carefully picked up a chip and nibbled on it, suddenly not as hungry. If my appetite came back, I could just snag some food from the kitchens at the mansion. They always set aside some snacks for employees during big events.

But that didn't do much to help my stomach now. It was in knots, just like my mind. The whole situation was so unexpected, I had no idea what to do about it.

If Declan had come just to ask me to a party, that would have been fine. But that wasn't what ended up happening. The second he saw Reid, he was determined to make him jealous. To wound him, using me as bait.

But Reid had no jurisdiction to say anything about my love life. He lost that chance.

"Declan Storms, huh?" Reid muttered a few minutes later. "You're dating Declan Storms, of all people?"

I took offense to the way he said that. He had no idea what happened between Declan and me or what we were doing.

I held my breath for a few seconds, calming myself so I didn't burst out with something I didn't want to say. "Not really dating. Just... hanging out, I guess." It was new to me, too.

Reid snorted, pointing the sandwich in his hand toward the front door. "Might want to tell him that."

I rolled my eyes. Yup, he was definitely jealous. Part of me was happy he was. It served him right for breaking up with me.

But I needed to get one thing straight.

"That's not the issue, Reid. You being home is."

Rediscovering Connections

EID'S BROWS RAISED, and he blinked a few times before pursing his lips. "Excuse me?"

"I didn't mean that rudely," I stated, not wanting him to think that. "But, you being here poses a slight issue. I was hired to house sit."

Reid nodded slowly, as if he still wasn't catching on.

"To *house sit*, Reid. Your parents hired me to stay here because no one was going to be home. Hired me to take care of the dogs. But now you're here, so *I* don't need to be."

The look on Reid's face didn't change. It was completely blank, like he comprehended what I said, yet didn't understand why I was making a big deal out of it.

"Reid!" Exasperation set in. I pushed my still damp curls away from my face.

He just shook his head and crunched on the last of his chips. Standing, he crumpled all his garbage into a ball and threw it away in the can under the sink. "Marlowe. If you leave, you don't get paid, right?"

I shrugged. Obviously, that would be the case. First things first, one of us would have to call the Bennetts and let them know Reid was on the island for the summer. Once they knew that, they would most likely pay me for the days I had been here so far, because they were fair and kind people, but then I would be out.

"Not a huge deal. Can't expect to get paid for a job that I'm not doing." I finished my lunch and wrapped up the remaining sandwich to put in the fridge. Even if I left, I knew Reid would eat it eventually.

Reid leaned against the counter, his arms crossed over his chest. Again, his muscles strained against the sleeves of his t-shirt and I couldn't look away. When did he get those? Did he start working out this year?

I finally looked up, finding him with the expression I used to hate. The all-knowing look. The one that said, "Marlowe, you're wrong and you know you're wrong. So I'm giving you a moment until you figure it out yourself."

I used to hate it because he was always right. It just took me a few extra seconds to get the lightbulb moment.

"Of course it's a big deal, Mars. First off, my parents trusted you. They—"

"They called me as a last resort," I interrupted. They hadn't chosen me for any specific reason other than that.

He shook his head, a curl escaping the bunch and falling over his forehead. He reached up and pushed it back, his hands combing through his hair as he did.

My heart skipped a beat.

"They called you because they trust you. But also, if it was as last minute as you say, then they probably were paying you some good money to drop everything and come stay here." He quirked his brow.

My eyes narrowed, and I pursed my lips, folding my arms over my chest in an effort to intimidate him. It was the only thing that used to work. Usually it made him laugh, in my lame attempt to look intimidating, but at least it got my point across.

This time, though, he didn't laugh. He stared me down until I broke.

I shrugged again. He wasn't wrong; the money the Bennetts were offering was more than I would make at the Seaside Cafe for the entire summer. I had already made a mental list of all the things I could do with that money. Namely, putting it toward college and a car.

"Again, not a huge deal. It wasn't like I was planning on the money. It was a nice bonus, but that's all. I still have my job at the cafe and at the mansion when needed. I'm good."

Reid frowned, his head tilted to the side. I couldn't tell what was running through his mind. Regardless of what he thought, my points were valid. There was only the small issue of working the Masquerade tonight. But before I could ask Reid if I could pack up and go in the morning instead, he had slipped his buzzing phone out of his pocket and swiped at it a few times before putting it to his ear and walking toward the backyard where the dogs were rough housing.

I took that as my cue to leave, too. As soon as I got back into the guest room, I groaned. I still had to do my hair and makeup, not to mention pack my work clothes in my bag. And because of all the craziness that happened, I now had less than an hour to finish before I had to leave. Reid's house was much further from the mansion than mine, and it would take almost twice as long to bike there. I had plenty of time when I was in the shower earlier, but that slipped away and I would have to rush.

I heard the sliding door open and Reid return, so I stuck my head out of the bedroom and called for him. "Hey, since the event is going to go pretty late tonight, is it okay if I pack up and head out in the morning? I don't have time to get ready, pack, swing by my house, and make it to work."

Reid appeared in the hallway and shot back the look he seemed to have permanently attached to his face now—one of confusion. "You're biking to the mansion? That's on the other side of the island."

I grimaced. "I know. I was going to change when I got there. If I bike slow, I won't sweat too much." But the worry in his eyes told me that wasn't what he was concerned with.

"I'll drive you." I opened my mouth to argue, but he held up a hand to stop me. "And what do you mean, pack up in the morning?"

Was this boy not paying attention to anything I had been saying this entire time? Honestly, from the moment he stood in the kitchen with a bat, everything I said seemed to go in one ear and out the other. It was like he didn't bother to digest my comments the same way I had been hanging on to his every word.

He had my entire focus, yet I was an afterthought for him.

"To leave, obviously. Reid, are you not understanding what I've been saying? You're here. Your parents don't need me to house sit anymore. The only issue right now is that I don't want to carry my bags home or to the mansion, not that I really have time to do either—"

Once again, he cut me off. Maybe that was the problem—he was so caught up in his own thoughts, he wasn't considering mine.

"You're not leaving, Marlowe."

Clues and Confessions

THIS BACK AND forth was giving me whiplash.

What was he going on about now? Why were we having this same conversation seventeen times and not getting any further than we did before he arrived?

"Are you holding me hostage?" I tried to joke, but he didn't laugh. I was at a loss. The only thing I could think of doing was cracking jokes. It was an old standby when I got nervous, but right now, it failed.

Reid stared at me with his dark brown eyes, like he was trying to memorize every detail of my face. They softened after a moment, one side of his mouth turning up in a half smile. A sharp pain hit my chest.

It was the same way he used to look at me. Before.

It was the same way I had wanted him to look at me for months. The way I wished he would FaceTime me before bed, answering the phone with that exact same look.

It was the same way I had dreamed of him multiple times since we broke up. Since he broke up with me.

I didn't want him looking at me like that. Not right now. Not when my confusion was at an all-time high.

Mostly, I didn't want him looking at me like that because it flooded my mind with memories.

Like the sun setting behind him as he walked a few feet ahead of me on the beach, his shoes dangling from one hand, looking over his shoulder at me. I had found a seashell the same color as the sunset and was holding it up for him to see.

Or the time I rambled on and on about the new Zane Hunter movie, gushing about the romance between the couple. He had listened intently, agreeing with my takes, and not even cringing when I talked about how emotional the mushy love scenes were.

Those were times he used this look. Back when we were happy. In love.

Not now. I didn't want him looking at me like that now. Not after he broke my heart in a million pieces, for reasons I still didn't fully understand.

"What about this…" he started, shoving his hands in his jeans pocket. It was only then that I realized how tired he had to be from his day of travel. It took almost an hour to drive from the nearest large airport, which meant his plane must have taken off at the crack of dawn. His t-shirt was wrinkled, which was completely abnormal for him. "What if you stay?"

I blinked, my gaze shooting up to his again. Stay? Stay where? Here? Did he really expect me to stay here now that he was home?

That was it. I was certain.

Reid Bennett had lost his ever-loving mind.

"Uhh…" I didn't even know how to respond to that.

"Look, my parents don't know I'm here."

"Who did you just call then?" I had assumed he called his parents to let them know he landed and was safe and sound. It was the obvious assumption.

Reid shook his head and waved his hand. "That was nothing. Anyway, they told me they were going overseas. I thought that meant the place would be empty."

Again, I blinked a few times, trying to figure him out. "What about Noodle and Fluff?"

That got a little chuckle from him. "As horrible as it sounds, I didn't really think about that. I guess I thought they left them with a friend or something. Either way, I figured the house would be empty, and I'd have the place to myself."

My phone buzzed on the bed in front of me, diverting my attention for a second. I ignored the message, but glanced at the time. I desperately needed to get ready, or I would be late.

"Listen, if my parents don't know I'm here, then what's stopping them from continuing to pay you?" Reid said, a brow raised.

I jerked at the bluntness of the comment and stumbled into the door frame.

"Stay here. Do the job. Get the money. I'll fess up eventually, but even if I don't tell them until closer to when they return, you still get the money. Or..." His face fell for a moment, but he lifted the corner of his mouth, masking his obvious disappointment. "Or, I mean, you can leave. I can handle the dogs and the house. But I won't tell if you won't."

"I would never swindle someone for their money," I blurted out. There was no way I would accept payment from the Bennett's for a job I didn't do. But that meant...

"If they don't know I'm here, they think *you're* here. So why not stay and make some extra cash?" Reid said, almost as if he were reading my mind.

"Stay... with you?" I whispered. I bit my lip, so completely unsure what was going on. Did he really think we should stay in a house together? For an entire month? If this was last summer, I would have said yes in a heartbeat. But that was then.

This was now.

And even though I had wanted to see what the summer would be like with him back on the island... I didn't want this. The closeness. The proximity alone wouldn't allow my heart to shut up. If it had its way, I would have leaped into Reid's arms the second he put the baseball bat down and not let go.

Good thing my brain was somewhat smarter. Right now, though, it was too conflicted to be of any use. I was glad Reid was back. Really. Our friends would be happy too.

But staying here? Could my need for the money outweigh the hurt in my heart and allow me to continue on with him sleeping only a floor away?

Reid's face fell again, but it took him an extra beat to cover it up this time. "I'll stay out of your way, I promise. Like I said, I thought the house was empty, so I was planning on lying low this summer anyway."

There was something in the way he phrased that comment that concerned me.

When Reid and his family first moved here, he didn't have the easiest time. His parents were newly rich, their company having taken off a year or two before. They had been looking for a summer rental on the east coast when their realtor got a surprise call about this house going up soon.

They bought it sight unseen and came to the island that following summer.

But Reid hadn't lived the same life as most of the Baysider kids. While a good majority of them were also summer-only residents, they had still grown up around money most of their lives. Reid hadn't. He didn't own the same stuff they had, hadn't shared in their life experiences.

Therefore, they rejected him. Though his address was the same as theirs, they didn't take kindly to him. That's how he ended up hanging out with Liam and Caleb and integrating into our group.

It made me wonder what he really planned on doing this summer. He usually stuck with us, but now that we were broken up... what had his plan been? He wanted to lie low, but did that mean avoid me? Avoid our friends?

I wouldn't have made him choose. I could be the bigger person and be in the same place with him if he wanted to hang out. Though the stabbing pain in my heart had yet to subside since seeing him a few hours ago, I would have done it.

Another thought hit me just then. I knew Reid was waiting for an answer, but I couldn't help but wonder.

If I hadn't been here when he first arrived, would he even have told me he was back? Considering I had to hear of his plans to stay home from his parents, part of me thought he wouldn't have. That I would have heard it from someone else, or not known until I saw him around the island.

I didn't realize I had been basically staring at him until he cocked his head to the side and cleared his throat.

"Um, okay," I squeaked out, still not exactly sure what I was saying. "Deal."

I had a job to do. I had money to make.

Money that I needed if I was ever going to get out of this town. Preferably with a car and to college, but money didn't discriminate. Once it was in my bank account, I could use it for whatever I needed.

"I have to get ready," I said before Reid could continue on. I would barely have time to dry my hair, much less make it look presentable.

"Just holler when you're ready and I'll take you over there." Reid turned and made his way back to the kitchen, rummaging in the fridge for another soda.

Without a second thought, I skipped to the bathroom and grabbed my hairdryer. Because of lack of time, and the need to slick it into a bun anyway, I pulled off the diffuser attachment and started brushing and drying.

Once I finished my hair and threw some simple make-up on, I headed to the bedroom to get dressed. Now that Reid was driving, I didn't have to pack my work clothes separately and wear my tank top and shorts while I biked. That was nice.

After smoothing my white button down into my black trousers, I slipped my feet into my all black tennis shoes and added the black belt. The uniform was simple, but totally not my style.

With one more check in the mirror over the dresser, I added a little lip balm and declared myself good enough with the time I had. A few of my freckles were darkening, popping through my already tanned skin on my nose. I didn't dare cover them, so my makeup consisted of mascara, a hint of blush, and some concealer for the dark circles under my eyes.

Reid must have let the dogs in, because Noodle flew into my room. If he was inside, that meant Reid was getting ready to leave, which meant I needed to go. He was always the punctual one, which came in handy when I was the late one.

"I'm coming!" I hollered toward the front. Reid didn't answer, but Marshmallow took the comment as an invitation to join Noodle on the bed. Happy that they were comfortable, I grabbed my bag and went for the door.

Just as I reached for the handle, my phone buzzed. I shouldn't have gone for it, knowing Reid was probably waiting by the door to the garage, but I slipped it out just to double check. If it was Grandmum with instructions for the event, then I needed to know, anyway.

But it wasn't Grandmum. It was the same unknown number that sent Eleanor's video message the other day.

The message I had all but forgotten about in all the hullabaloo with Reid and Declan.

UNKNOWN: Marlowe. Your game begins now. Follow the clues to the prize. But know, in true Eleanor form, the prize isn't the *only* prize. Keep that in mind.

UNKNOWN: Climb the stairs where memories run free, find the room where nostalgia's the key.

Hidden Messages

"Marlowe... I don't want to rush you, but we should probably get going," Reid called from the kitchen.

He was right. I had spent too long staring at the phone in my hand, trying to figure out what in the world this message meant.

The first question—what *game*? Eleanor left me a game to play? With clues? What was it, a scavenger hunt of sorts? She had mentioned something about a quest, but I guess I hadn't taken her *literally*.

Not able to spare another second, I jogged to the kitchen and out the door Reid held open for me. He blocked Noodle from following us into the garage and shut the door behind him as I slid into the passenger seat.

My mind was spinning.

Climb the stairs. What stairs? My house didn't even have stairs. Reid's did, but that didn't make any sense. Why would whoever sent this be talking about Reid's house?

But lots of places had stairs. How was I supposed to know which set of stairs? The mansion had a *ton* of stairs. Even a staircase that led to literally nowhere. It ended at a wall. Eleanor once said it was blocked off because it once led to part of the attic, and a few decades prior, someone had fallen through and the whole area was deemed unsafe. They never used that part of the attic anyway, so they walled it off. But the historical society, which somehow didn't include Eleanor, but her niece, Pearl, declared the staircase an original part of the home and unable to be removed.

That obviously couldn't be the answer, though.

"Everything okay?" Reid asked softly.

I glanced over at him, having almost forgotten he was in the car. The ride to the mansion wasn't long, but tourist traffic had us at a crawl.

"You're really quiet, that's all."

I nodded. "I'm fine. Just... never mind. It's nothing."

I could tell he wanted to push a little and get me to fess up, but he refrained.

Was that how it would be between us now? Awkward? Dancing around each other, tiptoeing in order not to cross any invisible boundaries?

We used to share everything, never really holding back secrets. But now... I didn't know what to tell him. Eleanor's original message said to tell only those that I trusted explicitly.

Had this been last summer, Reid would have known every single detail about the original video and the text message clue the second I received it.

Truthfully, I did still trust him. His breaking up with me didn't automatically make me lose that. It just... made it harder to justify. Sure, I could tell him, and I knew he wouldn't share it with anyone else, because he would know how important it was to me. He was that kind of guy.

I hesitated, though, unsure why. Something deep down told me to keep it to myself, no matter how it pained me.

"Hey, if this is about you staying..." Reid started, getting my attention back once more.

"No! No, it's not that," I blurted out. I had barely given that any more thought since he said it. Once I got the text, it flew out of my mind completely. "No, um, yeah, I guess it'll be fine. Are you sure you're cool lying to your parents, though?"

Reid Bennett was a lot of things, but he wasn't a liar. Any time he tried, his ears turned a deep crimson color.

He pulled into the Covington Estates employee parking lot like he had a million times before when he dropped me off for work, and put the car in park.

"It's not really lying, is it? Just... not telling the entire truth of where I am. Plus, they said they wouldn't bother me this summer, so I doubt they'll be calling much." He frowned for a flash, but looked up at me again. "I don't want to ruin your summer either, Marlowe, so when I say I'll stay out of your way, I mean it. Promise."

I couldn't help but grin a little. I thanked him for the ride as I slid out of the car.

"Give me a call when you're done and I'll come pick you up, okay?" he called right before I closed the door.

"It's alright, Grandmum will be there as always. Besides, it'll be pretty late when we're done breaking everything down."

He nodded and pulled away, and I headed inside, grateful for him driving so I didn't show up in a sweaty mess.

The employee entrance was a small side door on the south side of the mansion, leading directly into the storage rooms and the prep kitchens.

It looked like the catering staff had already arrived, the serving crew putting on their finishing touches. Unlike most events, where they would be in all black with a black half apron around their waists and a white bow tie, they were in full suits and long black gowns. They even wore masquerade masks. It was their job to blend in with the crowd, not to stand out and draw attention away from the guests.

The Mansion Masquerade was also one of the major events that extra housekeeping was called in for. Our duties included setting up the banquet hall, and cleaning all the main bathrooms and a few guest rooms in the East Wing.

I needed to put my bag down in a cubby, then find Grandmum. They always put her in charge of the housekeeping staff at events like this, since she had the most experience out of everyone. She was also the strictest one on staff. Even though I was her granddaughter, I didn't get let off any easier than anyone else.

As I made my way into the set-up room and through the prep kitchen, I ducked and weaved around the caterers and the waitstaff. I almost collided with Chloe, a girl in my grade with shoulder length dark hair and the brightest blue eyes I had ever seen. She had on an amazing dress, even if she was tripping over it a bit. That was, until she finished putting her heels on. She was normally around Emma's height, but with the four-inch heels, she now was almost as tall as me.

I started to say hello, but got interrupted. "No facial piercings!" a tall guy in a chef's coat yelled after Chloe, who then scurried to the cubbies.

I smiled and hurried off to find Grandmum. It wasn't hard—I followed the stern voice and went against the rest of the crew that was scattering off to various parts of the mansion.

"Hi," I said sweetly, giving her a big grin. She returned with her normal scowl, which made me smile bigger. It was like she didn't miss me at all, but deep down, I knew she did. If she didn't, she would have been chewing me out for being late.

And I wasn't even late. I just happened to be the last person into the room for assignments, but that didn't matter to Grandmum.

"First floor bathroom, east wing, and coat duty," she muttered, handing me both an assignment card and a basket of supplies. The card had a checklist attached for both setup and breakdown, and the basket held cleaning supplies and items for the bathroom. It weighed close to ten pounds, so I held it with both hands.

"How are you, Grandmum?" I asked before she left to find more people to scold.

"Lovely. The house is noise free, except for that darn cat that won't leave me alone."

I giggled. "Mr. Munchkin just wants a few treats now and then. Throw them out the window and he'll get out of your hair."

Mr. Munchkin wasn't my cat. I had no idea who he actually belonged to, but he visited daily. I made the mistake of giving him a treat once, and now I couldn't get rid of him. He probably was driving Grandmum crazy, tapping on the kitchen window every day.

Grandmum grunted. "Darn cat," she reiterated. "You're doing well, all alone in that giant house?"

I *almost* said that I wasn't alone, not anymore, but remembered at the last second that Reid was still a secret. Not that I expected Grandmum to go tattling to his parents. "Yeah. I'm okay. The dogs are there too, so it's not super lonely."

"Darn dogs." Grandmum wasn't really a pet kind of person. They were too messy, according to her. "Get to work now."

I gave her a smile, then headed to the East Wing to get started on my work.

After setting up, the actual event was rather dull. I took coats for those that had them, which were few and far between due to the warm weather. Mia Covington handed me a shawl, thanking me for taking it because she thought it was ugly and didn't match her dress, but her mother made her wear it.

Her mother was Eleanor's great niece, Olive. Mia's family were some of the only Covington's that still lived on the island. There were less than ten out of the entire extended family. Mia's house was on Covington Crescent, of course, right next to the mansion, but on the other side of the property lines.

While everyone else enjoyed the masquerade, I wandered around, thinking about the clue from earlier that evening. I still had no idea what stairs meant, even though I looked at every staircase in the mansion with a side eye.

The part about nostalgia had me hung up, too. The only nostalgia I was getting right now was for Eleanor. Her portrait hung over the fireplace in the room where I set the coats on a temporary coat rack. The painting was from her youth, where she was about twenty-one years old.

She was gorgeous, with pink bow-shaped lips and bright blue eyes, just like her grandmother.

It was times like these when Eleanor would randomly find me. I had a habit of strolling around the mansion while Grandmum or Mom worked, or exploring between setups and takedowns. Eleanor would wander with me, telling me stories about the mansion, growing up on the island, and everything between.

Sometimes we roamed so long and far that people had to come find Eleanor, as they needed her for whatever she had been doing before she saw me. I always apologized, but she would pat my hand and say, "It's been a pleasure, my little sunshine."

Before I knew it, another housekeeper came to find me, saying the guests were ready to go home. I rolled out the coat rack to the main foyer, handing items back as the owners came for them.

After a quick tidy of the bathroom that didn't seem to get used tonight, my job was over. I headed for my cubby to get my bag, then looked around.

The clock in the corner struck two in the morning when I passed it on my way to find Grandmum. She always waited for me to be done before heading home, standing stiff and tall next to the door to the employee parking lot.

Except... this time, she wasn't there.

Once again, I found myself stranded and left behind.

Island Revelations

"NO, NO, NO," I whispered to myself, cautiously glancing around to see if I knew anyone else who might still be here. My index finger began subconsciously tapping against my thumb as I tried to figure out what to do now.

It was late. Dark. And even though the Cove was a relatively safe place to live, walking across the entire island in the middle of the night wasn't the smartest idea.

Most of the adults in the kitchens were from the country club catering team, so they were out. Even though we worked a lot of the same events here at the mansion, I didn't know them well enough to ask for a ride.

I paced in front of the door, unsure what to do. Reid said to call him for a ride home, but it was *two in the morning*. There was no way.

Emma was probably still awake, but her parents didn't allow her to use her car past midnight. Same with Norah. And, like me, Caleb didn't have his own car.

I bit down on my lip. I could call Grandmum and see if she wasn't too far from the mansion yet.

With another thought, I realized that wouldn't work. She refused to answer her phone while driving, so she wouldn't even see that I had called until she got home.

There was one other person who said to call him after the event. Maybe Dec—

"Are you lost?" someone asked behind me, interrupting my thoughts. I paused, trying to place the voice before I turned around.

"Mia?"

She raised her eyebrows as I spun to face her. "What are you doing?"

I grimaced, unsure how to explain to her that I was stranded. "Uh... my grandmum left," was all I could spit out.

Mia Covington was a Crescent kid, but wasn't as stuck up or snobby as many of them. She was also what I called intimidatingly pretty. Like you knew it was natural, but when she was all dressed up like this, she looked like she belonged on a red carpet.

With her long brown hair almost down to her waist, her pale pink lips, and wide Covington blue eyes, she could have been a model. Add all that to her floor length, strapless sapphire dress, she was absolutely stunning. I couldn't pull off a look like hers to save my life.

"Oh," she replied, pursing her lips. "Do you need a ride?"

I shook my head, knowing where she was going to go with that sentence. My eyes widened as I said, "No, no, it's fine. I'll... walk."

She gave me the *look*, which was warranted, especially since I already had the same thought.

"It's two in the morning, Marlowe. Let me grab Mom's keys, and I'll be right back."

Once again, I stood by myself, dumbfounded that she even knew my name. The Crescent kids, especially the Covington's, all attended a private school on the mainland. Though we had grown up on the same island together, we had never really interacted.

I thanked her a million times, then apologized before mentioning that I was house sitting at Reid's, as Bayside Boulevard was on the opposite side of the island. She gave me an interesting look for a second before moving on and keeping up polite conversation.

She was so much like Eleanor, it pained my heart. I didn't tell her that, though; it would have been weird. But talking to her calmed me down, just like every time I spoke with Eleanor.

I extended my heartfelt gratitude as we pulled into the driveway. She once again waved me off and said goodnight. I watched as she headed back for the boulevard, then I turned to the house.

All the lights were off, as expected. I knew the alarm code, so that wouldn't be a problem. That was, if Reid set it. Did he leave it off so it didn't go off when I came in? I would have to set it no matter what, which was always a bit scary to do. Accidentally setting it off was a major fear, especially since the Bennetts weren't even in the country.

I used the key and opened the door, keeping an ear out for the telltale beeping of the alarm. It didn't come, so I was in the clear.

What I was not in the clear of were the dogs. Noodle and Marshmallow came sprinting toward me, sliding on the wood floor, crashing into each other and me. I bent down and pet them, trying to get them to hush up. Even though Reid's bedroom was upstairs, with the ruckus they were making, he was sure to wake up.

"Out! Go outside and get your crazies out!" I whispered to them, pointing to the back door. They seemed to understand and bolted for the door again, almost crashing into that, too.

As soon as I got them out, I turned to head to the guest room, but caught something out of the corner of my eye. A light coming from down the far hall, from the library.

Thinking Reid left it on, I started down the hall, only to be surprised when I found him sitting in the oversized armchair, angled away from me. I could clearly see him, but unless he looked up from his book and to the side, he wouldn't see me.

My heart leaped into my throat as I took him in.

Gray sweatpants. A faded black Star Wars t-shirt that looked familiar, but never looked like *that* on him. Glasses on his face. A book in his hand.

There was no doubt about my earlier question now. Reid must have been working out lately. He had become the definition of ripped.

As if he could read my mind, he lifted his arms and stretched, yawning at the same time. My jaw dropped as I caught sight of his four pack, which looked suspiciously close to becoming a six-pack sometime soon. I had never seen such a defined set of abs in my *life*. Most of the guys at school that flaunted their assets had great bodies, but more of a flat torso.

Reid's was... well, what I assumed the term washboard abs actually looked like.

He lowered his arms and cracked his neck side to side while yawning again. That's when I remembered who I was staring at and what time it was.

I gasped, which caught his attention. He fumbled with the book for a second before putting it on the side table and leaping to his feet.

"Marlowe! You have to stop scaring me like this," he said with a sly grin. He reached up and ruffled his hand through his curls, messing them up even more than they were.

Oh, he knew what he was doing. There was no way he looked like that, gave me a smile like that, and didn't know what he was doing to me.

"I'm so sorry. What are you doing up? You're never up this late," I basically whispered, not trusting myself to speak any louder for fear of what might accidentally slip out of my mouth. My mind was still set on his body. And the way his hair looked like he had been running his hands through it for the past hour. And his glasses, giving him that hot nerdy look that I loved so much. And—

No. *No.* I could *not* be thinking about Reid Bennett this way. Not anymore.

I tried to shake him loose from my brain, but all it wanted to focus on was his abs. The thought kept playing over and over on a loop.

At least I'd have some good dreams tonight.

Reid stood and shoved his hands in his pockets, rocking back on his heels. "Just making sure you didn't need a ride or anything."

I paused. The thought of calling him had crossed my mind, but he usually never stayed up too late. Even when we were dating, he went to bed before midnight. Add that to the fact that his plane probably left at sunrise yesterday morning. He had to be exhausted.

Yet... he waited up. For me.

"You... waited up for me?" I whispered again, my eyes meeting his now. My heart fluttered to a stop in my chest as his face softened and he nodded. He reached up and pulled on his right ear for a moment, and I frowned.

He only did that when he was nervous. Or uncomfortable. Was I making him nervous?

"Of course. I wanted to make sure you got back safely. Well, goodnight," he said softly, turning sideways to pass by me. I let him go, watching as he turned down the hall and headed toward the stairs.

It took me a moment to collect myself and let the dogs back in before heading to my room. The entire encounter lasted only a few minutes, but felt like hours.

Instead of being tired, my body was now exhilarated. On fire. Pumped up. Full of adrenaline. Sleep wouldn't be coming for a while, so after I changed, washed my face, and brushed my teeth, I laid in bed, scrolling on my phone mindlessly.

It was almost three now, and I had to work the afternoon shift at the cafe later. I needed to get some sleep.

Just before I put my phone on the nightstand for the night, it vibrated in my hand.

DECLAN: You up for the party on Monday, Crash?

I blinked, looking at the time stamp to double check that he just sent it now, and I hadn't missed it from earlier. Who texted someone about a party at three in the morning?

Especially after I specifically told him I would text him *tomorrow*.

But sure enough, it was a brand new message.

The first thing I did was check my work schedule. I kept a list of that on my phone too, for easy access, mainly. Logging into the website where the cafe posted shifts was obnoxious and unnecessary.

> **ME:** Maybe. I have to work that afternoon, but get off around seven.

> **DECLAN:** 372 Bayside. See you then.

Once again, he didn't offer to pick me up. Just like he didn't offer to drive me home from the cafe the first time we hung out.

I hadn't had many boyfriends in my life, but the stark differences between Reid and Declan were already starting to show...

The only problem was that Reid was no longer an option. At least Declan seemed interested in me, even if his gentlemanly manners could use some work.

Coastal Crossroads

MORNING CAME WAY too early again. It always did. As a night owl, the early morning sun streaming in my face was my version of a nightmare. Even though the Mansion Masquerade had been three days ago, I still felt like I was trying to catch up on sleep.

But Noodle and Marshmallow didn't seem to care about my abnormal sleeping pattern. They jumped on the bed at seven, knowing their food schedule by heart.

I yawned and stretched my arms above my head, then took out my hair tie. I raked my hands through my knotty curls as I brought them back down. Between the lack of hair care last night and the bun I slept in, my hair wasn't looking so hot this morning.

The first thing on my to do list was coffee, though. Maybe even a double dose—I could make some here while I let the dogs out, fed them, and possibly took a shower just to redo my hair. Then, I could bike up to Muggsy's for another cup.

I reached down to pet Noodle, but he had other ideas, taking off out the door with Marshmallow on his heels.

"Okay, okay, I'm up, I'm up. Man, you two are demanding. How do you even know what time it is? You can't read a clock." I stretched my legs, then dangled them over the side of the bed while I yawned one more time.

As soon as I put the dogs safely outside to run around, I headed toward the pantry to get their food. That's when I smelled it—the scent of freshly brewed coffee.

I paused at the counter, my gaze traveling down the length of the marble slab until I found the culprit. It shouldn't have been such a big mystery, but *I* hadn't turned the coffee-

maker on. Yet, it sat there, pot full of steaming hot, freshly made morning go-go juice.

There was even a mug sitting next to it.

Mr. and Mrs. Bennett were big coffee drinkers, so they opted for a maker with a large pot, instead of those one cup brewers.

I was grateful for that, because I could easily throw back three cups in a morning, and brewing a single cup each time seemed wasteful, not to mention time consuming.

Marshmallow pawed at the back door, begging to be let in, so I gave up on the coffee and went back to get them. I filled their bowls, and they dug in.

Out of energy at the moment, I plopped onto a bar stool and pulled out my phone. Emma had texted about switching shifts next week, so I answered her first, happily accepting the switch.

Grandmum hadn't sent anything. Part of me wondered if she even realized she left me at the mansion. Maybe she thought since I got a ride there, that I had a ride back. If I was still at home, she wouldn't have left without me, I was sure about that. It must have been an oversight.

I opened my texts again as a thank you from Emma came in, but that wasn't the one I clicked into.

The message from the unknown sender, with the clue to Eleanor's game, was what my finger landed on. After the Masquerade, I had completely forgotten. I felt guilty about that. Eleanor had set something special up, and I hadn't even thought about it all weekend.

"Climb the stairs where memories run free, find the room where nostalgia's the key," I whispered to myself, rereading the message over and over.

It *seemed* easy enough. But I found myself completely stumped. Was I overthinking it? Was there some hidden meaning I wasn't understanding?

Also, how many clues would there be? Was this the only one? And what did the first text mean, the prize wasn't the only prize? How many prizes were there?

Nothing made sense, and I knew I would continue to sit there and drive myself crazy until I got some caffeine into my system. Everything was better post-coffee.

I glanced up, staring once again at the coffee pot and the mug.

At the same time, Reid padded down the stairs. My attention drifted toward him, flashbacks of him in the library filling my mind.

He had on a pair of gym shorts and a plain white t-shirt now, another tighter fit one. He also had a small towel in both hands, rubbing at his damp hair. If he turned around, there would be wet spots on the back of his shirt, around his shoulders, because he always forgot to dry that area.

I snapped my mouth shut before I started drooling, because seeing him again right now didn't make anything better. Being attracted to him made all my emotions and feelings even more confused and sad.

"Good morning," he said, sounding way more awake and chipper than I felt. I waved and turned back around, exiting out of the text message. "Hey, a little déjà vu, huh?" He chuckled, glancing at the towel and back at me.

I rolled my eyes, remembering our first encounter with me in the towel. It seemed like a lifetime ago. "Funny."

"Coffee?" he asked, heading toward the pot and pouring a cup.

I gaped at him. Reid didn't drink coffee. He despised it. It didn't matter if it was hot or iced, a latte or even a frappe. The taste of coffee in any form made him cringe and gag. He preferred green tea or just water.

"You made coffee?" I questioned as he slid over the mug toward me, having put some half and half in it. I accepted it gratefully, but stared at him in amazement.

He glanced over his shoulder with a grin. "Yeah. I set it up almost two hours ago, but just hit on before I went in the shower, so it's fresh, I promise."

My jaw dropped. *Two* hours ago? I checked the clock on my phone to make sure I did the math right.

"Reid. It's only seven. What were you doing up at five?" Just thinking about waking up at five made my head hurt.

He shrugged as he grabbed the loaf of bread and popped a few pieces into the toaster. "Habit." I watched as he gathered the salt, a bottle of seasoning, an avocado, and the eggs from the fridge.

My jaw stayed open as my gaze followed him around the room, making breakfast. More specifically, my favorite breakfast—avocado toast with scrambled eggs on top.

A second later, a plate slid into view, the avocado toast done up perfectly.

"Thank you," I said softly, still unsure what was happening.

First, he waited up for me the other night. Then, he made coffee. Now he was making me breakfast?

He was acting like nothing happened between us, and that confused me even more. Was that how I was supposed to be acting? Being around him wasn't as hard as I assumed it would be, but things *were* different. Pretending they weren't would only lead to more confusion and eventually it would blow up, I just knew it.

Reid finished making the eggs, plating some for himself and serving me the rest. He sat next to me at the counter after filling a cup of water. Noodle booped his leg, and Reid dropped a tiny piece of scrambled egg for him.

"Plans for the day?" Reid asked a minute later.

I glanced at my phone, remembering that I was going to work on this clue today. I didn't know if there was a time limit or anything, so I figured the sooner, the better.

Part of me wanted to tell Reid about it, to get his opinion. I had no doubt he could solve it in no time flat, but was that even allowed? If I didn't solve the clue on my own, would that disqualify me from whatever prize, or prizes, there were?

"Work later. Dinner shift. Then..." I paused, not sure if I should remind him about Declan and the party. "There's a pool party." Reid's brows lifted in a hopeful manner. "The one Declan asked me to go to." And the brows slammed back down again.

His face hardened, his jaw twitching as he chewed the last bits of his eggs. He took a big gulp of his water, then blotted his lips with a napkin held a bit too tightly in his hand. He stood and made his way to the sink to wash his dishes, his spine straight, his back rising and falling with every sharp breath he took.

"Looks like you have your day planned, then," he said, not bothering to look at me.

My jaw dropped. Was this how it was going to be? Granted, maybe I should have left the Declan thing alone, especially after what happened in this kitchen the other day. But then again, it was my life. Reid broke up with me, and I was free to see other guys if I wanted.

"I guess I do," I answered, equally as annoyed.

I glanced up at Reid, finding him frozen in place between the sink and the island, his hands at his sides, shoulders slumped. I couldn't read the expression on his face, but it leaned more toward sadness, if I had to guess.

"You're going to a party with him. A pool party. A *Bay-side* pool party. Why him, Mars?" he said, softer than he had before.

I didn't really know what to say. For the time being, I gave him a nonchalant answer, trying to match his nonchalant, the past is in the past attitude. "Why not?"

It was dumb. It was vague. It didn't answer anything, for either of us. But at least it was something, because the way he was looking at me right now would have made me fold otherwise.

Reid's stare used to make me weak in the knees, and nothing about that changed. For a moment, I reconsidered staying at the Bennett's for the money. Reid said he would stay out of the way, but this morning was proving otherwise.

I didn't hate it. But I also didn't know what to do about it.

His eyes stayed glued to mine for beat, then he broke contact. I gasped, like I hadn't been breathing.

His frown pulled down his whole face. "You could do so much better, is all I'm saying. You're such an amazing, smart, beautiful, kind person, Marlowe. And he's... well, I just know you could do better. That's all."

Then he took off, heading back upstairs without looking back, both dogs trotting after him.

I watched as he went, but only one thing ran through my mind.

I did better once. I dated you...

BAYSIDE BOULEVARD WAS packed by the time I arrived promptly at eight. It had taken a while to bike here from work, on the opposite side of the island, with sore and tired legs from my shift.

Declan mentioned it was a pool party, so I had my suit on under my bright pink halter top and jean cut-offs. My ever-present belt bag was slung over my chest.

The noise only grew as I wound my way through the house and to the backyard, finding a large pool surrounded by dozens of people.

I had never been to a Bayside party before, and instantly felt out of place. Gennies had parties too, but not with a full DJ on one side and a buffet of snacks and drinks on the other.

Before I could try to pinpoint anyone, someone bumped into me from behind, sending me stumbling forward a few feet. Hands circled my biceps, stopping me from falling flat on my face.

"Hey there, Crash. Glad to see you're living up to your nickname."

I heard the smile in Declan's voice before I saw it on his face.

With a groan, I looked up, but I didn't catch his eyes right away. My gaze traveled over his bronzed torso, his pecs looking as hard as stone. His perfect chiseled surfer body gleamed in the sunlight. Even his shoulders were broad and wide, looking even bigger without a shirt on.

Finally, my eyes reached his, finding them twinkling. A brow lifted, having caught me ogling him.

My face flushed, but I stood to my full height. "This time wasn't my fault. Someone—"

"Jordan. Yeah, I saw. He never looks where he's going. Ignore him," Declan said, leaning in to talk close to my ear, as the music was so loud, I probably wouldn't have heard him otherwise.

His hands left my arms as he turned to the side, wrapping one arm around my waist and guiding me further into the backyard. The scent of the pool mixed with the saltwater off the beach.

I shivered at his touch, a small jolt coursing throughout my body, yet my gut still told me not to get too comfortable. This was a Bayside party, and I knew what that meant.

The other reason my worry radar was going off?

Grace, currently shooting daggers at me from across the pool. Being able to find each other no matter where we were was a long-ingrained sensation, one that came in handy when we were best friends.

Right now, though, I would do anything to stay on the other end of the yard from her.

Declan guided us to the food area, grabbed a few sodas

from a cooler, and gestured to some empty chairs around the pool.

He waved to a few people, but made no move to introduce me to any of them. Of course, I recognized most of them from school, but it still wasn't my normal crowd.

Right then, a shadow crossed over me as a few people walked between our chairs and the pool.

"Excuse me, who let you in?" a snide, nasally voice said. The undertone of the high-pitched voice could have been sweet, had it not been dripping with venom.

I lifted my hand to block out the sun and see who spoke, but it wasn't necessary. I knew who it belonged to.

"This is a Baysider party, in case you couldn't tell," Grace stated. The girls around her laughed. I kept my jaw tight, even though everything inside of me crumbled at her words.

"Then why are you here?" I retorted, throwing the sass right back at her. Two years ago, we would have been laughing while chiding each other, but now, the sass was lethal.

Her glossy lips snarled as she looked down her nose at me. I had to admire the way her bright pink bikini top popped off her dark skin, but I would never admit it. Not anymore. Even if it was an exact color match for the bright pink halter top I had on. It was like we were still on the same brainwave.

"Ugh. It's pathetic that you're basically, like, stalking me."

Stalking her? Because I showed up at a party I wasn't even sure she would be at? How was it considered stalking if I had barely seen her in the last year or so?

"Grace, don't be rude to my guest. She's with me," Declan announced, scooting over a bit and throwing his arm around my shoulders.

I shuddered a little, not liking the claim, but kept my seat and looked up at her.

Her lips flapped in disbelief for a moment as she shot a look across the pool. I followed her gaze, finding her boyfriend, Sean, watching. "With *you*, Declan? Did you lose a bet or something?"

If I hadn't been looking directly at her, I would have missed the brief flash of worry that crossed her face. She masked it quickly, but it made me narrow my eyes and wonder.

Everyone around us burst into laughter. Tears stung at the back of my eyes, but I blinked them away before they could fall.

"She's with me, Grace. And if I say she's cool, then you don't get to argue that, understand?"

I blinked, hard. Did Declan Storms just stand up for *me*? That was new, but now wasn't the time to argue against him.

Besides... it felt good to have someone have my back for once. Especially against my ex-best friend.

Grace flipped her oversized sunglasses onto her nose and stormed off. Declan sat back, looking smug, as if he had just won some sort of argument with her.

Feeling slightly uplifted from the way he defended me against Grace, I settled back in the lounge chair and took in the scene around me. As long as I stuck by Declan, it seemed like no one was going to bother me.

"What else are you up to this summer, Crash? Plan on running anyone else over with your bike?" Declan said a moment later, laughing at his version of a joke.

I didn't laugh, but I did crack a smile. "First off, that wasn't planned. You were standing in the bike lane, so really, it's mostly your fault." I plastered on a smile and looked up at him. "Just trying to figure some things out," I answered. My mind shifted to a few other thoughts while looking at Declan. Like what we were doing. What *I* was doing, hanging out with him at a Bayside party.

Reid's comments flashed through my mind, but I shut them down almost as fast. I didn't want to be thinking of him. He had moved on. I could too. And even if I didn't technically want to date Declan, it was still fun to have someone to hang out with.

"Whenever I need to work stuff out, I literally work it out. The gym is a great place to not only sweat, but sweat out your problems." Declan glanced over at me with the most serious look I had yet to see on his face. Like he truly thought he just solved all my problems by recommending I go to the gym.

"Oh," I answered, raising my brows and feigning interest. The mere thought of working out for fun made me cringe, but I didn't show him that. "That's not really my thing, but it looks like it works well for you." Based on his body, I figured he had a lot of things to work out in his mind.

"So, what is it?"

"What's what?"

"What you have to figure out."

I tucked my lips in. "Right, that." There was no way I was going to bring up my thoughts on him and Reid, so I went in another direction. While I wasn't sure if he could help me solve the clue, it seemed like he was interested enough to try. "It's, um, a scavenger hunt of sorts. I think."

"You think? You're not sure?" In a flash, he lifted his arm into the air and caught a ball that had come sailing our way. I hadn't even noticed it, but was grateful he did.

Declan whooped and hollered, then threw the ball back.

"Well, I haven't solved the first clue yet, so I'm not even sure if it's a real scavenger hunt or not. The instructions were... vague. It has to do with Eleanor Covington, though." I didn't want to tell Declan everything just yet. I didn't have a reason not to trust him, as he proved himself kind so far. But... I also didn't have a reason to trust him completely. "I can't really say more. But if I tell you the clue, do you promise to keep it a secret?"

A slow grin filled his face as he turned to look at me. "I promise. Your secret is safe with me." He put his hand over his heart, directing my attention once more to his chest. His tanned, toned chest.

Dragging my gaze away from his body, I unhooked my belt bag, took out my phone, and opened the text. I didn't show it to him, so he couldn't see any of the other parts, but read the clue out loud.

"Climb the stairs where memories run free, find the room where nostalgia's the key." I glanced up at him when I finished, finding his brows furrowed and his lip slightly snarled.

"Huh? Stairs? Key? What does it mean?" Within a second, he looked completely disinterested, as if not being able to solve it right away made him tune out.

"No idea. Like I said, still figuring it out." His immediate lack of interest sent up a red flag for me. Either he had feigned interest before, just so I would tell him something, or he never really cared in the first place. The quick turn-around made my head spin.

"Sounds hard."

I nodded and dropped my feet to the concrete below. "You know, I'm a bit more tired from work than I thought I would be. I think I'm going to go."

"So soon? You just got here." Declan popped to his feet next to me, but the sadness in his comment didn't match that on his face. His eyes were darting around, looking for something or someone other than me.

In the span of a few minutes, I had lost his attention completely. That was, if I ever really had it to begin with.

"Later, Crash," he answered before launching a ball toward Smitty.

I gave him a tight-lipped smile, then bent down to reach for my bag on the chair. That's when a loud roar echoed throughout the backyard.

Glancing up, I saw a herd of giant teenage boys rushing from the back patio straight toward me.

I shrieked and covered my head with my arms just as they reached me. I couldn't tell how many of them there were, but it was a lot. Enough for them to have to weave around me, leaving me standing helplessly in the middle as they rushed by.

My heart pounded in my chest. I wasn't sure why that had been so scary, but it was.

"Wait for me!" someone shouted.

I barely had time to look before another guy barreled his way down the pool deck. At the last second, his shoulder clipped mine.

Everything went into slow motion at that. He ran by with enough force to send me spinning, losing my footing. I reached my arms out, desperate for something to cling onto, but found no one.

In a last-ditch attempt to keep myself upright, I lifted my right foot and went to plant it firmly behind me.

Except there wasn't anything behind me.

Nothing except water, that was.

With my arms now pinwheeling, I fell into the pool with a giant flop, sending a spray of splashes everywhere.

Underwater, I couldn't hear the girl's shrieks. I couldn't hear the guy's snickers, and couldn't see the fingers pointed in my direction.

But the second I surfaced, the noise rushed at me like a bomb had gone off.

I looked up, hoping to find someone to help me out of the pool so I didn't look like the biggest fool ever.

Thankfully, Declan stood at the edge, his lips tucked in. He must have been biting down on them hard in order to keep from laughing, because his face was as red as a tomato. He reached down and offered me a hand, just like he had when he helped me up off the pavement when we crashed.

"Crash, I didn't give you that nickname so you would keep proving it right, you know," he said as soon as I was on solid ground again. Once I let go of his hand, he let the laughter go. "Sorry. Not laughing at you. Laughing *with* you."

But I wasn't laughing. I looked around, hoping to find someone with a towel, but came up short once more.

"I'm going to go," I whispered. I wasn't even sure if it was loud enough for Declan to hear over the music and noise from everyone around us.

I swiped my bag and stomped my way through the house, not even caring that I was dripping all over everything.

But I didn't let the tears fall until I got onto my bike and pointed it in the direction of the Bennett's.

THE WET BIKE ride back gave me time to think. Which was quickly becoming dangerous.

My mind flip-flopped the entire ride to the Bennett's.

Maybe I should pack up and head home. I clearly didn't belong on Bayside Boulevard.

Declan definitely flirted with me the day I crashed into him.

But now he acted as if he didn't really care?

Where did that leave me?

No Declan. No Reid. At least, not in that way.

If Reid was acting like everything was totally normal between us, then I should be able to do so, too. Reid and I had been great friends before we dated. The first summer he came to the island, he was like a lost puppy, trying to find a place to fit in. And he fit in great with our group.

His second summer with us we started dating, but it was casual. The friendship took precedence. We kept in touch often when he was at home and not on the island.

This past year? No communication at all. Outside of my birthday message to him, that was. The friendship dissolved the moment we broke up.

By the time I made it to the house, the sun had begun to set. Tonight wouldn't be the night to make any big decision about leaving. It would have to wait until the morning.

All I wanted right now was to get out of my wet clothes and into a warm pair of pajamas.

I didn't bother parking my bike in any sort of manner. As soon as I was close enough to the front door, I let it fall into the grass and took off across the front porch.

Slowly, I turned the knob, cringing when I heard the little click. I wasn't sure if Reid was home or not, but if he was, I didn't want him seeing me like this.

I closed the door behind me as softly as possible and waited. If the dogs were inside, they would surely come running any second. After a moment without noise, I started making my way across the kitchen.

Except my wet feet and the tile floors didn't mix. Not five steps in, I slipped, landing on the cold, hard tile with a thud.

It was the second time I had ended up on my back reconsidering my life's choices lately. I had to say, I wasn't a fan. I would much rather be upright and not in pain.

The fall had been so hard, it knocked the breath out of my lungs momentarily. Panic started to set in until I was able to take a breath. Once that happened, my brain realized just how much pain I was in. My head didn't hit hard, but it still ached, as well as my back and hips.

"Owww," I moaned, then planted my hands on either side of me in order to lift myself into a sitting position.

That didn't work either. All the water from my wet clothes had pooled under me, which sent me slipping once again.

"Marlowe?" The kitchen light flickered on, making me squint. Of course Reid would come in *now*. That seemed to be the theme for our summer—Reid coming in to save the day while I looked completely horrible. It wasn't so much a damsel in distress as it was a Marlowe in a mess.

"What happened? Why are you on the floor?" he said, rushing in and crouching beside me. "Are you okay?"

The worried look on his face killed me. Even though we weren't on the greatest of terms right now, especially since he knew exactly where I was coming back from, he still cared.

I opened my mouth to reply, but he cut me off. "Why are you all wet?"

My face flushed. Once again, I was in a position I didn't want to be in. First, in a towel. Now, soaking wet, in pain, on the floor.

"Stay there," Reid demanded. He jumped to his feet and ran out of the room.

This time, I was able to push myself up without slipping again. I scooted down a ways to avoid the growing puddle on the floor, and gently got to my feet.

I had just let out a large sigh when Reid returned, towel in hand.

"Here," he said, draping it over my shoulders and wrapping me up. "Now, what happened?"

But I just shook my head. As much as I was sure he cared, he didn't need to know the whole story. Plus, I *really* wanted to get out of these wet clothes. Between them and the air conditioning, I was freezing.

He stepped forward, as if he were to wrap me up in a hug to warm me. But at the last second, he dropped his arms and kept his distance.

"What happened?" he repeated. He stared at me, trying to decipher if I were going to lie or not.

I decided to tell the truth. "Nothing. I fell in the pool."

Reid's upper lip curled. "And no one there happened to have a towel?"

I bit my lip, trying to figure out how to get out of this without saying too much. I knew he was already mad about me going in the first place. He thought he had the right to be, but he didn't.

"It's a long story," is all I could come up with.

"That's how it's going to be?" he said, as if he had read my mind. I blinked, thrown off for a second.

"How what's going to be?"

He turned and leaned his back against the counter, crossing his arms over his chest. "You. And *him*," he said, as if it disgusted him to even consider talking about Declan. "Do the girls know about him? The guys? I can't imagine Caleb is too happy about it."

I stared at him in shock. Emma knew about Declan, but only the crash and him showing up at the cafe. I hadn't told her about the Bayside party yet.

Reid huffed, seemingly getting my answer from my lack of response. He dropped his hands and pushed away from the counter.

"Do you even know who Declan Storms really is? What kind of guy he's like?" His voice rose by the word, almost yelling.

I blinked. Blinked again. Did he really think I was that clueless? I was the one who went to school with Declan. Lived on the island year-round with him. Somehow, I had to think I knew Declan better than Reid, even if I barely knew Declan well at all.

"Sure. He's the kind of guy who came to have dinner with me on my birthday," I shot back, tightening the towel around my shoulders. My teeth clattered together and goosebumps broke out all along my skin.

Reid exhaled slowly and calmly, almost too calmly. He kept his gaze trained on me, his chin tilted down, his onyx eyes flashing with fire.

"If you only knew," he started, but I didn't let him finish.

"Knew *what*, Reid? You can't go around telling me to stay away from people just because *you* don't like them! You don't have the right to tell me who I can and can't hang out with anymore, remember?"

"I'm still your *friend*, Marlowe!" he bellowed. He was close to exploding, but I didn't even care.

"Friend? How can you call yourself a friend if you never called? Never texted? Never bothered to check in? With any of us?" I didn't mean to throw my friends into the mix, but it happened. It was true, and he knew it.

The second he left Covington Cove last summer, he cut off all communication. Obviously it was the hardest on me, but the others felt the loss too. If he really wanted to call himself our *friend*, then he wouldn't have done that.

The fire subsided slightly at that blow. I only half regretted saying it, though.

"Are you... mad?" I asked, wondering just what was going on with him.

He shook his head, his curls flying every which way. "No, Marlowe. I'm not *mad*. I just can't believe you, of all people, would be with him."

"What?"

Reid threw his hands in the air. "With him! Him, Marlowe! Of all people, you're with *him*?"

"I'm not *with* anyone, Reid!"

His comments took me by surprise. They were blunt, harsh, and unlike Reid.

But I stood by my answer. I wasn't currently looking for a relationship with anyone. I wasn't relationship material, it turned out.

The further I kept myself from people, the better. I was the girl who people liked, but couldn't love. I had been shown that again and again, first with my parents, then Grace, and Reid. Everyone I got close to ended up leaving, so keeping my distance was for the best.

At least, better for my heart.

So no, I didn't consider myself to be 'with' Declan. But a party was a party, and I wouldn't deny myself of having fun.

"I'm going to get into dry clothes," I said while Reid still stared at me in disbelief.

There were a million more things I wanted to say, but none of them would be right. I didn't even know what was right anymore.

Reid didn't have any say over who I hung out with. Who I dated.

So why did he care all of the sudden?

And why was my heart pulling toward him, just knowing that he *did* care?

Echoes of Eleanor

THE HOUSE WAS quiet by the time I got out of the bathroom. I jumped into the shower quickly, just to warm
up, then pulled on some warm pajamas from the towel
warmer.

I tiptoed out of the guest bedroom and down the hallway, not sure who or what I was going to find. Would Reid
still be as pissed off as he was a few minutes ago? Had he
calmed down?

I had. Once I had warmed up, all sorts of sense came
back to me. I hadn't meant to argue with Reid. We never
really had before.

Noodle and Marshmallow were asleep on the couch,
barely moving their heads to look at me as I passed them.
Reid must have taken them for a long walk or something,
because they were tuckered out.

As hungry as I was, I didn't head for the kitchen. While
in the shower, I remembered the clue I had wanted to work

on. The one that I had all but forgotten about lately, except for telling Declan.

Declan, who had shown exactly zero interest in helping me solve it. Making me extremely embarrassed that I had even brought it up in the first place.

Eleanor had said to find someone I trusted implicitly. That person hadn't been Declan. I had just been so wrapped up in what was going on, how he had just defended me against Grace, made me feel wanted and appreciated, that I made a mistake.

Hopefully, he had forgotten all about it by now.

I opted for the library. Maybe if I were around books and stuff, I would be able to think smarter.

It was a dumb idea, but at this point, I would try anything.

I avoided the chair Reid had occupied the other night and sat in the matching one in the corner. My phone stayed in my lap; I had already memorized the clue word for word.

Thinking outside of the box was my next step. I thought past the words itself and more about where they came from. Or *who* they came from.

Eleanor Covington. What kind of relationship did we really have? It was very maternal, even though Eleanor had never been a mother herself. She had been like a grandmother to all of us on the island, but for me, it was more personal than that.

However, the main part of our relationship had been within the confines of the mansion. Occasionally we'd see each other in town, but we really connected the most there.

Could that have anything to do with the clue? I had walked by a dozen staircases while working the Masquerade, wondering of their importance.

For Eleanor, the mansion and the entire island could be

considered nostalgic. She had lived there all her life and had been one of the only people remaining on the island that knew an original Covington. Though Genevieve had passed the year before Eleanor was born, she still grew up with Charlotte—

I sat up straight, thinking about Charlotte. Charlotte and Eleanor. Eleanor and me. How she—

"Am I seeing things?" Reid's voice interrupted my thought process and caused me to jump with fright in the chair.

My hand flew to my chest, my heart pounding behind my ribcage. "This is getting old. My heart can't handle it," I joked, even though he truly had scared the crap out of me. Every nerve ending in my body went into high-alert mode.

He seemed to be in a better mood. I didn't want to disrupt that by saying anything about earlier, so I opted for my standby of cracking jokes again.

Reid chuckled, his tone low and deep, sending shivers through me. "It's a big house. It's bound to happen. Unless you want to wear one of those little bell collars like cats do."

I narrowed my eyes and smirked at him. "*You're* the one doing the sneaking right now. Maybe you should wear one."

He let out another small laugh, and the tension in my shoulders relaxed slightly. "May I?" he asked, gesturing to the chair across from me.

Once again, the image of him raising his arms above his head, his abs on display, flashed through my mind. That chair held a memory I didn't know if I'd ever get out.

Or if I wanted to.

"Um, sure."

He sat down, crossing one ankle over the other knee and sitting back, his hands falling into his lap as he stared at me. "What are you up to? Reading anything good?"

I blinked a few times, then looked down at my empty hands. I held them up to show him I had no book in them, and he just laughed again.

"Guess not. Ever finish that Sage Patel novel?"

I scrunched my nose, trying to remember the name. "Oh, *Tarak*? Unfortunately not... sorry."

He shook his head and waved me off.

That had been the last book we buddy read together. All last summer, we switched off books, him picking one, then me. We would get two copies, read them, then discuss. It was the only way he got me to read, as I wasn't big into doing so for fun and not for a grade.

Thankfully, he usually chose really good books. They were mostly sci-fi or fantasy, or a mixture of both, but still captivating. I chose rom-coms, but he never complained. Not once.

But since we broke up... I hadn't picked up a book again.

"I'm sorry, Mars. For yelling. And everything I said."

All I could do was sit there and stare at him. I appreciated the apology, and of course I accepted it, but I was at a loss for words.

"What are you doing in the library then, if not reading?" he asked, changing the subject and saving me from sitting there in silence.

It felt like yesterday all over again. Sitting on the pool deck with Declan, thinking about Eleanor's clue, telling him because I thought he was interested.

The only difference is that I knew Reid would be interested. He would help. He wouldn't disengage the second it didn't sound fun for him, like Declan had.

I made a mistake telling Declan. But telling Reid wouldn't be the same mistake.

I took a deep breath and went for it. Reid was one of the smartest people I knew. I had just gotten a light bulb idea, and if I could run it past anyone, it would be him.

"If I tell you something, do you *promise* not to tell anyone?" I started. It was a stupid question, because I knew he wouldn't. The realization that I really didn't have to ask versus praying that Declan wouldn't say anything wasn't lost on me.

He mimed zipping his lips shut and throwing away the key, then nodded, leaning forward with his elbows on his knees, his gaze on me intently. He didn't have his glasses on yet, and the intense stare from his dark eyes held me captivated.

"You heard that Eleanor Covington died recently, right?"

He nodded again, but remained silent, allowing me to continue.

"I got a video from her the other day." His brows raised in surprise, but I kept going. "It... was really sweet. It made me cry, actually. But that's not the point. Right before I left for the Masquerade, I got another text from the same number. With a clue."

His jaw dropped at that. He shook his head, as if to clear it, then ran his hands through his hair. "Okay, back up. What?"

I rewound and caught him up to speed with everything that had happened since I found out Eleanor had died. Once we got to the clue, I pulled out my phone to show him.

"That's what I was doing when you came in. Trying to solve it. And I think I figured it out, but I want to see what you think."

Reid's fingers brushed against mine as he took the phone to study the message. A shock shot up through my arm. I sucked in a breath and held it while he fixed his eyes on the screen.

"It looks like we're dealing with a—actually, tell me what you thought first," he said, stopping himself as he handed me back the phone.

I clutched it in both hands and bit my lip. Suddenly, my idea seemed stupid.

"Well, I was thinking about Eleanor, and our friendship, and how it existed mostly in the mansion. Then I wondered what would be nostalgic for Eleanor, and Charlotte Covington came to mind. Then... Well, there's one staircase that leads directly to a room. Just one. All the others in the mansion come up to hallways. But this one staircase, it's not a main one. At the top is one specific room before opening into a hallway. I don't know if that makes any sense, but..."

Reid's eyes grew. He leaned even further forward, on the edge of his chair now, and reached out, laying a hand on my knee. I stared at it, his fingers burning into my skin. "And? What room is it?"

"Charlotte's playroom," I whispered. I cleared my throat before speaking again and tore my eyes away from where he touched me. "Normally, they only allow tourists to look at it from the door, but Eleanor brought me in there numerous times. She loved to show me around, telling me all about the toys, about Charlotte, about growing up in the mansion. It was one of her favorite rooms."

His face lit up. "Mars! That's genius! Honestly, an amazing catch. I was thinking of the stairs and key and maybe something under a staircase, but no, I think you've got it!"

I bit on my lip again and blushed, but my heart grew about five sizes in that moment. Reid was outstanding at giving compliments. And they were always genuine, too, not fake or superficial. If he praised you, he meant it.

"Wow, Marlowe. What a cool opportunity you've been given." Reid sat back and folded his hands behind his head, the smile on his face even bigger than before. "It's obvious that you were a huge part of Eleanor's life and she really loved you."

Tears prickled at the corner of my eyes. "I really loved her too," I whispered back, trying not to think of it too much, or I would probably start crying.

Eleanor was the grandmother I wish I had sometimes. Even though I loved Grandmum, she wasn't the maternal sort. She and I had a different sort of relationship than I had with Eleanor, and that was alright.

I wiped my eyes and glanced over at Reid. His face lit up, and he looked at me like it was the proudest moment of his life. But instead of sharing in his excitement, a yawn rifled through me. I covered my mouth and looked away, but a wave of sleepiness hit hard.

"I'm going to get some sleep," I said sheepishly.

Reid stood, but allowed me out of the door first. "Are you going to go?" he asked as we got to the living room, where he would head upstairs and I down the opposite hall.

"Go where?" I asked, not following.

"Charlotte's playroom. If it's a scavenger hunt like you think, wouldn't the next clue be there?"

Ideally, yes. But for some reason, my mind refused to let me hold on to the thought. What if it wasn't the playroom? What if I was completely off base?

"What if you don't try, Marlowe?" Reid said softly, his hand on my arm.

I hadn't spoken out loud. But he must have known what I was thinking, anyway.

"Yeah... yeah, I guess I'm going to go."

"Good," he said with a gentle smile. "Proud of you. Goodnight."

He started up the stairs, but I couldn't just let him walk away like that. My heart gave a pull as I opened my mouth.

"Reid?"

He paused and turned, one hand on the railing. "Yeah?"

My eyes met his, the dark brown framed by his long lashes. "Do you want to go with me?"

Reef of Regrets

CFFEE CNCE AGAIN waited for me when I woke up, and Reid descended the stairs with a head of wet hair. Why he had been showering so early in the morning, when last I knew he took night showers, was still a question I hadn't asked yet.

The only reason I was up was because I had to work. The morning shift was easy though, as the cafe never got super busy. Seaside Cafe was more known for lunch and dinner menus than brunch.

Reid offered to drive me, so he could pick me up after and head to the mansion together. He said it was too far to bike all around the island, not to mention silly when he had the car and the free time.

"You ready?" he asked, dangling the keys from his hand like he had the other night.

"Yeah. Thanks again for the ride."

Reid started the engine and backed out of the garage. "You don't have to thank me for everything, Marlowe.

Besides, biking to work, then to the mansion, and back to the house would be ridiculous. I mean, I know how much you love getting your exercise," he paused and shot me a knowing glance, "but if I have the means, then I'm happy to help."

"Noted. Did you know your parents left the car keys for me and a note to use the car if I needed?"

Reid let out a huff of a laugh. "Bet you still wouldn't have, though. You hate driving."

I shrugged and looked out the window. "Why drive when you can bike and enjoy the fresh air?"

"What if it started raining? What if you forgot sunscreen and came back with a blistering sunburn? What if you crashed? What if—"

"Okay, okay, I get it," I replied, laying my hand on his arm to get him to stop his disaster scenarios. I didn't acknowledge his third comment of crashing. It was still too soon. "I don't consider biking exercise though, just so you know."

"Noted," he echoed. "I'll see you at one?"

He pulled into a space and put the car in park, turning toward me. For a split second, I had the incredible urge to lean over the console and plant a kiss on his cheek.

Just like I used to do.

I blinked, gulping back my instincts and reaching for the door handle. "Yeah, one is perfect. Thanks again."

"Have a good shift!" he called after me as I climbed out of the car.

Emma stared at me through the restaurant window as I ascended the front stairs and came in through the door. We wouldn't be open for another twenty minutes, but once the opener came in, we didn't relock it.

"What was that?" Emma asked, pouncing on me the

moment the door closed. I eyed the pink headband pulling back her short, dark hair. It was cute, and I sort of wanted it.

I gave her an innocent look. "What was what?"

Her eyes grew wide, her lids completely disappearing and her thin brows skyrocketing. "That was Reid Bennett in the car. In the driver's seat. Smiling at you like a lovesick fool. What *was* that?"

I ducked under the front counter and crouched down to the bottom shelf, where I kept my apron and notepad. "That," I said as I stood, "was nothing."

Emma snorted. Like a full on pig snort. It was halfway between a gasp and a laugh, but ended up as a snort. I stared at her, waiting for her to come to her senses.

"If that was nothing, then what's up with you and De-clan? Word on the street is you two are getting cozy. Almost as cozy as you were in that car with Reid..."

My face dropped. What did *that* mean? Did she think I was dating both of them? Cheating on one with the other? Leading them on?

I had to clarify things, and quickly. "Listen. I'm house sitting for the Bennett's. And dog sitting. Reid wasn't sup-posed to be here this summer. He came back, but told me to stay so I could get the money." I gave her a look that told her how much money, without having to say words. And added a raise of the eyebrows that explained how much I could use that money. She held her hands up in surrender, understanding my unspoken words.

"And Declan... well, he and I need to talk, because I'm not even sure what's going on there."

I purposefully didn't mention his time at the Ben-nett's house the other afternoon, or what happened at the pool party.

Emma hummed, then ducked around me to set out tableware.

The shift flew by, the two of us keeping busy with our regulars and a few tourists who meandered in, looking like they just woke up while also ready to dive into the ocean on a moment's notice.

"You said you needed to talk to Declan, right?" Emma asked as I dried the last coffee cup and returned it to the shelf. The lunch rush had started, but our shift ended in a few more minutes. We didn't get assigned tables for lunch, since the girls on that shift arrived an hour ago. We were just around to help set up, clean up, and deliver food.

"Yeah? Why?"

She jutted her chin toward the front, where a group of guys sat by the window.

The group of guys being Declan and his friends.

"Looks like you might get your chance," Emma replied with a smirk. "I have to say, I haven't heard of him randomly appearing at the workplace of his girlfriends before."

"That's because his girlfriends never worked. And I'm not his girlfriend," I retorted, reminding her of a few necessary points.

Declan had never dated a Gennie, as far as I knew. He stuck with the Bayside girls, and even ventured over to the Crescents once. That didn't last long, though. She ended up with a guy from the private school and dumped Declan quick.

"Well, not-girlfriend, looks like he's waiting for you. He hasn't stopped glancing this way since he walked in."

"I'm not on tables. We're about to clock out," I argued, reminding her.

She rolled her eyes. "I didn't say *wait* on them, you doof."

The light bulb finally illuminated in my head. He wasn't here for me to serve him. He was here for... well, for me. "Oh. *Oh*. Right. Let me clock out first."

We rushed to the back, then stashed our aprons and stuff beneath the front counter.

"Hey," I said, walking up to the table. The guys smiled at me, which made me nervous but comforted as well.

"Crash! The star of the show!" Declan declared as he jumped to his feet and wrapped his arms around me tight, pinning mine to my side. It was awkward, but over quick.

"Star of what show?" I questioned when he let me go. I had quickly learned that nothing with Declan ever made a lot of sense, and if I wanted answers, I had to ask before his mind veered in another direction.

"The scavenger hunt!" one of the guys at the table announced way, *way* too loudly.

I whipped my head toward Declan and seethed. "You told them?"

His face lit up like a kid on Christmas morning. "You said you were having a hard time solving the clue, so I thought the more minds, the merrier!"

"That's not how the phrase goes," I muttered to myself. "And I asked you not to say anything."

"Why, so you can keep the Covington fortune to yourself?" a guy with the brightest blonde hair I had ever seen called out from the back of the table. It had to have been bleached. It definitely didn't look natural.

My eyes widened and my jaw dropped. "Are you kidding me? Declan!" I gasped when he grabbed my hand and brought it up to his chin. He batted his eyelashes at me, but I was too pissed off to fall for his flirting tactics.

"Yeah, if we help, we get a share of the prize money, right?" I didn't bother looking to see who said that. I didn't even care anymore.

"They need to *shut up*," I stage-whispered to Declan. I wanted to rip my hand out of his, but knew we were on display right now. The rest of the restaurant had to be watching this go down, especially since they mentioned the Covington name. "You weren't supposed to tell *anyone*."

Declan gave my hand a squeeze and put on his most charming grin. It didn't work this time, though.

"Everything okay over here?" Emma asked as she squeezed past the nearby table and stood shoulder to shoulder with me.

"It's amazing, thanks. Marlowe, it's not a big deal. Like I said, the more people thinking about it, the faster you figure it out, right? I was just helping."

"Helping? Are you kidding?" My breath started coming in shallower bursts now.

The bell over the door rang, jerking my attention away.

"Welcome to the Seaside Cafe. Please take a seat and someone will be with you shortly," Emma and I both announced in unison, as we were trained to do when we heard that bell.

"Crash, come on. Let us help you! The Covington fortune is at stake—"

"No! No! Declan, I specifically said to keep it a secret! Just between us! I didn't even say anything about a fortune!"

"And I think—"

"She doesn't seem to care what you think right now," Reid interrupted. He had been the one who came through the door, and now firmly planted himself on my other side, his arms folded over his chest tightly. "I'd let her go, if I were you."

Declan glanced down, assessing the muscles on Reid's arms, a sneer appearing on his face. But he dropped my hand anyway.

I paled, glancing between Declan and Reid, completely baffled. Reid seemed to have assessed Declan as some sort of threat based on the way he stared him down, his jaw tight, his breaths coming in short spurts. My chest tightened as a flush creeped up my neck and into my cheeks.

Whether it was embarrassment or something else, I wasn't sure.

Emma leaned forward and whispered, "You need to get them to leave. Mason is poking his head out and if he has to come over here, it won't be pretty."

My lip quivered and my hands shook. I was still fuming inside. I was scared that if I opened my mouth right now, all I would do was scream.

Who else had Declan talked to? I had trusted him with this *one* secret. There were four boys at the table, but somehow, I didn't think it was the only four he told.

I chanced a glance over at Reid, finding his chest puffed out further now, his eyes locked on Declan. He barely blinked.

"Just go. Please," I whispered, looking at Reid, but talking to Declan. I turned and faced him. "Now."

His eyes narrowed as he looked between me and Reid. Then, he signaled to his friends to get up, and they filed out of the restaurant in front of him.

"Seems like your superhero came to the rescue, huh?" Declan said as he pushed his way between Reid and me on the way out. "See you later, Crash."

As had become the norm, I was once again utterly confused as Declan left.

All I wanted now was for everything to go back to how it was a few weeks ago.

Before I crashed my bike into the most popular guy in Covington Cove.

Chasing Shadows

R EID DIDN'T TALK as we walked to the car. He did open the door for me, but didn't stick around to close it.

Truthfully, I was glad he didn't, because it looked like he would have slammed it so hard, it would have broken.

Since the guys were still mingling around the square, Reid put the car in gear and took off in the opposite direction. It wasn't the way to the mansion, but if I knew him, it was just to go around and not pass by Declan.

Reid was mad.

I was panicking. My chest still felt tight, my hands shaking as I laid them in my lap. The whole situation with Declan left me angry. Upset. Humiliated.

All the things Reid probably meant when he asked 'why Declan.' Like he knew better, and was hoping I did too. But I didn't.

I tried to swallow the lump in my throat, but it wasn't moving, which made talking difficult. Reid's hands gripped the wheel so tight, his knuckles were turning white, and he was chewing on the inside of his cheek so much, I worried about it.

Besides that, I had no idea what he was thinking. He always said the quiet part out loud, never shying away from giving me his opinion, even if it was brutally honest. That's what I liked about him—knowing I didn't have to hide anything. That I could trust him to tell me exactly what was on his mind.

"Reid?" I whispered a minute later, after he took a left on Harbor Street to head south toward the mansion.

"Are we going to the mansion? I could hang a right on Pine Avenue instead, and go back home."

"It's not my home, it's yours," I muttered, staring at the chipped polish on my nails. Reid inhaled sharply, but otherwise stayed quiet. "Yeah. To the mansion. Please."

He nodded once, keeping his eyes glued to the road. I could tell he wanted to explode. If this had been last year, he would be going *off* on me right now. Rightfully so, too. I should have stayed cautious about Declan from the start. What he did was a jerk move, and ambushing me in public with it was rude. He told his friends on purpose. I just couldn't figure out what that purpose was.

Whatever Declan and I had was done. I didn't trust people easily, yet somehow I had gotten caught in his little charming web.

"When we get there, how are we getting to the playroom?" Reid asked as he came to a stop at a light. We were only a minute or two away now.

I hadn't thought of that. Normally, I wandered and Eleanor found me.

But now, there was no Eleanor. Even though I worked there occasionally, I couldn't just walk right in and meander for no reason.

"I'll see if Lily is working. If she's giving a tour, maybe I can convince her to let us up there."

Reid nodded sharply again, still not looking in my direction. His mind had to be running a million miles a minute, but he didn't unleash any of the negativity toward me. I was sort of glad he didn't.

My excitement over solving the first clue had peaked last night. Knowing Reid and I were going to find the next clue had kept me motivated throughout my shift. I didn't want the whole Declan thing to overshadow the moment. I didn't want it to be a bigger deal than this.

Instead of going around the road toward the employee parking, Reid pulled into the visitor lot, where the tourists parked for their tours. We entered through the front doors, and were greeted by a college aged girl whose name I didn't know sitting at a desk a few feet away.

"Are you here for the tour?" she asked, glancing at a notebook on her desk.

"Sort of," I replied, giving her my most cheerful smile. "Is Lily Pierce providing tours today?"

The girl looked up at me, her brows knitted and lips pursed. "She is. Do you have a personal tour scheduled?"

"Yes," I lied, trying to stay quick on my feet. Reid shuffled next to me, looking everywhere except me and the host.

After flipping through a few pages in the notebook, the girl stared at us again. "I don't have any personal tours on Lily's schedule. Her next one is in thirty minutes, but it's a public tour."

I shrugged, like it wasn't my fault her list was wrong. "Maybe someone forgot to put it in? This is my friend, Reid. He's a summer kid and has never been here before. Can you believe that? I mean, us year-rounders come here almost every year for school field trips. It's crazy to think that he's never stepped foot inside."

My lies built up on lies, but I had to get inside and upstairs. Besides, we weren't really breaking any rules. I walked around the mansion so often, I knew the floor plan as well as my own home.

"Marlowe?" came a voice from the opposite side of the foyer.

"Lily! Just the girl we're here to see. Thanks so much for your help," I said to the hostess before grabbing Reid's hand and pulling him toward Lily.

Her dirty blonde hair was pulled back in a bun at the nape of her neck, and she held an apple slice halfway up to her mouth.

"Me? You're here to see me? Why?"

Her suspicions were valid. Though I knew her from school and we had worked together on a few projects before, we weren't really close friends. She was as close to a Gennie as a Crescent kid could get. While she lived on Covington Crescent Boulevard, her mom was a teacher at the elementary school, so she always stayed on the island for her education. Which was great, because she was also super smart and helped me raise a few grades with our projects.

I let go of Reid's hand and leaned in close to Lily. We were just about the same height, but her eyes were a deep sapphire blue and she had a scattering of freckles over her suntanned nose.

"Listen, I have something to tell you that's kind of a secret. Can you pretend you're giving us a private tour so the hostess girl will get off our back?"

Lily frowned, but after staring at me for a minute, she nodded. "Our tour starts here in the foyer. It's part of the original mansion, which includes..."

Once out of earshot of the hostess, Lily dropped the act and turned to me and Reid. "So what's up? What's this big secret?"

I didn't waste any time explaining the scavenger hunt, without giving *all* the details away.

"If I'm right, I think the clue is leading toward Charlotte's playroom," I finished, pointing up the stairs.

Lily cocked her head and narrowed her eyes. "But Charlotte's playroom is closed to the public. You can't go inside."

I tucked my lips in, my cheeks going slightly pink. I didn't want to name drop, but I had to. "You know I work here occasionally, right? My Grandmum works in housekeeping? Well, since the day I was born, I've come here with her or my parents, to work. Eleanor and I... we sort of became friends. When I was little, she would bring me to the playroom and let me look around or play with some of the dolls."

Lily's blue eyes widened. "She let you inside? She never let anyone inside."

My face had to be as red as a tomato now. Reid stepped forward, putting his hand on my lower back. The touch shocked me at first, but then put me at ease.

"Marlowe was special to Eleanor. They had a sort of relationship she can't really explain. I know it seems odd, and you have no reason to believe any of this, but we're asking you to trust us. We promise, no harm will come to the playroom and we'll be in and out as fast as possible. And we'll leave a tip and a glowing review with your manager."

My head turned slowly toward Reid. How he always knew the exact right thing to say at the exact right time was astounding. Here I was, prepared to beg and plead my way upstairs, when he came to the rescue with a few simple words.

Lily sighed and looked at her watch. "Alright. Just for a few minutes, though. Make it quick. And I expect the review to include how many family members you're going to be recommending."

"Every one I have," Reid replied with a smile.

The second we got to the playroom, I froze. "Reid," I whispered, leaning in close to his ear. "I have no idea where to look."

He nodded like it was the easiest thing to solve. "You mentioned dolls. Did Eleanor let you play with them?"

Of course. The dolls. I walked swiftly over to the far corner, where a bookshelf held Charlotte Covington's doll collection. They were over a hundred years old, but kept in perfect condition thanks to the Covington Historical Society.

Reid and I carefully picked each one up, looking behind and under them to see if they were hiding a clue.

"Someone's coming!" Lily whispered.

I stared at Reid in fear. We still hadn't found the next clue. He pulled on his right ear, but looked around the room, scanning everything he came across.

"The dollhouse."

I beelined over there, not even trying to figure out why he said that. Charlotte's dollhouse was an exact replica of the mansion as it was originally built. Over the years, more wings had been added, so the dollhouse was significantly smaller looking than the house now.

But it stood almost five feet tall and at least four feet across. It took up an entire corner of the room and was meticulously decorated to resemble the interior of the mansion as well. Eleanor said the contractors and workmen who built the mansion gave it to Charlotte as a present.

I didn't have to think twice about where to look first—the playroom on the top floor. There. A small envelope leaned against the far wall. I snatched it up and ran back to Reid and Lily. I slid out of the doorway and Lily reattached the red velvet rope that blocked off access to the room.

"You get it?" Reid muttered out of the corner of his mouth as another tour started our way. They must have come from Nathaniel and Genevieve's bedroom, which was the stop right before the playroom.

"And that was Charlotte's playroom," Lily said, turning and extending her hand toward the staircase, pretending to continue with our fake tour. She was good, I had to give her that. Believable, jumped right into action, and discreet. "Down the stairs, if you please."

We followed her directions, but when we reached the bottom, she stopped us. "There was something in the dollhouse, wasn't there?"

I nodded and held up the envelope. I didn't dare open it right now, though.

Lily's brows shot up her forehead, her doe eyes as wide as they could be. It wasn't quite a look of shock as much as it was wonder, mixed with a little worry. "Whoa."

I nodded. "Thanks for going along with it. And if you can do me a favor and not tell anyone... that would be great." I grimaced, remembering how well that worked for me the last time I asked someone to keep it a secret.

She nodded, her bun bouncing behind her. "No worries. But, if you want to get out of here without questions, I'd head through the employee entrance. We haven't been gone long enough to pretend we did a full tour, and Caterina at the front will question you. And then me." She cringed, but I laughed.

"Got it."

21

Waves of Uncertainty

I HELD THE ENVELOPE in my lap the entire car ride back to Reid's house. He seemed visibly less tense than he had been on the way to the mansion, which was nice.

Another clue had to be in this envelope. Would I be able to solve this one? Would it take me as long as the first one did? Would I let Reid help, like I asked in the library yesterday? Checking the dollhouse had been his idea. I came up with the playroom, but didn't have a clue what to look at once we got there. The only reason I had the envelope now was because of his quick thinking.

Reid pulled into the garage and turned the car off, but neither of us moved. We both stared straight forward, the air becoming thick.

I took a deep breath, wanting to break the tension, but also not sure what to say. Apologizing for Declan and his behavior didn't seem right, nor was it something I wanted to do. Thanking Reid for saving the day by suggesting the dollhouse didn't feel right either. He wouldn't want to be thanked for that, anyway.

The only other thing I couldn't get out of my mind was the look on Reid's face as he stared down Declan at the cafe. How he looked like he wanted to tear Declan apart, just for touching me, not to mention the stress Declan had caused before Reid arrived.

"Marlowe..." Reid started, cutting through the silence. By the tone of his voice, I could tell where the conversation was going to go.

I sighed and hung my head, awaiting his comments. Even though I loved that he was honest with me, it still hurt sometimes.

"I'm only saying this because I lo—because I care. But Declan Storms? Once again, why?"

My heart skipped several beats when he started to say what I thought he was about to say. But he corrected himself. He cut himself off before he got the word out.

He also didn't give me a moment to explain, not that I had come up with anything. At this point, even I was confused as to 'why Declan Storms.'

"You trusted him, Mars. You don't trust anyone. And you told *him* about the scavenger hunt, thinking he wouldn't tell everyone he came across? He's not a nice guy, no matter how charming he tries to appear."

These were all things I had realized too, and didn't need him pointing out to me. I came up with the same conclusions on my own and didn't need Reid driving them in. I could beat myself up perfectly fine, thank you.

I also could have come up with a million different retorts then, but I stopped myself before letting any out. There was no need to sling negativity back at Reid when all I wanted was to tell it to myself.

My bottom lip quivered for a second before I tucked it in, chewing on it so I didn't give myself away.

"I made a mistake," I murmured. Whether the mistake was trusting Declan, going out with Declan, or purely crashing into Declan in the first place was to be determined.

If this had been about anything other than a Covington scavenger hunt, I would naively assume that Declan was really, truthfully, trying to be helpful.

But that couldn't be the case anymore. There was no way he brought in all those friends for an actual brainstorming session. They wanted something. And Declan thought I'd just hand it over to him.

None of that answered Reid's question, though. Why Declan Storms?

I stayed quiet as bigger questions crossed my mind.

Why not you, Reid Bennett?

Or, more importantly, *why not me?*

"EARRINGS, CHECK. BUN, check. Lipstick, check," I muttered to myself as I glanced in the mirror. "Envelope, still untouched on the dresser. Check." I sighed, staring at the envelope I put there two days ago, after leaving Reid's car full of sadness instead of being giddy over finding another clue.

We hadn't spoken since then, not besides some hellos and goodbyes. I thanked him for still making me coffee every morning, though

I also hadn't heard from Declan since the cafe. He hadn't texted, and I didn't have the guts to message him myself. Not after what happened. The thought of letting it go, moving on with my life, and never talking to him again crossed my mind several times.

"Noodle! Off!" I shouted as I pushed him away from me. He had sprinted into the room and tried to jump on me as I sat on the bed putting my flats on. He had his paws on the comforter, full of grass and dirt. Reid must have let them go play in the backyard.

He had done a good job of living up to his promise of staying out of the way. The promise he made when he told me not to leave.

I had no idea what he was up to, but I was about to be late. Grandmum called me at the last minute to help work. The Covington family was having Eleanor's private funeral today, and that meant lots of people coming from all over the country. They were coming back to the island, and most would be staying in the mansion for the weekend. We needed to open more rooms and freshen everything up.

The celebration of life for Eleanor would be in another month or so, when the town could get everything together. More than likely, the entire island would want to show up, so large-scale accommodations needed to be made.

As I stood outside the employee entrance a bit later, I knew I wouldn't be able to get through this shift easily. Though I doubted I would see many people, just knowing the reason behind why I was getting the house ready was hard enough.

I had been in the mansion twice since Eleanor's passing, but this time, it felt more real. Especially with Grandmum on my case, making sure I cleaned every bathroom and guest room to utter perfection for the extended Covington family.

I made it through and only shed a few tears, mainly when I passed by the painting of Eleanor and found her niece, Rebecca, staring up at it. I didn't bother her, but I did pause for a moment, taking in the scene. Rebecca was now the oldest living Covington on the island. She was in Eleanor's shoes.

As soon as I finished all my duties and checked out with Grandmum, I headed outside to my bike. Digging in the backpack I brought with me, I quickly swapped out my work shirt for a tank top over my sports bra, stuffing the work shirt in my bag.

Right as I kicked off and started down the long, winding road that led from the mansion to Covington Crescent Boulevard, my phone jingled. It startled me, making me wobble, but thankfully I kept my balance and pulled over into the grass before grabbing it from my bag.

> **DECLAN:** Party happening now. Can you come, Crash?

I paused. My initial reaction was a resounding heck no. He also betrayed my trust. Like Reid had mentioned, I didn't trust people easily. By all means, I should have either ignored him, blocked him, or responded with a simple, one-word sentence—no.

I already had made an entirely new list in my phone of all the reasons I never wanted to see Declan Storms again. The first being the humiliation from the cafe. Numbers two through five were personal opinions on what I was now assuming was a facade he put on for people.

But before I could answer, another message came through.

> **DECLAN:** I'm sorry for what happened the other day at the cafe. I truly thought having more people to help figure out the clue would be for the best. I didn't realize my friends would be obnoxious beasts like that.

> **DECLAN:** Please forgive me? Come hang out. We'll have some fun, promise. Besides, I have something for you.

He what? Why would Declan Storms have something for me?

My phone buzzed one more time before I could answer Declan.

> **NORAH:** We're headed to the mainland to grab Liam and Livvy! We'll text you when we get back. Hope you're having fun working, lol!

She attached a picture of her, Caleb, and Emma all leaning into the center of Norah's mom's SUV. With all of them together, there would have been no way they would have fit in the tiny sedan she normally drove. The one she bought used for only a few thousand dollars and was being held together by hopes and dreams.

My heart fell. They thought I was still working, which wasn't a bad assumption, as I had just gotten off. But it meant they left me out of picking up Liam and Livvy. I would have loved to have joined them all, even if we would have been a little cramped.

Except... I clicked on the picture again and zoomed in.

It looked like the car would have already been cramped, whether I went or not.

Because sitting in the third row seat, looking out of the window, probably attempting not to be in the picture at all...

...was Reid.

I clutched the phone so tightly, my hand cramped. It was only a matter of time before he migrated back to the group. I just hadn't been prepared for how I would feel when he did, and I wasn't a part of it. I wasn't quite angry, but definitely hurt. It almost felt like a betrayal, even though it really wasn't. Being left out because they thought I was at work wasn't really being left out.

But still. It stung seeing him in the back of the car, like he was trying to hide from the picture. Did he not want me to know he was with them?

That's when I made my decision. If Reid could hang with them, I could hang with Declan and the other Baysiders. There was no one that said I couldn't.

ME: I'll be there in thirty.

Bayside Bonds

THIS BEACH PARTY wasn't in the same place as last time. We were further down, away from the pier, but closer to Richards Marine Tours and Repair, the Richards' family boat business that Caleb had a part time job at this summer.

But Caleb wouldn't be at this party; he was with the rest of my friends about to have an amazing afternoon together.

As if on cue, Micah Caldwell popped out from one of the bushes that lined the entrance to the beach.

"Watcha doin', Poet?" he asked, crossing his arms over his toned chest. He had his chin length shaggy dark hair pulled back with a hair tie, leaving his scruffy face on full display. On any other guy, it would look unkempt. But on Micah, it was sort of hot.

I would have narrowed my eyes and told him to move, but he wasn't trying to give me a hard time. His best friend, Preston Richards, won the title of biggest goofball last year, and Micah no doubt would win it this year.

The only thing that could potentially derail Micah was the fact that he was fast tracked for valedictorian too. It almost didn't make sense—how someone could be so completely crazy while also one of the smartest in the entire school. If it wasn't for Zoey Richards, Preston's sister, Micah would have it in the bag. The competition between them was intense, and I was glad I wasn't anywhere near that grade wise.

"Heard there was a party. What are you, the bouncer?" I teased, giving his shoulder a slight shove. I ignored him calling me Poet. Micah gave everyone a nickname, and if you didn't have one, he called you by your last name until he thought of one.

Unless he really didn't like you. Then he called you by your government name.

Two years ago, we had a project together in English, where he found out there had been a poet named Christopher Marlowe. From then on, I became Poet.

And though he was a Baysider, he never took to one group of friends besides Preston. We called Micah a jumper, because he flowed between groups of people. He was pretty close to Caleb, which is probably how he got the job. Micah worked at the Richards' boat business, too.

"How's our boy?" he asked, turning to join me on the walk to the party.

I stared at him, not sure who he meant. Did he mean Declan? Or was he talking about Reid? There was no way he didn't know that we had broken up last year, but maybe he heard Reid was back? It wouldn't have surprised me— Micah seemed on top of all the gossip.

"I meant Rebel, but the fact that you're contemplating that makes me wonder if there's another guy..." Micah said, bumping his shoulder into mine. Rebel was the name he gave Reid a few years ago. He had been hanging out with Caleb when Reid came in with Liam. When Micah found out Reid was a Baysider but friends with the Gennie's, he started calling him Rebel.

I rolled my eyes and shoved him away. "Get lost, Caldwell. I have someone to meet up with."

"I can see that. Declan Storms, huh?" he answered, his focus straight ahead, where Declan jogged his way up the beach, once again shirtless, with a big grin on his face. "Be careful with that one," Micah added before ducking to the side and heading the opposite direction.

What did *that* mean? Granted, I had already found out part of it. But Micah's warning seemed more sinister than that.

Declan finally reached me, not even out of breath as he slowed to a stop. "Hey Crash, good to see you."

I gave him a half-hearted smile, but didn't answer. Really, the only reason I came was because all my friends left me behind. And maybe part of me wanted to use Declan to get back at Reid... just a little.

"Come with me. I have something to show you," Declan said, extending his hand for mine again.

Without thinking, and mesmerized by the dimples in his cheeks, I slipped my hand into his and followed him down the sand. I paused for a second, taking off my black flats, and dropping them into my backpack.

I should have been smarter than this. I should have demanded an apology, an explanation as to why he told his friends. The real reason. If I had been more confident, I would have done all those things. But I wasn't.

"Where are we going?" I whispered, as if it were all a big secret.

He leaned in, the scent of sunshine and the ocean wafting off of his chest. "Just around the beach grass over there," he said.

Right as we arrived, the few people that had been standing around left. I ignored that, and put my bag down on the sand next to a towel he already had laid out.

"Let me go grab us some drinks," he said after I settled down. He turned and jogged back toward the beach grass.

A seagull landed close by a moment later, scaring me half to death. I waved my arms toward it, trying to shoo it away.

It flew back a few feet, but didn't leave entirely.

Taking in a deep breath, I attempted to calm my mind, attempting to push the thought of Reid and my friends out. I didn't know the circumstances, and it wasn't like they had purposefully left me out. They thought I was still working.

Besides, when Liam and Livvy came back, we would all hang out again. I had been living with Reid for a while now. I could handle being in a group with him.

It still pained my heart, though. I closed my eyes, breathing in the salt water air, and trying not to think of Reid stretching his arms over his head. Of him kissing me on this same beach last summer.

Of running, laughing, and laying in the sand, soaking up the sun.

Of the way his face looked absolutely heartbroken when he said we should break up.

A squawk forced my eyes back open. The bird from a moment ago had ventured closer, but now approximately ten of his best friends joined him. A quick glance up showed me even more of them on their way.

And they were all tiptoeing toward me, their beady little eyes staring me down.

My stomach churned. I *hated* seagulls. Their snappy little beaks freaked me out. The way they scampered about in the sand before launching into the air, circling unsuspecting beachgoers until they dive bombed them, grabbing their food. It was all calculated. Planned. They were shiesty characters, not to mention their ability to peck your eyeballs out of your skull if they wanted.

I glanced up the beach, wondering if anyone else was around to save me from the flock of doom, but came up empty. It was just me and the birds.

I shook my arms again, wider this time, in an attempt to get them all to scatter, but it was no good.

That's when I felt it—a plop of something falling on my head, followed by a dripping sensation toward my temple.

I didn't want to reach up and feel it. I really didn't. But instinct took over and suddenly I found my fingertips covered in a white goo.

"No... oh *no, no, no*," I whispered to myself. I jumped to my knees and reached back for my backpack, trying to see if I had any napkins or a towel or something I could use to wipe this off before Declan came back. I couldn't wipe it on his towel—that was so gross and he would definitely know it was me.

All I had in my bag was my work shirt. "Sorry, but desperate times and all that," I whispered to it, using it to wipe the poop off my face and hair. "Ew, ew, ew, ew."

Without a mirror, I had no idea if I got it all or if I just smeared it around.

It didn't matter, though, because a moment later, another plop hit my right shoulder.

My eyes widened. That's when I turned to look in every direction, finding at least two dozen seagulls circling me. The ones in the front were pecking at the sand by the edge of the towel.

Eating. They were eating.

I wanted to vomit. They waddled closer, enclosing me in their circle of terror.

Closing my eyes and praying I didn't find what I thought I would, I dug my hand into the sand and examined it.

Someone put *bird food* in the sand.

With one hand to my mouth, I rolled off the towel and to my knees, ripping it away from the beach to reveal what was underneath. I threw it over my shoulder, scaring a dozen birds away, but it didn't matter.

Bird seed littered the ground. The second the towel was gone, the seagulls dove in for the feast.

I screamed and leaped to my feet, clutching my bag to my chest as they flew all around me. One pecked at my toe, mistaking it for food.

"Ow!" I screeched, hopping away on one foot. My chest tightened and my vision began to tunnel.

That's when I heard it—giggles. My head shot up, finding a group of Baysiders by the tall beach grass Declan and I had come around, their phones out, trying to keep their laughs behind their hands, but failing.

"Oh my God, that was *priceless*," one said, staring at her screen.

"Did you get the scream? Tell me you got the scream!"

"Who cares about the scream? I got the second wad of poop landing on her shoulder!"

My head spun, my vision blurry now as I took in the scene around me.

Declan said he had something for me.

He apologized for telling his friends about the clue.

He came to take me for a birthday dinner.

He called me his girl.

And it was all, what, a prank? An elaborate, long drawn out prank?

My gaze shot toward the grassy area, the only way out of this part of the beach and to my bike.

I dug my toes into the sand, jumped over the pile of bird seed and seagulls, and pumped my legs hard to get through the group.

But a wall of tall, toned guys blocked my path.

"Move," I seethed, but they didn't listen. At least two had their phones out, still capturing my humiliation on camera.

Tears threatened to roll down my cheeks, but I wiped them away before they could. They didn't deserve that satisfaction.

"You got a little something on your forehead, Crash."

Declan.

I whipped my head around so fast, my hair hit me in the face. "*You.*"

The grin on his face no longer charmed me. It no longer made my heart pound or made me reconsider my decisions.

Right now, all I wanted to do was punch it off his smug little face.

So I did. Or, at least, I tried. At the last second, Declan darted to the side, avoiding my fist, leaving me careening forward.

A steady pair of arms caught me before I went toppling to the ground.

"Easy now," a male voice whispered into my ear. Adrenaline coursed through my body. I didn't want anyone touching me, talking to me, looking at me. I wanted to run far, far away and never see these people again.

And I still wanted to punch the stupid dimples off of Declan's face.

"Let's go. Don't say anything, just go," the female voice said. I didn't have to look to see who said it, but the shock that came from it stung all the same.

The more masculine set of hands lifted me to my feet, handing me off to the girl. "You're a jerk, Declan. Honestly, who does something like that?" he said, louder and away from my ear now.

"Aw, come on, Sean, it was a harmless prank on a Gennie. A hysterical one, but harmless! We've been planning it for weeks!" Declan responded in between taking deep breaths from laughing so hard. "Come back, Crash. I'm sorry! I swear, it was supposed to be funny! I thought you'd laugh!" But the way he wheezed from laughing himself told me he wasn't serious.

None of this was serious.

I didn't believe a word he said. I shouldn't have believed it in the first place. Someone like Declan Storms had no interest in someone like me.

As soon as we cleared the grass and made it back to my bike, I looked up.

Grace and her boyfriend, Sean, flanked my sides, their hands still on my arms.

Grace spoke first, her dark brown eyes flecked with green and gold trained on mine. "Hi."

Shores of Redemption

BLINKED, SURE I was hallucinating. No way did Grace and Sean just help me out of there, out of the humiliation from Declan and the Baysiders.

"What do you want?" I shot back, still unable to believe she was here on her own accord. The old Grace would have been.

The new Grace would treat me the same way she did at the pool party. Pretending like I didn't belong anywhere she was.

The fact was, she lived two blocks away from me. She was a Gennie, not a Baysider. But dating Sean gave her certain privileges that didn't seem to extend to others. Hanging with the Baysiders had made her into a monster, someone I didn't recognize.

This Grace though... This was more reminiscent of my best friend. The one who would fight and stand up for me. Who had my back, no matter what.

"Sean, get her bike in the truck, please," Grace said while still staring at me. "Mars Bar, let's get you in the car, okay?"

"I can ride."

Grace sighed, breaking our eye contact and looking down at her long, lean legs and perfect purple pedicure. "You're staying at Reid's, aren't you? That's on the other side of the island. It'll take you an hour, minimum, to ride there. And you're... not in the best condition right now."

Something hot and wet slid down my cheek, and I could only hope it was tears and not another seagull. I got my confirmation when big pools of water plopped on the asphalt below me.

Grace put her hand on my lower back, guiding me to her truck. It was old and beat up, the door trim rusted, but it worked.

"I'll go deal with them," Sean said after I climbed into the passenger side. "That wasn't cool. I'm so sorry you were chosen as their target this year. They tried to pull the same stunts on Grace, but I intervened. The second I saw you at the pool party the other week, I should have known. I can't apologize for them because they need to do the apologizing to you."

His words hit me straight in the heart. When Grace started dating him, she introduced the two of us hesitantly. Sean was one of the few year-round Baysiders that joined the Crescent kids at the private school off-island, so he didn't associate with Declan and his crew too much. Besides summer parties, that was.

At first, I liked him a lot. He was a genuinely nice guy. But once Grace associated more with the Baysiders and tossed me aside, I lumped Sean in with the rest of them and made assumptions.

I didn't know what to say, so I just gave him a small smile before he closed the door and jogged around to give Grace a quick kiss.

Grace climbed into the truck and jiggled the key a few times before the engine caught. When she started dating Sean, she had yet to get tangled in the Baysider world. But after the first few weeks, she completely changed, and I no longer was a part of her life. She dropped me like a hot pan, but I was the one that got burned.

The next summer, I started dating Reid, and thought it might have been an opening for Grace and I to reconnect, but all it did was alienate us more. Some of Sean's friends were the ones responsible for pushing Reid out, and that fact alone separated Grace and me even more.

But this... this crossed the line. And for some reason, Grace seemed to think so too.

"I'm sorry, Mars Bar," she said, using my old nickname. She called me the name of a candy bar I didn't even like, which she thought made it more ironic. "This is all my fault."

I called her Graceland, like the Elvis estate, which I said was ironic because she couldn't stand his music.

I didn't pull out her nickname now, though. I didn't say a word as we drove off. The only sound in the car was the rattling of the loose tailpipe and the turn signal when Grace took a left onto Bayview Boulevard.

Grace parked in Reid's driveway, turned off the car, and stared out the windshield.

"I know I can't change things, Mars Bar, but... I also know I was a raging witch with a b to you the last few years. And you didn't deserve it. It's just that… when I'm around all of them, I get swept up, you know? It's a crappy excuse. I just…," she sighed, dropping her hands into her lap. "I have no excuse. I shouldn't be making excuses for how I've treated you. And you have no reason to accept my apology or be my friend again, but just know I am sorry. I should have stopped them, like Sean said, when we saw you at the pool party. They always choose a girl to mess with, to be the victim of their prank each summer. I thought if I was rude to you that you would leave. But Declan claimed you, and that kind of scared me. They change guys every year, and knowing it was Declan… I mean, it's Declan."

She didn't have to elaborate for me to understand.

I gulped, the lump in my throat making it hard to swallow. These were all the words I wanted to hear from Grace. Except they were almost two years too late.

I never thought I would get an apology from her. I never thought the two of us could be in the same place again without fighting.

But here we sat, side by side, like we used to.

"Thanks for getting me out of there," I whispered. At this point, I didn't have anything else to say. I needed some time to think about what she said and how it changed things going forward.

First, though, I needed to shower and get all remnants of seagulls off of me.

I opened the door and slipped out, looking back at my bike in the pickup.

"I'll help," Grace said. She dropped the tailgate while I punched in the garage code so she could get my bike into the garage.

Knowing Reid wouldn't be home for a while, I thanked Grace, and told her I'd be fine, that all I needed was a long, hot shower, and to go to sleep.

It was barely seven, but I didn't care.

I watched as she backed down the driveway, lifting a hand as she waved goodbye. Then, I turned into the house, dropped my backpack on the floor next to the door, and pushed past the dogs.

They went outside, and I shuffled my way to the guest bathroom, shedding clothes as I walked through the room.

Once the shower steamed up the bathroom, I stepped in, letting the scalding hot water wash over me. I shampooed my hair four times, hoping I got everything out, and scrubbed my body, especially my shoulder and face, twice.

An hour later, the water turned cold. I stepped out, then used a hand towel to wipe a spot on the mirror clear.

Normally, I would comb through my hair and do some skin care, but tonight, I couldn't bother. I couldn't even bring myself to look in the mirror. I was too scared of what I would find.

I managed to get a pair of pajamas on, but didn't have the energy to dry my hair, so I wrung it out with a towel a few times before going to let the dogs in.

Cuddling two fluffy dogs in bed was exactly what I needed right now.

My entire body felt heavy, from my head to my feet. Like the adrenaline and anxiety finally wore off, leaving me with a shell of a body.

I wondered what my friends would do when they got back with Liam and Livvy. Would they all hang out for the rest of the night? Would they invite me over, or would they continue on their own?

Would Reid stay with them? Or would he come home, since he claimed to want to 'lay low' for the summer?

I snuggled down under the covers, leaving just enough room over my face so I could breathe. By the weight, I guessed Noodle had made himself comfortable next to my legs, and Fluff tucked herself up against my back. They created a sense of safety and security that I hadn't experienced in a while.

It also made me absolutely break.

Tears streamed down my cheeks, my breath coming in small gasps, trying to keep up with the sobs wracking through my body.

This entire summer had taken a nosedive, and I was the only person to blame for it.

Crashing into Declan had been one of the most embarrassing things in my life up until now. Falling for his elaborate prank topped the list, even higher than the seagull issues.

At least with the seagulls, people felt bad for me. People being Grace and Sean, but it counted.

I highly doubted anyone felt sorry for me for being played by Declan Storms. They had probably all been in on it from the start. He and his friends hatched this little plan of stringing me along and leaving me out to dry and I fell for it.

I would *never* trust a Baysider again.

They were nothing but trouble. Even Grace had seen that. They played with people's emotions for fun, like they didn't have enough of their own entertainment. They had all the money in the world to do whatever they wanted, yet preying on the innocent occupied their time.

The saddest part was I fell for it all, hook, line, and sinker. Just having someone show me the slightest amount of attention sent me following along like a puppy, chasing after them, begging for more.

That was my problem. I desperately wanted to gain people's attention, to get them to show any sort of affection my way. I craved it; I needed it like I needed air.

Yet, time after time, I was let down. Humiliated. Left behind. Abandoned. Rejected.

I was Marlowe Mitchell, the girl no one could love.

My tears soaked through the blanket and top sheet now, pooling on the pillow under me. Noodle moved to rest his head on my knees, pressing into my legs, comforting me. It helped.

I sucked in a deep breath, trying to get a grip on my tears, but it was no use. The dam had broken, and I needed to let it all out. The weight of the past few weeks had caught up to me.

Being embarrassed by Declan.

Grandmum, Mom, and Dad all forgetting my birthday—again.

Grace being Grace at the party, yet taking me home tonight and apologizing. That one I needed to replay in my mind when I wasn't such a blubbering mess.

Even thinking about Eleanor got to me. Knowing I would never see or speak with her again. The scavenger hunt I was pretty sure I was going to fail at.

And most of all... Reid. Seeing him again after not talking for close to a year. After losing him in my life when he had been a constant.

Then there was the one thing I had yet to admit to myself that finally broke through with all the tears.

I still loved him, even if he had broken my heart.

That last realization really cracked everything open. My tears ran harder as my chest heaved with every breath.

Noodle shifted, his body going rigid next to me. I lifted my head just enough to see him staring straight at the door.

"Marlowe?"

Anchored Affections

HE SECOND OUR eyes connected, he rushed in. His face paled, his eyes going wild as he scanned my face, finding only a blubbering mess.

"Marlowe? Are you okay? What happened? What's wrong?" He raced through his questions while still searching me. Or, as much as he could see, since most of me remained hidden under the covers.

I watched as Reid tore his gaze away from me, stood up straight, his face steeling. "Noodle, Fluff, out. Go," he commanded. They listened right away, leaping off the bed and scurrying out of the room. He closed the door after them, then turned back to me, his voice softening considerably. "Marlowe? Are you hurt?"

I shook my head and sloppily wiped my nose with the back of my hand.

Reid reached forward, his thumb brushing against my cheek to wipe at the tears still running. I blinked and a few more spilled out. He kneeled at the side of the bed, trailing his fingers down my cheek and holding the side of my face in his hand.

"Mars? Talk to me. You're scaring me." His voice quivered just slightly enough for me to catch it.

"I'm fine," I squeaked out between deep breaths. The moment he touched me, my sobs subsided, but I couldn't fully catch my breath or stop the tears from falling. My brain didn't shut off because he came in; if anything, it made it worse seeing him sitting here, staring at me like he used to. Like he cared so deeply, that when I hurt, he hurt.

"Panic attack?" he asked gently, in the same calm, soothing voice he used to when he would try to talk me out of one. I shook my head. Even though I was pretty sure I had at least the start of one at the beach, it wasn't what was happening now.

But thinking of all the times he comforted me in the past made me start sobbing again. It hadn't been often, but enough for my mind to jump to each memory, replaying them on a loop.

I squeezed my eyes shut to try to block it all out, but it didn't work.

A second later, the bed dipped and a taut, muscular arm wrapped around me, the other sliding beneath the pillow under my head. Reid shifted, pulling me close, resting his chin on my shoulder.

"Whatever happened, Mars, it's going to be okay," he whispered softly into my ear. "I'm here. I'm sorry I wasn't here earlier, but I'm here now. For whatever you need, my lo—Marlowe."

That only made me cry harder, but true to his word, he didn't move. He tightened his hold and buried his face into the crook of my neck, moving with me as my body shook with sobs.

I let it all out—crying not only for the circumstances I had somehow found myself in, but for myself too. For trusting people I shouldn't have. For not trusting those I should. For making mistakes, when everyone around me had pointed them out. Tears streamed down my cheeks, representing what I had gained and lost in my life.

It was my breaking point, and everything had to go.

Once I had shed all my tears, I attempted to match each one of Reid's deep breaths, using them to calm myself down. He waited patiently, staying still until I was ready.

When I moved, he loosened his grip, propping himself up on one arm as I turned around. Once face to face, he lifted his other hand and wiped the tears off my face again.

"There she is," he breathed, a hint of a smile on his lips. "My beautiful Marlowe. What do you need?"

I wanted to talk about how he almost called me "my love" a few minutes ago. How he almost said it the other day. And when he changed it at the last second, it shattered my heart into a thousand pieces.

I would do *anything* to hear him call me 'my love' again. I had never heard someone outside of a Zane Hunter movie say it. Every time Reid said it, it filled me with a certain kind of happiness I had yet to replicate anywhere else.

If it was on the tip of his tongue, then he must have felt that way too, right? It couldn't have just been me.

However, I didn't want my burdens to be his burdens. He had already told me how I could have done better than Declan. He tried to warn me away, and I didn't listen.

I couldn't tell him about what happened earlier tonight. Reid wasn't an 'I told you so' kind of guy, but I knew he would think it. I would have if I were him. Anyone would. The entire island could have pointed to a blinking neon billboard that told me to stay away from Declan Storms, and I still would have been too dumb to figure it out.

Instead, I just pointed to the bathroom, wanting to splash some cold water on my face and see how horrible I looked, how puffy my eyes must have been.

Reid dropped his legs over the side of the bed, then held my arm as I did the same. He walked me to the bathroom as if I couldn't do it on my own.

But I didn't hate it. It was so typically Reid that it made me want to burst into tears again. I never thought I deserved someone so amazing like him, even when we were together. He was too good for me.

When I got to the sink, he let go, backing out of the bathroom and closing the door behind him.

My eyes were indeed swollen. The amber color popped against the red eyes and blotchy skin around them. They looked rather pretty on their own, but the rest of my face was a mess.

I washed up in the sink, then ran a washcloth under the cold water, pressing it into my skin and eyes to attempt to tame the redness and swelling. Most likely, it did nothing, but at least it made me feel better.

All I wanted to do now was sleep. I didn't have to work tomorrow, so I could sleep in as long as the dogs would let me. Maybe I could sleep the entire day away. If I slept all day, I wouldn't have to face anyone.

Not Declan.

Not Grace.

Not even Reid.

I opened the door to head back to bed. I needed to swap out pillows, as the one had to be soaking wet by now, between my hair and my tears.

I stopped after taking a single step out of the bathroom. My gaze hit the pillows first. They were both brand new, not the same ones I left on there a few minutes ago.

Then I saw Reid. He sat on the side of the bed facing the bathroom, one ankle crossed over the other knee, his hands wringing in his lap. He looked up at me as I came closer.

The sheer panic had left his eyes, but the worry hadn't. He searched my face, as if trying to find answers to his unasked questions.

"You changed my pillows?"

He glanced over his shoulder and shrugged. "Just grabbed some from the closet and changed them for you," he said, like it was no big deal.

But it *was* a big deal. It was a huge deal. It was a small, miniscule detail that most people would never think of.

But Reid Bennett had never been like most people. He always thought of the little things, always put the needs of others before himself.

That's when it hit me that he was here. At his house. He didn't go out with Caleb and Liam and the crew. He came home instead.

It wasn't because of me, but in my delusional state, I wanted to think it might have been.

"What do you need, Mars?" he asked softly as I turned and sat on the bed next to him. He was significantly taller than me, so where his feet hit the floor, mine didn't quite make it.

I sighed quietly. Whatever I told him, he would make happen. No matter what. I needed to tell him the truth. It pained me to keep secrets. I never had before. We had always been so open with each other, that hiding something from him physically made my chest hurt.

He wouldn't judge me. I knew that with all my heart. The only judgment would come from myself, which would hurt just as badly.

"You were right," I whispered, staring at my hands in my lap. There was no other way to start this conversation.

Reid heaved a breath of his own, his shoulders sagging. "I'm guessing whatever it was, I probably don't want to be right."

I opened my mouth to debate that, but he beat me to the punch. "You're hurt, Mars. Whatever it was you think I was right about made you upset. I have never seen you this distraught. So no, I don't want to be right. I never want to see you miserable at the expense of my opinions."

His words were like a knife to my heart. No matter what happened between the two of us, Reid still cared about me. Deeply, it seemed. Even if we weren't together, we weren't in love, he loved me enough to not want me hurt.

That's what he was saying when he told me I was better than Declan Storms. That's why he was so concerned that I was dating him.

He didn't want to see me get hurt. It was like he knew what would happen.

And in hindsight, I should have known too.

"I was so stupid, Reid," I started, a few tears popping up in the corner of my eyes again. I didn't have enough energy to wipe them away, so I let them fall, each one tumbling into my hands. "I should have known better. I just got so caught up."

The similarities between that statement and the one Grace made earlier tonight hit me hard. We weren't so different after all.

I enjoyed the attention. Having someone show an interest in me again made me feel valued. Pursuing Declan even after Reid came back to the island had been a conscious decision. Going to the beach tonight had been out of spite, out of jealousy, out of feeling inferior, inadequate, and insignificant to Reid and my friends.

Most of all, I desperately wanted to feel love again. And though I knew it wouldn't be with Declan, even from the first moment I crashed into him, my mind deceived me, playing tricks on me and thinking that being with him would provide the same serotonin boost I used to get with Reid.

That was what was on my mind. But they were thoughts I could never express to Reid.

If he told me the same, I would be *gutted*. Just thinking about him with another girl made me want to vomit. I couldn't tell Reid the reasons I had been with Declan up until now. Even if Reid had moved on, like it seemed he had, it wouldn't be right to rub it in his face like that.

So I left that part out and continued on. "It was just… dumb. That's all. I made horrible mistakes and I'm probably overreacting and—"

"Stop it," he blurted out. He reached for my hands in my lap, holding both of them in one of his. "That's not you, Mars. I won't let you talk about yourself like that. You are not dumb. You are not stupid. Something happened that most likely was out of your control. I'm not going to let you beat yourself up about it."

He squeezed my hand once, then let go, leaving me feeling isolated once more. I couldn't make him understand how everything was always my fault. He hated when I spoke badly about myself, and that was all I could do in this moment.

Exhausted, both physically and mentally, I turned and crawled back into the bed. I pulled the covers up to my chin and stared at him as he stood, staring down at me.

"He humiliated me, Reid. It was all a big joke that I wasn't in on."

His jaw tightened, one hand clenching at his side. The muscles and veins in his forearm flexed as he did. "Who?"

He wasn't asking for verification. He was asking for confirmation.

"Declan," I breathed. Just saying his name filled the room with tension.

Reid gave me one curt nod, then stood. "I'm sorry, Mars."

I could sense the rage coursing through him. He chewed on the inside of his cheek as if he wanted to say more, but held back, probably for my sake.

"Get some rest," he added, before walking away.

Instinctively, I reached out and grabbed his wrist, pulling him back to the bed. He glanced down at me, taking in the tears and my gross, splotchy face, and frowned.

His whole face softened as he lifted a hand to stroke my cheek.

"Can you stay? Please... just stay with me?"

Cresting Waves

I AWOKE THE NEXT morning of my own accord. Not from the sun streaming through the window, because I forgot to close the blinds. Not from Noodle and Marshmallow jumping on me. And not because of an alarm.

I awoke to absolutely nothing but silence. The blinds were closed, even though I didn't remember doing so. The bedroom door was closed too, so the dogs couldn't come in even if they wanted to.

And Reid was gone.

My eyes widened. He stayed. He hadn't even hesitated when I asked. In an instant, he had pulled the covers back and slid in, wrapping his arms around me, and settling my head on his chest.

That was the last thing I remembered—the rhythmic beating of his heart lulling me to sleep as he gently stroked my hair.

He had whispered something as my eyes started to close, but I couldn't remember what it was.

But he wasn't here now. The side of the bed he slept on was empty, cold, as if he had been gone for a while. Did he spend the entire night, or did he just wait for me to fall asleep?

Rolling over, I checked the time on my phone, noticing it had been plugged in.

First, he changed the pillows. At some point, he must have closed the blinds, so the sun didn't shine on my face this morning. And he charged my phone. I didn't even remember leaving it on the nightstand to begin with.

It was nine in the morning. Well after the dogs demanded breakfast. I shot up, but then remembered Reid was home. Though I was being paid to take care of them, he would have dealt with them by now.

I took my time getting dressed. No amount of makeup was going to cover the mess that was my face. Everything was puffy, my eyes thankfully not bloodshot anymore, but the swelling had yet to go completely down. I splashed some cold water and dried it with a towel. My hair was a mess, since I slept with it wet, so I threw it into a low ponytail and grabbed a Covington Cove High baseball hat from my duffel bag before making my way out to the kitchen.

Noodle and Fluff greeted me, jumping off the couch and sliding their way across the wood floors. They were always crashing into each other when they skidded, which made me laugh.

That felt good—laughing. The two of them always made me happy. Maybe today I would take them for a long walk down the beach. They loved chasing the waves and galloping in the sand. Fluff got all sorts of disgusting afterwards, but it was worth it.

The coffee maker was on, a mug left next to it. Reid, again.

But that wasn't all. A plate of eggs and avocado toast sat beside the mug. And a bud vase with a single, bright yellow sunflower.

My favorite flower.

Alongside all of that was a handwritten note. I recognized Reid's handwriting right away. Not that there was any question of who it was from.

M—

Hope you got some good rest. I'll be in the library. Here for whatever you want to do today.

—R

It brought a smile to my face as I reached for the plate. I set it on the island, then got some creamer for the coffee and settled down to eat. I had no doubt he would still be in the library, but the hammering in my head demanded sustenance and caffeine first.

The hangover from a long night of crying was way worse than any other type.

Once I finished, I put my dishes away, refilled my coffee, and made my way down to the hall.

My heart pounded, not sure what I was going to find. Would things be awkward? Last night had been so... intimate. Like the old us.

But we weren't the old us anymore. No matter how normal Reid tried to make things seem.

"Hey," I said, leaning against the door frame and taking a sip of coffee. Reid turned, lowering the book in his hands to the table next to him.

His eyes softened, a half-smile appearing on his lips. I couldn't tell if it was pity, sadness, or concern that crossed his features.

"Good morning," he answered, gesturing for me to come inside. I took a seat on the chair opposite him, but didn't put my mug down. It gave my hands something to do, something to focus on, so I didn't freak out.

"Are you okay?" he asked, staring right at me.

I nodded. "Mostly, I guess."

He didn't say anything, leaving me to fill the silence.

"You said you'd be around for whatever today? Did you mean that?" I blurted out, feeling a bit ridiculous. He wouldn't have said it if he didn't.

"Absolutely. What do you want to do?"

"Figure out the next clue. But also maybe take the dogs for a walk on the beach. Do you... do you want to come?" I lifted the mug to my lips again, taking a small sip.

"Absolutely," he repeated, putting his hands on his knees. "Back to the beach it is."

I paused, my brows furrowing. "Back? What do you mean, back?" If he already took the dogs for a beach walk, then we could do something different.

But Reid just tilted his head and looked at me like he was the one confused. "I go for a run on the beach every morning. I thought you knew?"

So *that's* why he was up so early taking showers. I hadn't asked, and since so long had passed, I thought it would be weird if I did. Which, obviously, I was right; he assumed I knew what he was up to already. "Oh. No, I didn't. You run every morning?"

He stood and shrugged. "Most of them, when I can. Running on the beach is a lot different than on the pavement at home, but a run is a run. Helps clear my head, you know? Sometimes I follow it with a weights workout, sometimes not."

There it was. The confession of the muscles. Running plus weights apparently equaled a hard, toned, muscular body. I wasn't mad about it, that was for sure.

"Well, we can do something else if you don't—"

"Nope," he interrupted, shaking his head. "You want to walk on the beach, we're going to the beach. I'll get the leashes. You get the clue?"

Five minutes later, our toes dug into the sand, the dogs on their leashes in Reid's hand.

"When did you start running every day?" I asked, feeling a bit like I was violating some sort of privacy agreement we both unintentionally entered on.

"When I got back home last year," he admitted. The knife in my heart twisted. He meant after he left the island at the end of the summer. After we broke up. "Working out became an escape for me. I didn't start intending to do it all the time, but it worked its way into being a habit, I guess. A way to get out of my own head."

I remembered back a few years, to the first time we kept in contact outside of the summer.

That was when he told me that what happened on the island also happened at home. When Reid first came to Covington Cove, the Baysiders ostracized him for not being like them. He had been a newly rich kid, not a lifelong one, and had lived a completely different lifestyle from them. So they kicked him to the Gennies, where, thankfully, he was way happier.

But back at home, they did the opposite. His friends thought he was too good for them. He was a rich kid now, with a summer vacation home, parents that flew around the world for business at the drop of a hat. The kid who moved into a new, giant home on the other side of town.

His friends at home rejected him for being rich. The Baysiders rejected him for not being rich long enough. There was no middle ground for someone like Reid. He was alone.

"I'm glad you found something you like to do," I said, trying to put a positive spin on it. "It's definitely working for you, I'll say that."

My face turned beet red as I realized what I said. I just admitted to admiring his body, his newly acquired muscles.

But Reid laughed and thanked me. What he didn't do was ask about Declan, or what happened last night. And I didn't offer it, but I did say one thing.

"Want to hear something crazy?"

He nodded, looking over at me, his dark eyes full of curiosity.

"Grace and Sean saved me from the Declan thing yesterday. And Grace drove me back here, my bike in her pickup. But that's not the craziest part."

Reid just continued to stare, his brows rising with each sentence I made. He didn't know Grace that well, just that she had been my best friend. To him, she was more Baysider than Gennie, even though she grew up a Gennie.

"She apologized. Said she got swept into the Bayside life and lost herself."

"What did you say?" Reid asked, tugging on the dog's leashes as we turned around to head back.

"Nothing yet," I shrugged. "Didn't really think about it too much last night." I purposefully didn't mention the connection I made between how Grace had acted and how I had with Declan.

"Well, that's been a long time coming. I know you missed her a lot."

He was right. I missed her something terrible. I wasn't sure our relationship would ever be the same as it was, but I would love to have her back as a friend, at least.

"I wonder if she knows about the clues. If the Baysiders spread the news about it by now. I wasn't really supposed to tell anyone, but..."

Reid stayed quiet, but I knew what he was thinking. Probably about how much he despised them, and that they were going to ruin everything for me.

Either that, or he was still stewing over the fact that I told Declan. That I ever associated with Declan in the first place.

But I was at peace with it. Whatever happened, happened. More than likely, the story about the seagulls would be the top gossip for a while, and my scavenger hunt of sorts would be forgotten.

We reached the house and Reid used an old towel left by the back door to wipe the wet sand off the dogs.

"What now?" he asked, looking up at me from a crouch.

I grabbed the envelope from my pocket and held it up.

"Clue two," I said, wanting nothing more than for him to help me figure it out. "But first, candy."

Pier of Revenge

T HE FACT THAT Reid didn't even question my statement warmed my heart. He had always been great at going with the flow, to follow my lead whenever I said random things.

In this case, I was craving some Cove Candy sweets, and knew it would be the best way to get over all the craziness from the last few weeks. There was nothing a good Sea Salt Caramel Pearl couldn't cure. The bag full of tiny, rolled caramels infused with sea salt within and a sprinkle on top was my addiction.

The bell jingled over our heads as we entered the shop, instantly filling me with regret.

Since I started staying at the Bennett's, I hadn't checked in on Mrs. Ruth. It had been almost two weeks. The last time I did was the day Mrs. Bennett called to ask me to house sit.

"Sam! Is Mrs. Ruth in today?" I asked, basically sprinting to the counter.

He smiled at me and pointed to the back room where the candy was made. Mrs. Ruth wasn't allowed to make it herself anymore, but that didn't stop her from supervising as much as possible.

I slid behind the counter and pushed through the half door, finding just who I wanted to see. "Hi, Mrs. Ruth! How are you? I haven't seen you in so long!"

She scoffed and waved me off until the peppermints were done being cut. Once she approved the evenness of the candies, Elliot, the newest candy maker, bagged them and tied it shut with a twist tie.

"Don't spout such nonsense, Marlowe. You were at my house the other week."

I blinked, not realizing she knew I had been there. "But how—"

"Who else brings me blueberry muffins and croissants from Seaside? No one. Just you."

My smile stretched across my cheeks. I was absolutely bursting with pride. "Well, I know they're your favorite, Mrs. Ruth. Actually, I'll be working tomorrow. I'll bring you some more, okay?"

"If I'm sleeping, just—"

"Put them in the fridge. I know. You had some gorgeous flowers on your table when I was there. Who were they from?" I leaned against the door frame, crossing my arms over my chest. I could hear Reid and Sam chatting behind us.

"My secret admirer," Mrs. Ruth called back.

Sam chuckled and leaned over the half door. "They were from Eleanor. Don't you lie."

Mrs. Ruth sneered and coughed. After dabbing her mouth with the pocket square she kept in her hand at all times, she said, "Darn girl sent me flowers, then up and died on me before I could call her for a proper thank you."

My jaw dropped. I blinked, not sure what to say. Normally, I loved her bluntness, but that... was it too soon? It felt like it was too soon.

But Mrs. Ruth waved me off. "Oh, hush. When you get to be my age, dying is a joking matter. It's the latest trend now—everyone's doing it. Just wish we had some prior notice, is all."

All I could do was nod, still flabbergasted. "Well, Mrs. Ruth, I have some Pearls to buy and a pier to walk. I hope you have a day as fabulous as you are." I leaned down to give her a hug, which she returned with one arm and a sigh. "I'll stop by with the food tomorrow."

"Sam! Give Marlowe her Sea Salt Caramel Pearls now," Mrs. Ruth said, talking to her son instead of me. Our conversation had been dismissed, so I walked back to the main shop, shaking my head.

I never knew what to expect with Mrs. Ruth. She constantly surprised me and I loved it.

Sam hooked me and Reid up with a full scoop of the pearls and refused to take my money. He said if he did, his mother would have his hide, even though he was a grown adult. I didn't doubt it, so I slipped my wallet back into my pocket and we left.

We turned down the next street, both of us subconsciously heading toward the pier without talking about it. We walked side by side, enjoying the candy in the mid-morning sun.

"Have you read the clue yet?" Reid asked as we approached the entrance to the pier. Tourists dotted the walkway, but it wasn't overly busy.

I shook my head, a curl escaping and bouncing in my face. Reid's hand twitched, like he wanted to reach out and fix it, but at the last second, he shook his head and dug into the bag for a Pearl.

"Nope. Haven't touched it yet. Do you want to read it?" I reached into my back pocket and pulled out the small envelope. Considering the initial text message was only two lines, I didn't expect a long letter or anything. Honestly, I didn't know what to expect.

"It's yours to figure out, Marlowe. I'm just here to help if you need. What do you think it all leads to?"

"No idea. The text before the first clue said something about the prize not being the only prize. So that means there is a prize, but not what. And that whatever it is, isn't the only prize. Not vague at all, right?" I laughed at the absurdity of it all, and Reid joined me.

"Not at all. Go ahead, read it. Let's see if we can get this one."

"You mean get it faster than I did the first one? Let's hope so because if there's a lot of these, it might take all summer."

Reid rolled his eyes. "You're so hard on yourself. You figured out that last clue perfectly, Mars. I have no doubt you're going to get the rest just fine."

The confidence he had in me outweighed my own often. Sometimes, I relied on his to push me through. Like right now.

I handed him the Pearls for safekeeping while I slid my finger under the envelope and took out the index card size cardstock.

"Follow the path where seagulls play, where friendships are guarded, and where footprints leave their mark. Your next clue will not be found in the dark."

I stopped walking suddenly, my brows furrowed in confusion.

"Sorry!" a person exclaimed as they bumped into me from behind. Reid grabbed my arm and pulled me out of the way as I apologized to the lady headed down the pier.

"You're going to get run over," Reid said with a chuckle. "Can't stop like that in the middle of the pier, Mars. Now, read it again?"

I hadn't stopped looking at the card, reading it over in my mind. I repeated it out loud one more time for Reid, then looked up at him to see what he was thinking.

"Got anything?"

He chewed on the inside of his cheek, his gaze glassy and off to the side. I could tell he was going over it, just like I was.

"Well, one thing's for sure. The seagull part isn't funny," I muttered to myself. "Too soon."

Either Reid didn't hear me, or he ignored my comment in favor of working out the clue. "The only thing that jumps out first is the part about the dark. Wherever it is, it seems like we can only access it during the daytime."

I nodded, taking the candy back and resuming my munching. "That's logical."

Before I could continue to decipher the rest, a loud seagull caw came from down the pier a few yards. A caw that was too loud to be from an actual bird.

It hit again, finally drawing my attention. Reid's too.

A group of people huddled together, leaning against the pier railing a few yards away from us. Two of the guys were running and flapping their arms like wings and cawing.

At me.

The rest of them were standing around, the girls trying to hide their giggles behind their hands, the guys outright doubled over, laughing.

Declan Storms and company.

Reid tensed next to me. I reached out, brushing my hand over his arm in an attempt to diffuse him.

It didn't work. The more the boys kept cawing, the more he stood up straight, his arms clenching at his side, his jaw tight.

At the same time, my chest tightened, especially after I saw who was with the group.

I couldn't panic now. Now was *not* the time for my anxiety to flare up. I had to keep my wits about me and not let them see how much they affected me. Besides, the way Reid was acting, I more than likely would have to pull him down the pier before something happened.

Reid raised a hand and raked it through his hair, his biceps flexing as he messed up his curls. His nostrils flared as he took in a deep breath.

"Watch out everyone. Check the skies. We might be under attack soon!" Declan shouted in my direction.

My jaw dropped for the second time this morning, but it wasn't out of awe. It was out of sheer shock. The audacity that boy had. How did I not see it before?

He grinned an evil grin, the dimples not bothering to show this time. He was now only a few feet in front of me, as he and his friends made their way over while I was in a stupor, watching the ones pretending to fly.

One of them cawed loudly, right in my ear. I flinched and ducked, which only made everyone around me laugh harder.

Reid pushed me to the side, getting right up in the guy's face.

"Careful!" Declan said. "You might end up with crap on

your head. Like she did. What does that make this Gennie maid? A crap—"

But he didn't get to finish his insult before Reid's fist connected with his face.

I gasped, my hands flying to my mouth. "Reid!"

I wanted to tell him to stop, but it also was the same thing I had wanted to do to Declan the other night, too. Except he had ducked out of the way and I had gone sprawling.

Reid reeled his arm back, ready to punch him again. I called out before he could. "Reid! Stop!"

I grabbed his other arm with both hands and tugged him toward me, away from Declan, who was now trying to manage the blood pouring out of his nose.

"You broke my nose! You'll pay for that!" Declan shouted, but it came out a bit mumbled, like he had a cold.

I restrained myself from laughing. He was right—Reid could be in a lot of trouble. Declan was a Baysider, but more than that, his parents were lawyers.

Reid shook out his right hand, flexing the fingers. I wondered if he had broken any of his knuckles with the force he had put behind that punch.

He wound one arm around my waist, pulling me into him this time. I stayed tucked up against him while he stared at Declan with the most sinister look I had ever seen.

"You come near Marlowe again, and the next punch will leave you on the ground," he seethed. He tightened his grip around me.

Declan glared at Reid. "You don't know what you got yourself into, Bennett. You just ruined your life."

Instead of trembling, like I was, Reid threw his head back and barked out a laugh. "Sure, Storms. You think that now. I'm not worried. Not with what I know."

They were head to head, Reid having a few inches on Declan.

"You—"

But Reid cut him off. "What I know is that you're not untouchable, Storms. You might have forgotten about Gabrielle, but I haven't."

The look he gave Declan was definitely one of confidence, not of worry. My gaze ping-ponged between the two of them. Clearly, they both know what Reid was talking about, even if I didn't.

Declan was furious, but didn't say another word.

Someone had grabbed him a few napkins, and he shoved them under his nose, still trying to stop the bleeding.

Reid lifted his arm from my waist, settling it around my shoulders as he turned both of us to leave.

"Clinic's around the corner. Feel free to tell them *exactly* what happened," I added over my shoulder before I looked away and left.

Charting New Paths

REID'S ARM DIDN'T leave my shoulder until we got to his car and he opened the door for me. I let him stew all the way back to the parking lot, but once we pulled out on the main road, I had to know.

"What do you know about Declan? Who's Gabrielle?" I blurted out.

He didn't even bother looking at me before turning at the light. His breaths were still labored and his shoulders remained tight.

"Nothing that needs to be discussed," he answered curtly, like it physically pained him to be talking right now.

My face fell. Reid was *pissed*. Rightfully so, but still, it worried me. He was the kind of guy who wouldn't hurt a spider in the corner, and yet he just punched Declan Storms in the face so hard, he broke his nose.

Reid hadn't even blinked when Declan threatened him. Whatever he had on Declan was enough for him to not worry about getting in any trouble.

And he did it all for me.

I couldn't tear my eyes off of him the entire drive back to his house. He clenched his jaw so tight, I worried for his teeth. Occasionally, he snarled, like he was thinking about something and didn't like it.

My heart sank with every block we passed, realizing what was happening.

If I had left the Bennett's house when Reid arrived, we wouldn't be in this situation. We wouldn't have gone to the pier. I wouldn't have had Reid stay with me while I cried my eyes dry last night.

And I probably wouldn't have gone to the beach with Declan. The only reason I did was because I was angry with Reid and my friends.

If we had separated on the night of the Masquerade, Reid and I wouldn't be so closely intertwined. He wouldn't be dragged into my drama, into my personal life.

We would have stayed strangers, just like we had been the past year.

In short—once again, it was all my fault. All Reid had wanted to do was lie low this summer, and this was the opposite of that.

"Why are you so mad right now, Reid?" I whispered, as he pushed the button to open the garage door. He didn't pull in; instead, he parked on the driveway and turned off the car.

We both sat and stared out the windshield for a moment. Every time I had been in this position lately, it ended in confusion. With Reid outside the mansion—confusion. With Grace, right here—even more confusion.

Nothing was going right this summer. Everything was upside down and so far out of my control, I didn't know what to do about it. I either caused it, or I was the problem behind it.

Yet, I felt like I had done nothing at the same time. Sure, I crashed into Declan Storms and set off that entire situation. But, looking back, it appeared as if he already had something planned. I just happened to be the moron who got sucked in first.

Reid shook his head and leaned back, shoving both hands into his curls and tugging. Then, he slammed a fist onto the steering wheel, making me jump.

"He *hurt* you, Marlowe. He's a jerk who deserved what he got."

I stared at him, watching as his face changed from outright anger to concern and worry. I reached out, placing my hand over his on the steering wheel. He didn't flinch at the contact, which gave me hope. Finally, he turned and looked at me, his dark eyes full of fire.

"He hurt you," he repeated, in a low whisper this time, like it strained him to even say.

I frowned and tucked my lips in, thinking. "Physically, I'm fine. He didn't do anything except embarrass me. All that's hurt really is my pride..."

Reid laid his other hand over mine, grasping tight, like I was a life raft that could save him from drowning. "What did he do, exactly? From the first moment."

The pure desperation in his voice twisted the knife in my heart. The one that wedged itself there the second he ended things last summer, that dug deeper when I saw him in the kitchen with the baseball bat.

The one that edged close to making me break.

The knife that knew I was still in love with Reid. No matter what happened.

It was when the knife got removed that I would fall apart completely.

"Let's just say, I didn't have crashing my bike into someone like Declan Storms on my bucket list this summer," I started, trying to crack a joke to lighten the mood. It didn't work, and the mention of Declan's name made Reid grimace.

I told him what happened when I crashed. How Declan brought flowers and came to dinner for my birthday. About the parties. The texts. The beach.

Every minute I continued the story, Reid's face grew more and more strained. His hands clenched over mine.

"You told him the clue?" he asked when I finished. It wasn't so much of a question as it was a statement, like he already knew I had, but couldn't believe it himself.

I cocked my head, not sure why that was the one item he jumped to. Reid had walked in on the situation in the cafe, surely overhearing enough to understand the context.

But that wasn't what he was upset about. Being with him at the pool party was clearly the issue, not what I said.

"I'm sorry," I whispered, silently begging him to look at me instead of out the window.

He shifted and caught my eye. "You have *nothing* to be sorry for, Mars. I'm the one who should apologize. For everything."

He dropped my hands and reached up, pushing a curl away from my face. His hand skimmed against my cheek.

And he left it there. His dark brown eyes held all the words he couldn't say as he cradled my face in his hand.

I leaned into it, the warmth comforting.

This. This right here was home for me. Where I felt the most loved. The safest. Where I knew that, no matter what, someone had my back. I knew Reid would go to the moon and back for me if he needed to, without hesitation.

This is where I loved him. Where I knew he loved me. Or, at least, he used to.

"I missed your birthday," he breathed, the sadness over-taking everything else in his voice.

"Everyone forgot," I replied, not meaning to make it sound like he should pity me, but more to comfort him that it wasn't just him. I tried to brush it off like it didn't matter, but he saw right through me.

He shook his head just once, just an inch. "I didn't *forget*, Mars. I had a million messages ready to send, but I deleted them all. I didn't think you wanted to hear from me. So I didn't send them."

My heart felt like someone had just ripped it out of my chest. I could picture him sitting on his bed at home, typing and deleting over and over again. In the end, he probably ended up chucking his phone into the beanbag chair on the opposite side of his bedroom.

"It's okay," I whispered, not knowing what else to say. I didn't want him to be upset. Not about me. I wasn't worth his sadness. He deserved all the happiness life could give him, not me bringing him down time after time.

He shook his head again, never breaking eye contact with me. "It's not. But I'll make it up to you."

He leaned in closer, so close our foreheads were almost touching. I breathed in his scent, one so uniquely Reid that it instantly brought me back to every summer we spent together. A mixture of coconut sunscreen and his cologne—green apple with water lotus and cedarwood, he once told me.

I closed my eyes and leaned into his hand, tipping my head forward slightly. I waited, my heart pounding, my soul wanting.

Just when I thought his lips would meet mine, I let out a tiny little gasp, a breath of excitement, of need, of yearning.

But then, my eyes flew open as his hand fell and he let out a long, frustrated breath. He scrubbed his face, then opened his door and got out, slamming it behind him.

I sat stunned for a moment, then scrambled to follow, chasing him into the garage, where he stopped next to the door to the adjoined gym.

"I'll be in here for a while if you need me." But his tone said 'don't need me.'

I waited until the gym door closed before heading into the house.

There was no doubt in my mind that he was about to kiss me. If I had been braver, I would have grabbed his shirt, pulled him closer, and kissed *him*.

But I wasn't brave like that. Not anymore. Not when my heart and my mind were at war, not sure what to do about Reid.

Half of the problem wasn't even his problem. He had gotten so worked up about Declan, about what he did, even though he didn't know what it was. He *punched* Declan in the face for crying out loud.

Although that seemed to be a long time coming, and I wasn't entirely sure it was all because of me. There were other underlying reasons behind it.

I dropped my half-full candy bag on the kitchen counter, then joined the dogs on the couch.

"What do you think, Noodle? Is Reid overreacting? Do you think this entire summer is ridiculous? Do you, by chance, have a time machine?"

He didn't answer, but jumped up and licked my face instead. Marshmallow leaped on the couch, settling on top of my feet.

"Gee, thanks, guys. You give such great advice." I laughed as Noodle licked me again. "Here I was, thinking that staying here might have been a mistake. Being this close to Reid... it seems to cause problems. He's getting involved with my drama, and it's not what he wants. That much I know for sure. He broke up with me, remember?"

Noodle nudged my arm. I lifted it, and he wedged himself next to me, snuggling up between the back pillows and my side. It was a tight fit, but he didn't seem to care.

"You're both making it difficult to want to leave, do you know that? You and the money, I guess. As shallow as it seems, it's still good money..." I trailed off, staring outside at the water. "One more question—I should have kissed him, right?"

Sands of Forgiveness

DIDN'T KNOW WHAT to expect the next morning. I hadn't seen Reid since he ducked behind the gym door last night. I had rummaged through the fridge, collecting random things to eat for dinner, then stayed in the guest room by myself.

I had to work a double today, brunch and lunch, so I was up relatively early compared to my usual sleep in time. After throwing on my work clothes, slipping my feet into the most comfortable tennis shoes I owned, and normally only wore on double days, I headed to the kitchen to feed the dogs.

It had become a routine for Reid and I lately. He disappeared bright and early, and while he was taking his morning shower, I fed the dogs and let them out. We never spoke about it, but it was the habit we fell into.

But I didn't make it to the dogs right away today. The second I stepped into the kitchen, a small, red box pulled my focus away from wagging tails and drooling tongues.

I had become so accustomed to seeing a mug waiting, that the deviation of something new completely captured me. Tentatively, I made my way over, glancing left and right to see if anyone else was around.

Obviously, Reid left the box. It was small but rectangular, a white ribbon glued on to look like it was tied, but it could still be easily opened.

So that was what I did. I opened the box with shaky hands, unsure as to what could be inside. It looked like a jewelry box, but why would Reid have left me jewelry?

My answer came the second the lid was lifted.

Happy birthday, Mars was written on a small slip of paper on the inside.

"I didn't forget, Mars. I'll make it up to you." Reid's comments from last night rang through my mind.

He didn't forget. He had a million messages he wanted to send. And, from the looks of it, even a present.

Trembling, I moved the paper to the side. Then I gasped, finding the present within.

A delicate gold chain with a few charms in the middle. Two small stars and one circular object. I couldn't place it at first, but upon closer inspection, it hit me.

Mars.

It was the planet Mars. Just like the name he called me.

I tucked in my lips and bit down to stop a sob from escaping. He hadn't forgotten my birthday. In fact, had he sent me the messages he said he wanted to, or had sent this, the entire day could have turned in a very different direction.

With my hands still shaking, I managed to gently lift the necklace out of the box and put it around my neck, my fingers clasping over the charms.

This present meant the world to me. I couldn't even put it into words. There was no thank you enough that could convey how much this small, thoughtful gesture meant.

Not that I had anyone to thank at the moment. Creeping over to the stairs, I didn't even hear the shower on upstairs. Either Reid was somewhere else in the house, or he was gone.

Did he not want to be around when I found it? Did he want to just leave it and not talk about it?

Either way, I wore it with pride, then hurried to feed the dogs and get ready for work. I didn't know if I would even see Reid today, or what to say if I did. But that didn't matter now. Because now, I knew his true feelings.

At least, I thought I did.

SOMEHOW LIVING WITH Reid was slowly making me into a morning person, and I wasn't sure how I felt about that just yet. Waking up when the sun had barely made its ascent seemed criminal.

I yawned and stretched, silently asking myself if it would be possible to go back to sleep. When the dogs attacked, I knew that chance had become zero.

"Okay, okay, I'll get you fed. It's probably too early, but I'm guessing you don't care."

After getting my morning routine done, I threw on a tank top and shorts, tossing my hair into its signature half up bun as I walked down the hall.

The house was quiet. The only time I saw Reid over the past three days was in passing. We exchanged pleasantries, but nothing more. The day I found the necklace, he had glanced down at my chest, seeing me wear it, then back up to my eyes. His dark ones had lit up, and I expected him to say something, but he just nodded and went out the door.

It was more awkward than ever now. Especially since finding the necklace the next morning. And after what happened in the car.

Or, what *didn't* happen.

Since it was so early, it seemed highly likely that he was out running. I didn't know for sure when he left or got back, but considering the dogs were with me right now, I had to assume he was gone.

I made it to the kitchen and dropped food in the dogs' bowls before I instinctively looked over at the coffee. Except today, it wasn't on. I didn't get a chance to inspect closer before the sound of the back door opening distracted me.

Well, it distracted me for a moment. Once I saw who came through, I was distracted for a whole other reason.

Reid Bennett walked through, all six foot something of him, bronzed, sweaty, and *shirtless*.

I didn't dare blink, knowing that if I did, the hallucination would disappear. Instead, I kept my eyes trained on him as he wiped his face with the t-shirt in his hands, his chest heaving with each deep breath. He hadn't seen me yet, so I continued to watch as he paced in a circle, his hands on his hips, looking down at the rug beneath him.

Even his curls were damp, plastered to his forehead in little ringlets. As he turned, his back faced me and I now knew what inspired Michaelangelo to create David. The way the muscles on his back rippled with each breath, how they stretched, glistening in the sunlight as he craned his neck from one side to the other...

Still with his back to me, he reached up, lacing his fingers together behind his head, opening his chest to suck in more air. His triceps, biceps, and any other -ceps in his arms flexed, and his shoulders rolled, literally leaving me breathless.

I always thought of Reid as handsome. He had caught my eye the first time Caleb brought him to the cafe to hang out with us.

But this... this was an entirely new Reid. I had never been attracted to overly muscular men, but for some reason, his were just perfection. There was definition on top of definition without being bulky. All I wanted to do was run my hands over his shoulders, down his arms, and trace each individual ab, which were now more pronounced than they had been the other day in the library.

Finally, I blinked, gulping down all my thoughts as I turned back to the coffee pot, trying to put all of my focus on the machine. Before I could do anything, a hand reached around me and pushed the on button.

Reid stood right behind me, his arm slowly retracting as a sly smile adorned his lips.

"I set it before I head out. Turn it on when I get back. It's ready by the time I'm done showering," he said in a low voice, his warm breath tickling my ear.

Holy heck, what is this boy trying to do? His voice sent shivers from my head to my toes, lighting me up in every area possible.

My lips flapped open a few times as my brain attempted to remember the English language. I only regained consciousness when he stepped back a few feet, still looking at me as if I were his favorite candy.

I licked my lips, my mouth parched. Reid closed his eyes briefly, before sucking in a deep breath and leaning against the counter behind him.

"Good morning. You're up early," he said softly, even though there was no one in the house besides us. He tossed his damp t-shirt over his shoulder and crossed his arms over his chest. His muscles tightened as he did, making me weak in the knees.

I shrugged, trying to be as casual as he was, but failing. "You're chipper than you've been lately," I countered, trying desperately not to stare at his bare chest, at the biceps that bulged over it.

He just nodded, his face solemn. "Sorry. I got a little in my head." His eyes snapped to mine. "But know one thing, Marlowe. No matter where we stand, I will *never* let someone hurt you like that. I will not step aside and allow people like Storms to use you. To walk all over you. To hurt you in any way, physical or not. It will not happen while I'm around."

I stopped breathing, watching the fire burn behind his eyes. I always knew Reid would have my back no matter what, but now? Now I knew what he was capable of and how determined he was to keep that promise.

I nodded, taking his words to heart. Wanting to lighten the mood, I said, "Thank you for the necklace," I whispered, reaching up to touch the charms. His eyes followed my hand, staring at the chain around my neck.

"I'm sorry I missed your birthday, Mars," he whispered hoarsely. He cleared his throat and pushed off the counter, running a hand through his hair.

There was no answer to that, so I changed the topic once more, to something we would both enjoy. "We never finished the second clue," I said while patting the counter behind me for the mug. I needed something to do with my hands.

Reid kept his focus on me for another beat before looking down at his still sweaty torso. He gestured to it. "Think I can hit the showers before we dissect? I'm afraid I wouldn't be too great of company before then."

I grinned. "Sure. I'll make breakfast today."

Reid stepped toward me before pausing. If this had been last year, he would have leaned over and kissed my cheek before running off.

Today, he just gave me a small smile before jogging upstairs.

I fixed us an easy breakfast of yogurt parfaits, making him a green tea and finally pouring my coffee. He came down quicker than I thought he would, his hair wet and his t-shirt stuck to the still damp part of his back.

The back that held more muscles than I could name.

"So the only part of the clue I really remember is the part that says we need to go during the daytime. Do you have the rest?" he said, sitting on the stool next to me.

He had said his peace about Declan. There was nothing further I could ask. There was no more clarification needed. We were moving on and leaving all of that behind.

I slid my phone across the counter to him, having taken a picture of the clue last night so I could refer to it without needing the paper close by.

Reid reached over and grabbed a paper and pen, sliding them toward me.

"What's this?"

"For you."

"For what?"

A small chuckle left his lips, followed by a smile. "For you to make your list, Mars. The list I know you've already made in your head. We didn't really discuss the clue yet, but I know the second you read it, you started a new list."

I pursed my lips and narrowed my eyes at him playfully. "First of all," I started, acting as if I were about to argue with him, "you're not wrong."

His smile grew, then he took my phone in his hands and looked at the picture.

"Follow the path where seagulls play, where friendships are guarded, and where footprints leave their mark. Your next clue will not be found in the dark," Reid read out loud. He sipped his tea, deep in thought.

"Still a bit salty about the seagull thing. Do you think someone's messing with me?" I asked, scraping the bottom of my bowl to get the last bits of yogurt. "The coincidence is a little odd." I twirled the spoon in my mouth.

Reid stared at me for a moment before clearing his throat and looking back at the phone. "No. Um, I mean..." He just shook his head, his shoulders hunched over the counter, showing off how tightly his shirt wrapped around them and hugged his biceps. It was all I could focus on this morning, apparently. "No. We got the clue before *that* happened, remember? A coincidence, yes, but I don't see it being related. It would be too elaborate of a play."

"What if I was supposed to find something during the seagull attack? What if there was a clue under the—"

Reid held up his hand to stop me. "No. Really, with how dumb Declan is, I don't think any of them are involved. Remember the cafe? They all said they wanted a piece of the prize. Why would they say that if they were in on it?"

I twisted my lips and sighed. "Well, that's all I got. Seagulls play around the shoreline. No idea where friendships are guarded. And footprints can leave their mark anywhere. Maybe... maybe in cement? Know of any sidewalks going up lately?" I rested my chin on my hand, pouting slightly. The clues weren't as easy as I hoped they were going to be, making me feel kind of dumb.

"I don't. But great thoughts. You're thinking outside the box. I didn't even think about that for footprints."

I turned the phone over, not really wanting to discuss the clue right now. Ever since he left to go shower, one thing had been on my mind.

"Reid?"

He hummed, lifting his brows as he sipped the rest of his tea.

"Are we going to talk about what happened?" I never had a problem being direct with him before, and I wasn't going to start now.

"What happened when? Where?"

I gave him a pointed stare. He was stalling, and he knew it. "You. Me. The other night. In the car." Did I honestly have to spell it all out for him?

He had held my face in his hand.

He had leaned in.

He had almost kissed me.

And I'd be lying if I said I hadn't been desperate for him to actually do so...

Beyond the Breakwater

R EID'S EYES NARROWED. "I'd rather not talk about Storms at all, thanks."

I wanted to roll my eyes at him, but I closed them briefly and groaned inwardly instead. "That's not what I'm talking about."

He froze, his mug lifted halfway to his mouth before he lowered it slowly. Heat flushed into my cheeks as I thought about the car all over again.

"Reid..." I started, almost wanting to change the subject now. But I couldn't. I brought it up. I had to see it through.

His face gave nothing away. Not a single clue as to what he was thinking. I couldn't tell if he regretted what happened, if he had been happy with it, or where he stood at all.

But then... he licked his lips, tucking the bottom one in, and taking a big, deep breath before closing his eyes for a brief moment.

He knew exactly what I was talking about. And it affected him the same way it affected me.

I wanted to jump off of my stool and launch myself at him, wrapping my arms around his neck and kissing him until the name Declan Storms was a distant memory.

Yet, I stayed still. Waiting. Wondering if he would make another move.

He looked up and moved his mug away from him, resting his forearms on the countertop instead.

"What about the night before, Reid?" I prompted, wanting him to think of all the times recently that he acted like a boyfriend, not a housemate. I wanted him to remember how much he loved me. How much I had loved him.

I needed him to know that I still loved him. I just couldn't figure out how to express it without getting my heart shattered all over again if he didn't feel the same way.

His eyes searched mine, like I held all the answers he was looking for. "You scared me, Marlowe. I came home expecting you to be at work, where Norah said you were. That's why you didn't come with us, right?"

I nodded, not wanting to interrupt him. And not wanting to tell him the truth of why I went to the beach in the first place. How jealous I had been. How I let my emotions make decisions for me, which lead to horrible repercussions.

"When I came in and heard noises, I figured you had just gotten back. But when I realized what was going on... my heart *dropped*. My entire world stopped. I didn't know what to do. I thought you were physically hurt and I went into some sort of autopilot. And then... when I saw you laying there absolutely broken... Marlowe, I..." He trailed off and my heart ripped open all over again. The agony on his face was devastating.

I reached over and laid a hand over his, which he grabbed and squeezed like he was siphoning all my energy to save his.

"I have never seen you so upset, Mars. And there was nothing I could do about it, which made it worse. I wanted to beat the crap out of Storms, but... but you said stay. So I stayed. No question about it." He lifted his eyes to mine. "I promised you once that I would always be there for you, Marlowe. Whenever you need me, no matter what. It's a promise I'll never break."

I remembered his promise. He made it last summer, when a huge thunderstorm hit the island and I freaked out, my storm anxiety at an all time high. I hid in my closet as the wind whipped against the house, rattling the shutters. Then, out of nowhere, like a superhero, Reid appeared, soaking wet in my doorway. He had hurried over and sat next to me on the closet floor, wrapping me up in his arms and covering my ears. He had launched into a comical story in order to distract me from what was going on outside. It was then that he had also said those same words—"I'll always be here for you, Mars. No matter what."

Did promises like that hold true when we weren't together?

Reid stayed silent, now looking down at the rings on my fingers, examining them as if he had never seen them before. "I'm sorry I wasn't here earlier. And I'm sorry for being the one who hurt you, too," he whispered.

"You didn't..." I started, before realizing what he was talking about. He apologized for not being here earlier in the summer for my birthday. The crash with Declan. To stop it all before it even began.

But he was apologizing for hurting me last summer. When he broke up with me.

He let go of my hand and pushed his hair off his forehead. A tiny water droplet fell, splashing onto the counter next to my arm. He squeezed his eyes shut, like he was in pain, before responding.

"Mars... I... Honestly, nothing this summer is going according to plan. Once I got word that the guys at home were all headed to Beckham's family cabin on the lake for the summer, I spiraled."

My heart plummeted. Every thought about me, about him and me, about the two of us, flew out of my mind as I pictured Reid back at his house. Alone. This wasn't about me anymore. I had been focused on myself for so long now, that I never stopped to think about him and the circumstances leading up to his unexpected arrival. "They were all headed to the cabin, and you..."

"Weren't invited. Yeah."

"So you..." Full sentences weren't needed anymore. We were both on the same page, playing catchup with each other.

"Threw a bunch of stuff into a suitcase and booked the first flight to the Cove." He paused, his eyes searching the kitchen now instead of me. He took a deep breath before continuing. "I wasn't thinking. I just knew that I couldn't stay home anymore. My gut instinct said to get to the Cove and figure out my life when I got here. I blocked everything else out."

Just when I didn't think my heart could shatter into any more tiny pieces, I was proven wrong once again.

"You blocked it all out? Reid, you blocked *me* out. All year. I could have been there for you. I *wanted* to be there for you. The first thing you could have done when you came here was to find me."

He dropped his head into his hands, his fingers pulling on his curls before he slid them down and scrubbed at his face. "I screwed everything up, Mars. I know I did. You don't even know how many times I grabbed my phone to call you. To send you a text. I just... I couldn't. It hurt, Mars. And I know I have no right to say that, since I was the one who broke up with you, but it's true. But please, *please*, don't think that I didn't think about you. All the time. Every hour of every day."

How could he say that? "Were you even planning on seeing me when you got here? Or would you have avoided me?"

"I was going to see you. I just didn't think it would happen as soon as I walked in the door." He gave me a sheepish smile, like he had been caught doing something bad.

I didn't fall for it. As much as he claimed it pained him to think about me, I had been hurt a million times worse. "You—"

But I couldn't finish before both of our phones lit up with a new text message.

Liam had used the old group chat. The one we had the last few summers with me, Reid, Liam, Livvy, Emma, Caleb, and Norah all on it.

> **LIAM:** LIvvy and I have our first shift on the tower today. We get off at three. Meet on the beach later?

Emma replied right away.

> **EMMA:** Marlowe has a lunch shift. But I don't. I can come by at two and get some good lay out time before you and Liv get done. Maybe you two can guard me ;-)

> **LIAM:** You're weird, Emma.

> **EMMA:** You missed me, Liam.

The two of them were forever flirting, but never went past that. It was fun to watch, though.

Reid stared at the phone in his hands, a look of pure shock on his face, like he couldn't believe he was still in the chat. Then he glanced at me, holding the phone up like a question.

"What do you say, Mars? Beach day?"

I didn't want our conversation to end just because we got interrupted. Reid was using it as a diversion. We had so much more to discuss. So many repressed emotions coming to the surface that needed to be addressed. The almost-kiss from the car the other night required a conversation. What was happening between us called for a long, drawn out discussion.

We both needed a bit more closure in order to move past, and unfortunately, it seemed like it wouldn't be right now.

The part I wanted to talk about had been long forgotten. The urge to kiss him had passed.

I stared into his eyes, seeing a little bit of the light and joy return.

My heart ached for him, knowing the normalcy he craved. The friendships he needed. I wouldn't be the one to take that away from him.

"Sure. Beach day. We can swing by the cafe first and get—oh wait. Emma's right, I am scheduled to work. Let me see if I can switch shifts with someone, but maybe grabbing food from there isn't the best. We can hit—"

"Gennie's. I'll call in an order for all of us before we leave and we can pick it up on the way over."

There we were again, on the same wavelength.

"A beach day sounds fun," I finally gave in, patting his arm in approval.

"The beach it is." He lifted one side of his mouth in a small smile, then dropped it, his eyes widening.

"What is it? What's wrong?" I rushed, not sure what caused his sudden change in mood.

"Marlowe. The beach. Livvy. Liam. Guarding. The clue..."

30

Harbor of Hearts

"**Y**ES, I'LL TAKE your next two Friday mornings, promise. Liz, you're the best, thank you!" I said a few hours later, at a normal person's morning time. I put the phone on the coffee table and fist pumped. "Got it covered. We're going to the beach! I mean," I paused, lowering my arms, "not that your attendance depended on me or anything."

Reid tilted his head from beside me on the couch and lifted a brow, silently telling me he wouldn't have gone if I didn't. Why, I didn't know. But the thought was sweet and so utterly Reid.

After he explained his theory about the clue, I jotted it down on the paper he had given me, adding my own thoughts to it as well. Then, we ventured into the living room to hang out for a while. I wasn't sure what to do with myself, having never really been awake so early before. But Reid had been more than content chilling on the couch, watching some trashy TV, and reading. I mainly watched TV and scrolled through social media for a while.

"I'm going to take the dogs for a quick walk before we head out to gather supplies. Be back in a few." He threw me a smile and headed to the garage to grab their leashes.

I picked up my phone to head to the guest room and throw some stuff in a bag, but paused when I saw Reid's phone still on the table.

"Reid—" I called, swiping it into my hand and looking up. But he was gone, most likely going through the garage door to the backyard.

With a shrug, I put it down, knowing he'd come back for it after the walk. But as I did, the screen lit up, and I froze.

The picture on his background... was *me*.

Me, on the beach, last summer. At sunrise. The brilliant blues and pinks lit up the sky as I looked over my shoulder, my hair flying around, and the biggest smile stretching across my face.

My amber eyes reflected the colors of the sky, shining with an immense amount of joy.

I collapsed onto the couch, staring at his phone, bumping the screen again when it turned off.

I remembered that moment like it was yesterday, yet I never knew he had taken a picture. It could have been one of a million times I looked at him, as we had walked the entire length of the beach from Seaside Cafe to the Crescent houses and back. We wanted to see how far we could go from the second the sun peeked over the horizon until it was completely out of the water.

It had been twice, but we had also gone slow in some parts searching for shells, raced in others, with him tackling me and stopping to make out a few times. I had sand in my hair for the rest of the day.

My finger reached for the picture, wanting to touch it. When it brushed against the screen, the phone came to life and opened.

Reid didn't have a passcode. He didn't have facial recognition. Nothing stopped the phone from opening straight into the last app he was in.

The notes app.

More specifically, a single note he had either been looking at or adding to.

My breath caught in my throat, my heart screeching to a stop.

The note wasn't *just* a note. It was a list. Like the dozens I had in my phone right now too.

Except this one was titled. I didn't always title mine; sometimes I was in too big of a rush, sometimes I just didn't care. The contents always told me what it was about, anyway.

But Reid titled his.

"My Love."

I glanced around, feeling as if I were invading his privacy by looking at this. Technically I was, but my pause didn't last long. Mainly because, like the background, the list was about *me*.

I couldn't help myself—I had to read it.

Bullet points separated each individual item, starting with: When you smile at me, my entire world lights up, like fireworks set off from within. From one single smile.

Then: The little lines that form between your eyes when you're focusing on something super hard, and how they slowly disappear as you come to a realization, eventually replaced by a megawatt smile.

After that: When you go out of your way to do things for others. To make them happy. To make them feel included.

When you start to get anxious and panic, your shoulders hunch in, like you're trying to hide. But when you see me, you curl up into my arms and let out a deep, long sigh.

The list went on for a few scrolls, so many things on there that I would never have realized. But I instinctively went down to the last one.

Had he been adding to the list? Deleting something from it?

My answer came from the last two entries: The way you gasp so softly you probably think I don't hear it, right before I kiss you.

How your whole body shakes and shivers every time I whisper in your ear.

I almost dropped the phone reading those last two lines. Gasp? Like the little breath I had in the car the other night, when I *thought* he was going to kiss me?

And how did he know about the shivers? About how he affected me when he was that close, like he was this morning when he reached behind me to turn on the coffee?

They were definitely questions I didn't think I'd get answers to, unfortunately.

The other thing on my mind was how he just told me how hard it was to text or call, always stopping himself, but then he had *this* as his background? He had to see my face every time he picked up his phone. He had notes about me that he constantly updated.

I, too, had a picture of him as the background of my phone once. A picture of us, more specifically. But the day he broke up with me, I had biked to Norah's house in a mess of tears. She had changed my background to a group shot, sans Reid, to remind me of who would always be there for me. I hadn't realized until later that night when I went to call Reid out of habit and saw he was officially gone.

A lump in my throat formed. I looked at the picture of myself one more time before sliding the phone away and pushing off the couch.

MY HEART SPED up the closer we got to the beach, remembering what happened the other day on the pier.

As if he could sense my nerves, Reid glanced over and grinned. "This is going to be fun, right? It's been forever since I had a classic beach day. We got the food, Caleb's bringing the volleyball and net. It'll be fantastic. It'll be great," he repeated, as if he were trying to convince himself as well as tell me.

I nodded, tucking my lips in. I didn't want anything to bring this day down. Reid deserved to be with his friends, in a place he loved and felt included. Just because his friends at home deserted him didn't mean we had to do the same. *I* wouldn't do the same.

If he could move on and stay friends, then I could, too. At least, for the summer. In the end, he would leave again, and who knows what would happen. But that was a then problem, not a now problem.

Everyone had already arrived by the time we showed up. Emma and Norah laid out on their towels, Emma putting sunscreen on Norah's back.

I glanced around, checking out the scene as I whipped a towel flat, letting it glide to the ground next to Norah.

"You won't find them," Emma said, staring at me from beneath her signature red heart sunglasses. I caught her eye drifting down my neck, finding the necklace from Reid. She just gave me an eyebrow raise and didn't say anything.

I picked up the sunscreen she was using, finding it way too low in SPF. Even though I kept a good base tan year round, I still didn't use anything under fifty, especially in the summer.

"What do you mean?" I asked, slathering myself with the sunscreen I brought myself.

Norah propped up on her elbows, glancing between Emma and me, depending on who was talking.

Emma shrugged and tugged her wide brimmed straw hat over her head, tilting it down in the front so she could lay on her back and have it cover her face. "You're looking for the Baysider jerks, right?"

I nodded.

"They won't be here."

I blinked, staring at her. Norah snorted, knowing exactly what Emma was doing and finding it hysterical. I, on the other hand, did not. "Emma. Just spill. You don't need me to beg."

She broke into a grin, shadowed by the hat. "Sean warned most of them away," she started, purposefully pausing because she knew I was going to butt in.

"*Grace's* Sean?"

"Who else?" she answered with a smirk. "And that's not all. He said anyone who has an issue with Reid Bennett, with you, with *us*," she gestured to the three of us, encircling her hand wider to include the guys and the twins on stand a few yards away, "is to stick to the Bayside beaches. And Sean's word gets followed, if you know what I mean."

I knew. We all knew. He may have been a Baysider, but his family was one of the oldest Bayside families, and he was a year rounder. It gave him a lot of seniority.

Teenagers were a weird breed. We thrived by the unwritten rules we put forth, blindly following those who asserted themselves as leaders.

"Oh," Emma continued, getting our attention back on her, "and because Reid decked Declan in the nose and now everyone knows he's Mr. Muscles or something. And not to be messed with, unless they want to meet the same fate."

Norah audibly gasped at that comment. "*Reid Bennett* punched Declan Storms in the nose? Reid knows how to *punch*?" She sat all the way up and whipped her head around until she spotted Reid with Caleb, putting up the volleyball net. "Holy crap, look at him."

I didn't follow her line of sight. If I looked, I wouldn't be able to tear my eyes off of him, and it would get weird. "He knows something about Declan, but he won't tell me what it is."

"I cannot believe all of *that*," she waved her hand up and down in Reid's direction, "has been under Reid's clothes this entire time," Norah said, as if I hadn't even spoken. "He had one heck of a glow up this year. Wonder what changed."

I pressed my lips together, knowing exactly what had changed, why Reid now ran on the beach at five o'clock in the morning and dove into the gym every day, too. But I kept it to myself.

The feeling of someone watching me hit me then. I looked over and found Emma intensely staring, one finger pushing down her glasses as she looked over the top of them.

"You showed up together," Emma said flatly, keeping her voice neutral. "What happened to Declan? Why did Sean put out the warning?"

I watched as Caleb and Reid did a jumping high five when they finally got the net up. Caleb tossed the volleyball to Reid, then reached up, gripped his shirt behind his neck, and pulled it off in one big swoop.

His muscles rivaled Reid's, but Reid had the height and the lean torso on his side. Caleb's dark skin shone in the midday sunlight, highlighting his shoulders and abs. Both boys instantly gained the attention of the other girls on the beach.

Norah turned, so we were all facing the water and the boys now. She leaned forward and placed her arms on top of her bent knees. "You didn't hear? Marlowe was the subject of their prank this year. Declan was chosen, and somehow our sweet, innocent Marlowe got caught in the crosshairs. Seagulls, and all that."

She didn't elaborate, thankfully. I didn't need to relive the whole thing. Just the mention of seagulls made me glance around, to see if any were in the vicinity. Luckily, there were enough people around us that the birds stayed away.

"You were *what*?!" Emma screeched, causing Reid to hesitate and glance our way. Emma waved him off, and he returned to the net with Caleb on the other side.

I stared at Emma incredulously. "You really didn't know? You know everything. I assumed it was the talk of the town by now." I explained the seagull prank in as little words as possible.

"And *you* knew?" Emma said, glaring at Norah between us. "I'm losing my touch."

She simply raised her shoulders. "I saw the video right after I dropped Reid off the night we picked up the twins from the airport."

The night I asked Reid to stay with me.

"What a summer you've had, kid." Emma muttered, adding a little sigh at the end as she leaned back on her hands, tipping her face up to the sun slightly. "So where do you and Reid stand?"

I didn't answer her. Mostly because I had no idea how to answer that question.

But also because deep down, I knew what I *wanted* the answer to be. Every feeling I had for Reid had resurfaced in the past few days. I wanted to experience them all over again.

I couldn't admit that to *anyone*, though. Not when Reid was giving me such mixed signals. First, he acted like everything was fine and normal. Then, he stayed with me while I cried, and almost kissed me in the car. I had no clue what was going on with him or where we stood relationship wise.

"Whoa... looks like the guys have a fan club," Norah whispered a few minutes later.

I looked up and saw what she was talking about–a flock of girls surrounding the net where Reid and Caleb were playing.

"Can we call dibs because we knew him first? He totally Longbottomed, but we were friends with him before. That means something, right?" Emma pushed her sunglasses onto her head, staring at the scene in front of us with awe.

A bubbling sensation started in my gut, and my heart skipped a few beats as I watched Reid throw the ball in the air and jump to serve. Caleb dove with his arms outstretched, connecting with the ball, but not enough to get it over the net.

The girls all jumped and clapped, and Reid ate. It. Up. He grinned in their direction, taking a bow. One girl asked him to flex, but thankfully that's where he drew the line.

Caleb, however, had no boundaries, and stumbled over, flexing every arm muscle he could as soon as he was standing.

I didn't realize I was still staring until I felt eyes on me once more. This time, it was Reid. He caught my gaze and started to smile, but that's when I stopped.

The clue. Reid said the beach sparked an idea about the second clue.

"I'll be right back," I said, jumping to my feet and heading toward the game.

Norah let out a wolf whistle and yelled, "Go get 'em, tiger!"

31

Footprints in the Sand

REID'S GAZE NEVER left me as I jogged over.

As soon as I reached him, he immediately pushed through the throng of girls surrounding him. I got a few side eyes, but ignored them.

Reid reached for my elbow, leading me away from the crowd before he spoke.

"What's up? You okay?" he asked when we were in a quieter place. I glanced over my shoulder, seeing Norah and Emma watching us intensely.

"Yeah. I just... um..." I momentarily forgot why I had run to talk to him, now realizing he was once again shirtless in front of me. I cleared my throat, my mouth going dry.

But I wasn't the only nervous one. Reid reached up and pulled on his ear. His eyes told another story, though, and I watched as they skimmed down my body. I had on what I thought of as an old bikini, a plain black one from last summer, plus my jean cutoff shorts. There was nothing special about it, but Reid seemed just as eager to look at exposed skin as I had been to look at him.

A chill ran through me as his eyes returned to meet mine. "Do you, um, need some sunscreen? Your face is getting a little red."

Immediately, it flushed even more, probably appearing like I had the worst sunburn of my life. It wasn't the sun, though.

"What's wrong?" he whispered, his voice hoarse.

I blinked a few times, trying to remember. "Oh! The clue! Remember you said you had a theory about the clue and being at the beach. About lifeguards? That you'd tell me when we got here so you could show me instead of trying to explain it?"

His brows furrowed, as if he couldn't comprehend the subject change I just threw at him. But after a moment, he shook his head and grinned.

"Right! Remember the line about friendships being guarded?"

I nodded. It was the line I had the most trouble figuring out. He told me to add 'lifeguard tower' to my theory list, but didn't want to expand until we got here this afternoon.

"Well, Emma's text made me think of something." Reid turned, shielding his eyes from the sun, and pointed toward the lifeguard tower, where Liam and Livvy were about to get off duty. "She said something like, you guys can guard me."

The lightbulb went off. "Oh! Whoa, you're right! Friendships are guarded—the lifeguards! They're literally our friends."

"That, and the seagulls playing, and—"

"Footsteps! Wow, how did we not get that sooner? We practically live here. Well, technically I do, but you know what I mean," I said with a laugh.

Reid knocked his shoulder into mine. "The clues are clever. They require thinking out of the box and inside it at the same time. But you got that first one while I struggled, remember? I know you would have connected these dots soon enough."

I flushed again, turning to face the water so he couldn't see. "So... we need to get to that tower. But what if it's like Charlotte's playroom and the location isn't the real spot? We can't just go rummaging around everything up there."

"There's only one way to find out," Reid answered with a sly smile. He extended his hand to me, palm up, in an offering of solidarity. "Follow my lead."

We walked hand in hand toward the tower, passing by a slack-jawed Norah and Emma, until we reached the guards.

Once we got there, he let go of my hand and made a twirling motion with his finger, like he was going to circle the tower. I nodded, understanding what he meant, and we went separate ways.

I waved up to a guard when I approached the front. "Hey, is someone going to let the twins go soon? We've been waiting, like, forever!"

He shook his head and laughed at me. "Marlowe, you've been here for less than ten minutes. I'll let them go as soon as they finish their reports."

I pretended to pout. "But Liam is such a slow writer," I joked back.

Knowing Reid and I only had another minute or so set me off on my quest again. I casually glanced out of the side of my eye to see Reid still circling the tower in the back, scanning the underside of the deck and all the poles for an envelope.

I did the same on my side, trying to look casual about it, but probably failing. We met in the middle, on the opposite side from where we started.

"Anything?" he asked, sounding hopeful.

"Nope," I said, popping the p at the end. "Only that the twins will be down in a second."

"So it's definitely like the dollhouse in the playroom. What are we missing? We're here during the day. The footprints are in the sand. The seagulls meant the beach..."

I narrowed my eyes and looked around, following the wooden posts up to the base of the tower. One of the two lifeguard chairs extended slightly off the side, a ladder coming down from it for easy access to the beach.

"Friendships are guarded," I whispered, mostly to myself. That was it. Friendships were guarded because our friends were the guards. Literally, they would guard us from the chair.

Without warning, I sprinted around the corner again and pounded up the stairs. My breath came in small spurts now that I was on a mission and full of adrenaline.

"Marlowe? What are you doing—" Livvy said, stepping in front of me.

"One sec!" I exclaimed, sliding past her. "Sorry! Ignore me!"

I didn't look back. I just continued to the chair she usually occupied. She liked the right side of the tower, and Liam liked the left. If it wasn't here, then his spot was next, but I had a feeling...

And I was right. Bending down, I stuck my head under the lifeguard chair and found a small envelope taped neatly to the seat toward the back. It couldn't be seen from the sand; only if you were looking for it.

"Yes!" I cried. Instead of taking the stairs down, I swung my leg over the chair and climbed down the ladder, skipping the last few rungs, and jumping in the sand.

A pair of big, muscular arms greeted me, keeping me upright, then circling around me. Reid pulled me in close and lifted me into the air, twirling me around.

"You're a genius! Again! You are absolutely amazing, Mars."

As soon as he put me on my feet, we both realized what we did. We had gotten swept up in the hunt, overjoyed by the result. He jumped back a foot, brushing his hands on his thighs as he cleared his throat a few times.

"I mean, great job. Are you going to look at it now?"

I tucked a few escaped curls behind my ears. "No. Not with everyone around." With that comment, Reid pulled at his ear again before looking over at them.

They were all staring. Livvy and Liam had joined the group, Caleb sitting on the volleyball in front of Norah.

"This should be interesting," I mumbled, shoving the envelope in the pocket of my shorts, glad I still had them on instead of just my bikini.

Reid stepped closer to me and gestured toward them. "You don't have to say anything you don't want to. It seems like Emma probably knows something is up from the way Storms acted in the cafe. But has she asked about it?"

I shook my head. I didn't think of it before, but she hadn't said a word. She was great about keeping private things private, though.

We started toward them, and I watched as everyone turned and looked at Emma at the same time. Her face was stern, the kind of expression that said don't mess with me.

She was warning them. Of what, I wasn't sure, but it was probably something I would be grateful for.

The second we got back, Liam tagged Reid in for a game of volleyball with him and Caleb, grabbing one other guy from the beach a few feet away. The four of them went to play while the four of us girls laid out on our towels.

No one said a thing about what they saw. Not from the moment I left to right now. It was like it didn't happen. Even though I knew they all had to be dying to ask, I was grateful they didn't. I would tell them in due time. Probably either when it was all over, or I had other news to announce...

Not twenty minutes later, Livvy was asleep. Norah placed an extra towel over her so she didn't burn. Emma had dove into her book, ignoring the entire beach somehow.

I hadn't done anything but stare. The crowd of girls had come back, especially after Liam joined the game. All four boys on the makeshift court were a sight to behold. I would never think more of Liam or Caleb, just like Emma flirted relentlessly with Liam but would never make a move. Reid on the other hand...

I had already been there. I had him once. But that was before he looked like *this*. Last summer, he wouldn't have been on the court flirting with all the girls. He would have scored a point, then come to give me a kiss instead.

But now... he seemed to play harder and better with every compliment someone shouted at him. When he scored against Caleb again, he flexed his biceps, allowing a blonde to reach out and hang from it for a second.

He lowered his other arm to help her regain her footing, his hand trailing over the small of her back while she looked up and beamed at him. He returned the smile, and suddenly, I felt like vomiting.

"I'm going to go," I said out loud to no one in particular. Emma was in her own world, and Norah had been watching a group of Baysiders come close, see us, then turn around. Maybe it was her intense stare, maybe it was them remembering Sean's warning, but they hadn't come any closer.

"Going where?" she asked, not bothering to look at me while I gathered up my stuff.

"I forgot I have something to do. Just gotta go," I said quickly, unable to make up a lie at this point. It took all my energy to gather my belongings as quickly as possible and not look over at Reid. If I did, I for sure would lose my lunch. I had taken a few nibbles of the food Reid had ordered from Gennie's after finding the clue, but even those small pieces threatened to make a reappearance.

"Forgetting something?" Norah said as I got to my feet. I looked down at her, then at the spot I had occupied, finding nothing left. "You came with Reid. He drove," she pointed out, literally pointing at Reid.

I didn't follow her direction. "Oh. No big deal, I'll nab a tourike. I have my card with me."

The thought of being seen riding a tourike, the rent-a-bikes all the tourists used, across the island made me cringe, but it was better than interrupting Reid in his flirt-fest.

At the main beach entrance, I entered my details and grabbed a bike, settling my bag over my shoulders and turning toward Bayside Boulevard.

What in the world was wrong with me? If Reid could act like all of this between us was perfectly normal, why couldn't I? Why did it make me physically ill to see him smiling at those other girls?

There was only one reason why, and I knew what it was. I just couldn't bring myself to think it again. Not after seeing Reid on the beach like that. If I had thought our almost-kiss in the car had meant something, I had just been proven wrong.

All I had to do was hold out until his parents came back. Then, I wouldn't have to see him every day. I wouldn't have to live with him, with him doing all the little things I loved so much. The way he remembered my lunch order. Making me coffee every morning, even though he hated it. All the things.

That was it. After I left his house, it would be like every other summer when we hung out. I would see him occasionally, when we were with the group. We could be normal friends, like we always had been.

And at the end of the summer, he would go back home. Across the country.

Leaving me once more.

Except this time, it wouldn't hurt as much. He wouldn't be breaking up with me under the defense of being far away.

We would say our goodbyes and move on.

Hearts Entwined

THE COOL AFTERNOON breeze blew through my hair, drying the sweat that dotted my brow. A shiver flashed down my spine, but I didn't think it was from the weather.

Flashes of Reid flirting with the girls on the beach kept popping up in my mind, no matter how hard I tried to push them down. As I turned onto Palm Grove Drive, a tear escaped, rolling down my cheek before I could wipe it away.

Had I left because of overwhelming jealousy? Yes.

Was there anything I could do about it? Not really.

I had no claim on Reid anymore. Though my friends would never, it didn't mean other girls couldn't go for him. He was free to flirt and date and do whatever he wanted, just like I had been when I thought Declan Storms was interested in me.

Except, I had fallen into his foolish games and came out on the other side broken spirited and broken-hearted.

Reid was smarter than that, though. He was smarter than me. His strength of character was also stronger than mine. While I messed up my life by entangling with a Baysider jerk, he still stuck around.

I didn't think I could do the same. If Reid brought another girl back to his house, if he started dating someone else, no amount of money from the Bennetts could make me stay.

Because I was still in love with Reid Bennett. Even if he didn't love me, or love me as more than a friend, at least I wasn't lying to myself about my own feelings anymore.

Another tear escaped, thinking about Reid not loving me. The knife in my heart twisted so hard, a physical pain erupted in my chest, causing me to wobble on the tourike. I righted myself before I fell off and into the street, which was lucky, as a car passed by at the same moment.

"Marlowe?" a familiar voice called from the car.

I whipped my head toward the sound, as it slowed down enough to keep pace with me on the bike. Though I only had a glance, I didn't need it to tell me who sat in the driver's seat.

Reid.

Pressing on the brake handles, I rolled to a stop and put my feet on the ground. The last thing I needed was to fall off in front of Reid. The scabs on my knees from the last time I fell off a bike had just healed.

"What are you doing?" Reid asked, leaning over the center console, and looking straight at me with confusion on his face.

My blank stare must not have given him much to go on. I also couldn't come up with a good lie on the spot, so I told him the truth. "Biking back?"

Reid nodded, then drove away. I stood there, frozen and confused. He pulled over to the curb and got out of the car, walking back the few feet until we stood face to face.

"What happened?" he said softly. "Why did you leave without me?" The sadness in his voice broke me. He took my departure personally, as if I had purposefully left him.

Which I had. Just not in the way he was thinking.

My brows crinkled. I absolutely was not going to tell him I left out of jealousy. And I couldn't bring myself to tell him my true feelings. It wouldn't be fair to him. He broke up with me last summer, making it clear where his feelings laid. Just because I couldn't get over him now didn't mean he deserved to be burdened with it.

"It's not what you think," was all I could mutter.

"Then what happened, Mars? One second you were there, then the next you were gone. It took a full two minutes for me to get the girls to spill on where you went."

I shook my head, brushing my hand behind my neck to unstick the sweaty curls from it. "I just... um, I wanted to head back and work on the new clue. You were having fun, so I didn't want to bother you."

Reid blinked, as if I said the stupidest thing he ever heard. "Okay," he started, drawing it out a little, like he was still thinking. "So let's go back and figure—"

"No!" I stated, a little louder than I should have. Reid flinched and frowned. "No, I mean, I don't want to ruin your day with your friends. You and the guys were having a lot of, um, fun on the beach. Playing volleyball and stuff."

I was pathetic. I couldn't lie to save my life, and there was no way Reid didn't know that right now.

But all he did was shake his head, still staring at me with a look in his eyes I couldn't identify. He reached out and took my hand in his and stepped closer.

I stared at the ground, unable to meet his eyes now. Whatever he was going to say most likely would break my heart in the most Earth-shattering way possible. I couldn't handle that again.

All I wanted was for him to be happy. He didn't need to deal with my drama anymore. He tried to warn me, and I didn't listen. I learned my lesson. Even though he said he wanted to lay low for the summer, I saw how much fun he was having on the beach. How excited he had been when the text from Liam first came though. The way his face lit up when he and Caleb got the volleyball net together and started playing.

It's what he needed. What his soul needed. If anyone could understand what it was like to be left behind, to be rejected by those you thought were your friends and family, it was me. I would be the last person to let Reid down, and if that meant stepping aside while he moved on, then so be it. I wouldn't get in the way of his happiness, even if it meant sacrificing my own.

"Marlowe Mitchell," he said so softly I almost didn't hear him. I lifted my eyes to meet his, finding them soft, his lips slightly upturned. My heart pounded, my palms becoming clammy again. My face had to be on fire, but he didn't say anything. "You don't get it. Where you are, I am. There is no me on this island without you."

BY THE TIME I rode the tourike back to the nearest docking station a block away, and Reid drove us back to his house, I was covered in sweat and sand. All I wanted to do was take a shower and down a large glass of lemonade.

Reid took our bags from the backseat and followed me inside.

"I'm going to shower off really quick," I said, my face still flushed with a bit of embarrassment.

What he said back on Palm Grove Drive had not left my mind since. I repeated it over and over, which wasn't helping my mental status. I was in love with Reid Bennett. Madly in love. Deeply in love. Truly, head over heels in love, again.

By the way he had been acting up until now, I assumed he thought of me only as a friend.

For Reid, the island and I went hand in hand. For me, this was my home. A home made better by Reid.

In a week or so, his parents would come back, and I would be leaving.

At the end of the summer, he would fly back home for the year.

And I would be left in the same position I had been last summer.

I couldn't do that again. My heart wouldn't be able to handle it.

"Before you do, why don't we hang out by the pool for a while? It's pretty warm out. We can look over the next clue out there?" He tugged on his ear before rubbing the back of his neck. He looked at me from beneath his long, dark eyelashes I envied so much, a hint of hope in his onyx eyes.

I really did want to see what the clue said. We figured out the second one in only a day or so. Maybe this one could go just as fast. I still had no clue how many clues there would be total, so right now, the faster the better.

"Sure," I said, grabbing the envelope out of my bag and following him outside.

I took no more than two steps past the sliding door before Marshmallow darted out from behind me, crossing right in front of me making a beeline for Noodle.

I tripped over her, flailing my arms as my legs twisted up underneath me. Flashbacks to all the other times I had fallen this summer raced through my mind. I wouldn't have called myself a clumsy person, but my track record was about to disprove that.

It was like I was in slow motion, careening toward the ground, sure to land directly on my face.

But I didn't. Somehow, I was suspended in midair, halfway to the patio.

With a muscular pair of arms encircling my waist.

My lashes fluttered as I inhaled a sharp breath.

Without a word, Reid lifted me to my feet easily. He kept one hand on my back, the other now snaking up my arm.

Reid's forehead was inches from mine. My breath grew shallow as he locked eyes on me.

"Marlowe," he breathed, barely loud enough for me to hear it.

I couldn't answer.

I didn't need to.

In the next moment, his hand reached the side of my neck, grasping forcefully until my chin tilted up.

His lips brushed against mine, so gently, so soft, so cautious.

I gasped the tiniest of gasps, but didn't back down.

Reid must have taken that as a sign, because in one motion, he used the hand on my back to draw me flush against him, his other hand firm on my throat as he kissed me. His lips pressed against mine desperately, like he had been searching for me his entire life.

My hands rested cautiously on his waist, dancing along his waistband until my fingers scraped against his skin.

He groaned and tightened his hold, trying to get closer, even though there was no room between us. His thumb stroked my throat, my jawline, his fingers digging into my hair. His whole hand fit around my neck, pulling me toward him in so he could kiss me harder.

A thousand sparks flew through my body as he kissed me, igniting every last nerve ending and lighting me up. My fingers clutched at his waist, trying to hold on to him and root myself in this spot forever.

It was past and present, dancing together in a whirlwind of emotions. His kiss was like coming home on a warm summer day.

I stood there, my head spinning, completely lost in time and space. After what seemed like a moment and a year later, a jingling sound broke out, and the next second, Reid and I were wet.

Noodle had jumped into the pool, then stood next to us and shook himself dry, leaving the two of us dripping.

I jumped out of Reid's arms, instantly feeling cold and distant. All I wanted was him wrapped around me again.

I lifted a hand to my lips, still tingling from his kiss. He stared at me like he was trying to figure out what had just happened, and what to do now. His tanned cheeks paled as he blinked and looked away, a frown replacing the sly grin that had been there a moment ago.

We needed to talk. We needed to figure out what this meant and what to do from here.

But before I could say anything, Reid turned to the wicker chest behind him on the patio and grabbed a towel, offering it to me.

"Ready to work on that clue?"

Beacon of Hope

HE HAD LOST his mind. Reid Bennett must have gone absolutely insane. He wanted to work on the clue *now*? After *that*?

All I wanted to do was jump back into his arms, wrap my legs around his waist, and have him hold me while I kissed him into oblivion. I wanted to kiss him long enough to make up for all the lost kisses in the past year. I wanted to kiss him as long and as hard as I could, never coming up for breath again.

But... that would also overly complicate things.

Reid used another towel to wipe himself off, then announced he was going to go grab some lemonade and a snack.

It was like he lived inside my mind sometimes.

As soon as he left, I collapsed into one of the pool lounge chairs a few feet away, grateful for the soft, plush cushions under me. I didn't lay back, though. I stayed right on the edge, my elbows on my knees, my foot bouncing a mile a minute.

As much as I wanted to go straight back to kissing Reid, it would create problems.

Mainly because I didn't know how he really felt. Was he just caught up in the moment like I was? The proximity getting the best of us, causing us to fall back into the routine we used to hold?

Or did he still feel the same way about me as I did about him? I started to spiral, trying to connect dots I didn't know were comparable.

First, his jealousy over Declan. Was it jealousy, or did he say all those things because of his hatred toward Declan? He told me I could do better; I immediately thought of him when he said it, but was that what he meant?

Then there was the other night in the car... how we had come so close to doing what we just did on the patio. I genuinely believed he was going to kiss me, and when he pulled away... Why did he pull away? Why did he have to go to the gym to workout after? It was almost as if the thought of kissing me brought on so much frustration that he couldn't even handle it without an escape.

But his words... I could never discount his words. Reid wasn't someone who said things lightly. Everything he said, he meant. When he said he wanted to text me, but stopped himself. When he thought about me constantly, but didn't go through with calling.

What he said about the island being nothing without me. Or something like that.

And my picture on his phone? A picture I didn't even know he took. One he had to see multiple times a day. What did *that* mean?

I wanted to allow myself to believe it. I wanted to let myself have hope once again. But as much as I tried to convince myself I wasn't still in love with him, it was just as easy to convince myself that he wasn't in love with me.

That proximity played its part, and it was playing it well. As soon as I left the house, things would be different. As soon as he left the island...

I dropped my head into my hands, sand shaking out of my curls as I did. I needed to talk to my friends. Emma would know what to do about this. She would probably tell me to cool my jets and hightail it right out of this Bayside mansion, bringing me back to reality as a Gennie, at home with Grandmum.

"Found some of those crackers you like. The really salty ones. Figured they'd go good with the lemonade," Reid said, a giant smile on his face. He put the tray on the table behind the lounge chairs, then parked himself in front of me, mimicking my posture, his knees brushing against mine.

"Thanks," I mumbled, but didn't reach for a cup or a cracker. My mind was so muddled, I didn't know what to do with myself.

But I was acutely aware of every inch of skin currently touching Reid's. Our knees rested against each other, and his hand brushed over my arm as he went to grab a cup.

He downed the lemonade in three gulps, acting like he hadn't had a drink in a week.

"You have the envelope?" he asked, clasping his hands together in his lap and staring at me.

Why was he acting like we hadn't just shared one of the best kisses of our lives mere minutes ago? How was he able to turn off his emotions so quickly?

I took a deep breath and pushed all my questions and feelings down. We had a clue to solve, and I wanted to do it as fast as possible.

"Where shadows dance on moonlit waves, follow the beam to what you crave."

Here we go again. More nonsense that hurt my brain. The situation with Reid and my emotions already occupied enough room; trying to unravel the mysteries in these clues took up space I didn't have.

"Shadows on moonlit waves... so, boats?" Reid suggested. "What else could be tall enough for the moon to create a shadow?"

"The beam could be a boat's spotlight? Or..." A thought occurred to me. "Like the Richards' boat yard. You know, Richards' Marine Tours and Repair? They have that giant spotlight to help bring in the boats for their night tours, remember?"

Reid nodded. "That makes sense. Great catch."

I beamed, but instantly frowned. "Actually, it doesn't. Considering how hidden it's been the past two times, *where* would it be? They keep like dozens of boats there, between the tour boats, storage, and the ones being repaired."

Reid pursed his lips, chewing on his cheek as he thought. His hands had dropped, one resting on top of my knee now. I stared at it, my heart fluttering in my chest.

"Hmm. That's a good point, too. So far, the clue has been hidden within the hiding place, not out in the open. And the Richards' boat yard is huge."

"Follow the beam... what else has a light that casts a beam?" I tore my gaze away from his hand and looked up. "Oh!" I gasped, staring right at the Bennett's decor. Outside the back door, there was a small alcove where they kept the wicker bins of towels, pool toys, and dog stuff. They also had some nautical decor, like most people on the island.

Which included a lighthouse.

"The lighthouse!" we both exclaimed once Reid followed my line of sight.

"Moonlit waves," he said.

"Follow the beam of light!" I added.

He lifted a hand up to high five me, which I did. But instead of dropping his hand, he curled his fingers around mine and brought my knuckles to his lips.

"Still a genius, I see," he whispered, holding onto my hand.

My heart swelled with pride. Even though I didn't feel like I technically figured it out, and it was because of the decor, I accepted his compliment with ease.

"Should we go?" Reid asked a second later, letting my hand finally go.

I stood, finding sand dropping out of my shorts as I did. "Yes. But... I really need to shower first." In all the rush pre-kiss and post-kiss, I almost forgot how gross I was. Sand coated my legs still, and it fell from my hair where it wasn't sticking to my neck in a sweaty mess.

Though Reid had his shirt on now, I knew his torso would be the same. Sweat and sand, diving after the volleyball and all, could only truly be removed with a good scrub in the shower.

Reid nodded and gestured to the house. "Let's clean up and then we'll go."

As soon as I got to the back door, Reid's phone rang. I turned and looked over my shoulder as he slipped it out of his pocket, his face draining of all color when he read the screen.

"It's my parents."

Confronting Truths

I SHOT EMMA A look of desperation from across the restaurant the next morning. We both had the first shift, but she had shown up late, meaning I had to set up the cafe alone while my brain exploded.

She had hurried in, tying her apron around her waist as a slew of customers followed right behind her. We got caught up with coffee and pastry orders as the kitchen started working on eggs and omelets.

She mouthed *sorry* to me while wiping down a table a couple had just left. She pocketed the cash tip and collected the plates.

"Need to talk to you," I whispered as I hustled by her with a tray full of orders. For a Tuesday, it was abnormally busy. Of course it would be, on the day that I needed to speak with my friend alone.

"Grace came by the beach after you left. Looking for you," she replied, talking so fast I almost missed it.

I smiled at George, one of our regulars, as I handed him his coffee and omelet with a side of super crispy bacon. "Here you go, George. I may have thrown some of those pieces of bacon back on Cook's grill for an extra minute while he wasn't looking. It's right to our liking." I winked at him, and he chuckled. We both agreed that bacon should only be consumed when it had a good crunch to it.

After three more tables left and we finally hit a lull, Emma and I settled in a booth by the front door, where we could see the rest of the cafe and anyone who came in the door. I started rolling napkins around silverware while Emma took a cleaning spray and wiped down the laminated menus, then dried them with a rag.

"Grace, you said? What did she want?"

But Emma shook her head. "Nope. Not starting with that. Rewind, restart. What happened yesterday?"

I shrugged. I didn't know exactly which moment she was talking about and didn't want to lead into the wrong part of the conversation first. "What do you mean?"

That got a small giggle out of Emma. "Okay, you're being vague like me. Sure. I can play that game. What I *mean*," she said with emphasis, leaning in closer to me, "is that the second Reid noticed you weren't next to us anymore, he sprinted over like his butt was on fire."

I thought back to when he found me on Palm Grove Drive, his brows pinched together in worry. How he said it took two full minutes for the girls to tell him what happened.

"And when he realized you left, he was distraught. And you know I don't use the word distraught lightly."

I rolled my eyes at her, securing a napkin bundle with a small rubber band. "He was not."

Emma's jaw dropped, and she blinked a few times.

"What planet are you living on, Marlowe Mitchell? Because it can't be this one. You cannot be on the same Cove I am and not see that Reid Bennett still has it *bad* for you."

I tucked my lips in and blushed something hard. Emma gave an approving hum, like she knew what was going through my mind.

After letting out a deep sigh that rumbled through my bones, I looked up. Then, I spilled. I told her how Reid chased me down. How concerned he looked. And what he said, while holding my hand on the side of the road.

After Mason poked his head out and told Emma to keep her squeals to herself, she covered her mouth with both hands, choosing to stomp her feet in excitement instead.

"Mars! This is fantastic!"

I frowned, not sharing in her excitement. "It's not, though."

Her face fell, her brows furrowing. "What do you mean it's not? You love him. He still loves you. What's wrong with that?"

I settled the last napkin bundle in the basket to my right, piling up the rest of the silverware I didn't use and stacking them together too. Then I leaned back in the booth and pouted. "Because he broke up with me, Emma. He doesn't really want me. He's just caught up in the nonsense because we're in the same house and around each other all the time."

Emma snorted. "You have got to be kidding me."

Crossing my arms over my chest, I glared at my friend. "No. I'm not. Remember *why* he broke up with me?"

The smirk she gave me said she wasn't buying into my foolishness. "Because he was stupid."

My face crinkled. "No, because—"

"Because he was scared."

"Emma, no—"

"Because he was stupid and scared and so out of his mind in love with you that the thought of *not* being with you terrified him into thinking that breaking up was the best option. He wasn't dumb, but he was head over heels in love, which made him dumb. He couldn't see past his overwhelming feelings for you long enough to know that you were better together than apart, and distance would be no challenge for the two of you. Because you're Reid and Marlowe, the best, cutest, strongest couple Covington Cove had ever seen outside of Nathaniel and Genevieve Covington themselves."

How she said that all in one breath astounded me.

A few heads turned our way, but neither Emma nor I moved. I blinked, trying to process everything she said. Most of it made sense.

It was too bad most of it wasn't true.

"Emma, this is Reid Bennett we're talking about. Classic nerd. Straight-A student. Future lawyer or doctor or engineer or president or something. The *smartest* guy we all know." I had to point out that fact, since it negated the ones where she tried to say he was stupid.

She raised an eyebrow. "That's all true. But there's being book smart and then there's love smart. And everyone knows the smarter the guy is with books, the dumber he is when it comes to love. They try to compartmentalize things, try to make everything logical. And if there's something love isn't, it's..." she trailed off, waiting for me to finish.

"Logical," I mumbled. "But—"

"But nothing. He may be the smartest guy you know, but he's the stupidest when it comes to love. That boy was shakin' in his boots when he came back last year. Or his sandals. But whatever."

I forced air into my lungs, remembering last year. "He came to the island early for my birthday."

Emma nodded, her smirk turning into a smile. "I know. We all knew. You didn't, but we knew his plans. He was downright terrified."

"But I thought—"

Once again, she cut me off. "You thought he was all cool and collected. That when you showed up at the beach, finding Reid there instead of us, that it was a big surprise and he had all his wits about him."

I nodded, not really knowing what else to say. For my birthday last year, I got a text from Norah in the morning, asking me to meet her on the beach. I had already been grumpy, as I hadn't heard from Mom or Dad, and Grandmum had been called to the mansion early.

When I arrived, I didn't find Norah. What I had found was a full picnic set up in the sand, with all my favorites from the cafe and Cove Candy spread out.

And Reid, watching the waves crash on the shore, his hands clasped behind his back.

My body had gone into shock then, tears streaming down my face. He wasn't supposed to show up for another week, something we had talked about extensively. We had been talking all year, and I had been counting down the moments until he arrived.

When he had finally turned around, I had broken into a run, digging my feet into the sand, my calves burning. I had leaped into his arms, which he wrapped around me tight, his face burrowing into my neck as he spun me in circles.

The moment he put me down, he had cupped my cheeks and kissed me for what felt like an eternity.

Then he had asked me to be his girlfriend and told me he loved me. He said he always loved me and only waited to tell me that until he could see me in person.

And I told him I loved him right back, no hesitations.

"He recruited us weeks before he showed up. Norah and I gathered all the supplies. Liam and Caleb picked him up at the airport and brought him straight to the beach. Almost didn't make it in time because Liam got off on the wrong exit and—"

I held a hand up, not needing to hear the rest. Just thinking of Reid's lips quivering as he kissed me on the beach brought back the memory of last night, on the pool patio.

"Girl... you're holding out on me. What are you thinking about?" Emma leaned forward and rested her elbows on the table, her chin propped up in her hands.

I licked my lips, then bit the bottom one. "Last night... when we got back from the beach... Fluff kinda tripped me up, and I landed—"

"In Reid Bennett's arms, where he leaned down and passionately made out with you, stealing every ounce of breath in your body?" she finished for me.

I paused, not exactly sure how she came up with that, but nodded, as she was essentially right.

Not even Mason could stop her squeal. It was so loud it covered most of the bell jingling behind me.

She glanced over my shoulder and smiled, but didn't get up. It was probably a regular heading to their normal table.

"Welcome to Seaside Cafe. Grab a table and someone will be with you in a moment," we automatically said together.

Then she continued, staring straight at me. "So, does this mean you're officially back together?"

I shook my head, keeping my voice low when I said, "No. His parents called right after, and I didn't see him the rest of the night. I actually borrowed the car to grab Mrs. Ruth some food from Gennie's and drop it off. I haven't seen or spoken to him since."

It was a little white lie, as I had spoken to him after we kissed. About the clue. But I didn't bring that part up. I promised myself I would tell the group once it was all over.

"And this morning?" she inquired, her eyes narrowing as she looked behind me.

"Coffee pot was on. He left a mug for me, but I didn't see him before I came to work."

That brought a mischievous smile to her face. "Reid doesn't drink coffee."

I couldn't help it. My lips quirked. "He goes for super early morning runs on the beach. He sets the coffee and starts it when he gets back, so I have some when I wake up."

Emma waggled her eyebrows. "We all know how you are without your morning caffeine. Glad to see that boy is proactive about the situation. And," she said, pointing over my shoulder, "I can't believe I'm about to say this for the second time in less than a month, but you have a surprise waiting for you."

I whirled around, my heart dropping, expecting Declan again.

But seated at the table in the back was none other than Reid Bennett.

Cliffside Contemplations

H E HAD HIS hands wrapped around a mug of tea by the time I returned from clocking out and putting my apron away. I wondered if Emma had brought it to him, if she had said anything.

When he shook his head if I asked if Emma stopped by, then I knew. That girl was practically a vault. She wouldn't reveal a single thing to anyone, ever, if I didn't want her to.

She was the best kind of friend to have.

I slid a plate to Reid as I sat down across from him. We had his favorite strawberry chocolate marbled cheesecake in the back, and I snagged a slice before Mason noticed.

"Thanks," Reid said, unwrapping the fork from the napkin bundle I swiped on my way over.

"What are you doing here?" I asked, cutting right to the chase. If this was last year, it would be almost a daily occurrence. Sometimes he would drop me off at work, if I had already been out with him, or he would pick me up. Either way, he would always stick around for a bit, grabbing a slice of cheesecake, some tea, or a full meal. He had become a regular, mainly when I was on shift.

Reid shrugged and ignored my question, as if his answer didn't even matter. "Did you work on the clue more last night? I didn't see you..."

I nodded. "I think I have it. Want to hear my theory?" After he had disappeared, I gave the clue some more thought. The first two had gone deeper than our original solutions. If the answer was the lighthouse, then *where* in the lighthouse was the question. The beam is what sold me—it had to be up inside, by the actual light.

I had left the actual paper list back in the guest room of his house, but I remembered what it said.

"After I say something," Reid answered, his face turning solemn. He pushed the plate away and clutched his mug instead, tighter than normal. "My parents called last night."

I stared at his long fingers wound around the bright coral ceramic Seaside Cafe mug. "I know."

He let out a frustrated breath, which made me look up and catch his eye. They weren't sparkling right now. There was no hint of joy behind them.

There was sadness. Concern. Worry. And maybe a little anger, based on the way his upper lip twitched.

"They're coming back in three days."

My jaw dropped. I quickly closed my mouth, trying to regain some sort of control. *Three days*? They were supposed to be gone for the rest of the week, at least.

"They weren't expecting to hear that I was in town, but they saw some of my credit card charges from here and that's why they called. I didn't tell them I've been here the whole time." He gulped and stared into his tea.

"Charges... you mean they haven't seen the airfare fees or anything? They didn't connect those dots?" It must have been nice not to have to worry about every dollar and where it was going. One thing I learned on this island was the Crescents and the Baysiders never looked twice at prices. They didn't even blink when handing over their cards.

Reid shook his head. "I used their miles. Didn't charge them a dime."

"Sneaky," I whispered, sort of in awe.

"They asked about you."

My gaze snapped to his, my heart plummeting to the floor. Did he tell them I had been staying there and conning them for their money? I had tried to do my best and keep up with the dogs, feeding them, taking them out, and all of that. And even though Reid was cleaner and more organized than I was, I made sure the kitchen and living room were kept tidy, as well as the guest room and bathroom. Working in housekeeping gave me some skills, even if it wasn't my favorite thing to do. I wanted to earn the money.

"They told me to do this," he said, picking up his phone. He swiped in, clicked a few things, then put it down.

A moment later, my phone chimed. Reid and I locked eyes as I slipped it out of my bag.

Once in my hands, I swiped it open and finally broke eye contact. A little red dot sat on top of my Venmo app.

I had a payment.

I swallowed, my hand shaking a bit as I clicked into the app, then gasped.

"You earned every cent and more, Mars," Reid said as my brain tried to process the number in front of me. It was about one and a half times the amount Mrs. Bennett originally told me. "They also said to 'let the poor girl go home and stop holding her hostage.' Their words, not mine."

I couldn't stop looking at the screen as a sad smile tugged at my lips. "Oh."

Let the poor girl go home. I laughed internally at the hostage part, remembering what I had said to Reid when he first showed up.

But the 'go home' part outweighed the happiness from the joke.

Leave the Bennett house. Leave Reid.

Leave behind whatever it was we had just started again...

My heart flip-flopped in my chest, the beating going all sorts of out of order.

"But," Reid started, talking in a lower voice now, "like I said, they won't be back for three more days."

I put the phone face down on the table in front of me and sucked in a deep breath. Three more days. I nodded, understanding what Reid was trying to say.

I should stay. For three more days.

It gave me three more days to figure out what to do about the us situation.

Three more days to keep kissing him whenever I wanted. If *he* wanted.

I jumped when something brushed against my hand. Reid had reached across the table and laid his hand on top of him, his thumb brushing over my knuckles. "Tell me about the clue. What did you figure out?" he said, snapping me back to reality. He knew exactly when and how to distract me before I spiraled down the anxiety rabbit hole.

I didn't want to talk about the clue. I wanted to talk about us. About what happened by the pool yesterday. About what almost happened in the car the other day.

About what I was feeling. About what I wished for.

Once again, I shoved it all down and ignored it. If that was what he wanted, then fine. Besides, it would delay the inevitable heartbreak.

"So we figured it had to be the lighthouse, right?"

He nodded, still staring at me. I shifted in my chair, becoming uncomfortable. What if I was wrong?

"Well, the dollhouse and Livvy's guard chair made me realize it wouldn't just be, like, out in the open. Looking at the clue, it said something about the beam and about craved. I thought, what would a sailor crave when getting close to shore in the moonlight? The light. The beam." I couldn't hold back the grin that appeared, feeling rather proud of myself. It seemed so simple, but also complex at the same time.

"So, you think the envelope is up at the light source?" The solemn features of his face disappeared, the little wrinkle between his eyes lessening as he looked at me. I nodded, and he cracked a full smile.

He grabbed his keys and phone off the table and stood. "Want to go on an adventure?"

36

Lighthouse Liasions

WE LEFT REID'S car and my bike behind, choosing to walk to the lighthouse instead. It was a short walk, only about five to ten minutes, depending on how crowded it was.

The lunch rush was about to start, so the area around the cafe was getting busy, but the further away we ventured, the less populated it became.

Neither of us spoke for a little while, a sort of quiet tension settling between us. I knew what was on my mind—our kiss. If he was thinking the same, then his face certainly wasn't showing it. He was the epitome of calm on the outside.

About a block before the lighthouse, a tourist on a tour-ike took a corner too sharply and careened straight at me.

Me, being oblivious to life and lost in my own head, didn't realize it until it was almost too late. But Reid, being the utmost attentive person I had ever met, grabbed my hand, and pulled me out of harm's way before the tourist crashed into me.

Déjà vu and all that.

When he yanked on my arm, it sent me barreling into his chest, his other arm wrapping around my shoulders protectively.

"Are you okay?" he whispered directly into my ear, sending an all body shiver shooting down my spine.

I gulped. "Yup. Thanks to you."

He didn't respond, but rubbed my back once and let me untangle myself from him as the biker sent his apologies.

We were almost to the lighthouse before I realized Reid was still holding my hand. I bit my lip, suddenly overly aware of my fingers intertwined with his, my now clammy palm, the way it felt heavier than ever before.

Could he feel my pulse through my wrist? The loud thumping in my chest surely translated down my arm. I couldn't remember how to breathe correctly as I stared more at our hands than I did where we were going.

"We're here," Reid said, gesturing to the lighthouse. He waggled his brows up and down. "Where do you want to start?"

I shrugged, trying hard not to move my left arm, so I didn't draw attention to it. Maybe he didn't realize we were still holding hands. If I moved, he would notice, and he would let go. "The only way is up, I guess."

"Perfect. After you," he said, opening the old wooden door at the bottom. Once I walked through, he let go of my hand so I could grab the rail on the spiral staircase that led to the top.

Instantly, my heart dropped. A part of me wanted to call the whole thing off, just so he would hold my hand again.

After the first few stairs, a tingling sensation hit my back.

Reid rested his hand on my lower back, helping guide me up the stairs like a true gentleman. I sucked in a deep breath and tried to steady myself, but every nerve ending exploded like an arcade game, going completely haywire at the slightest touch from him.

When we reached the top, we separated, heading to both sides of the massive beacon, looking all around it.

Five minutes later, we stared at each other in defeat.

"It's not here," I said with a frown. I had been so sure that I cracked this clue. It made the most sense. Everything pointed to the lighthouse, and specifically to the beacon.

Reid narrowed his eyes and crossed his arms over his chest. "We're missing something. Let's think again."

"Can we think while back at the bottom and outside? I'm kind of getting claustrophobic up here."

He nodded, but instead of sending me down first like he had sent me up, he took the lead and started down the spiral staircase. He paused on the fifth step or so, glancing over his shoulder to make sure I was coming.

We both winced as the bright mid-day sun hit our eyes as we exited through the small door.

"Should we look around out here, just in case?" Reid asked. As soon as I made it to the doorway, he reached for my hand again.

I nodded, using my other hand to pull my sunglasses out of my hair, settling them over my eyes. All use of the English language escaped me at this moment as I focused on his hand in mine.

This time, it had been intentional. He didn't grab it to save me from my ultimate doom. He purposefully intertwined his fingers into mine and held tight as we started around the base of the lighthouse.

Reid, being closer to the building, kept an eye out for anything on the outside, and I scanned the surrounding area. Next to the lighthouse was a small park, where people could come and toss a Frisbee, or have picnics. A few benches were spread out to enjoy the view of the coast.

We made an entire loop before coming back to the original door. I sighed and pouted. "I was so sure," I mumbled.

Reid glanced down at me and frowned. He enveloped me in a hug and cradled my head on his chest.

I wrapped my arms around his torso, breathing in the scent of him that used to bring me comfort. Now, it just confused me. I wanted to melt right into him, to have him take away all my worries.

"I was sure too, Mars. It made sense. You came up with a brilliant solution. You did amazing considering the vagueness of the clues." He leaned his cheek against the side of my hair, then turned slightly and planted a soft kiss on my temple.

I squeezed my eyes shut and counted to five before deciding to be brave and go for it.

Leaning back a few inches, I looked up at him. "Can you do that again?"

He cocked his head. "Do what? Tell you how fantastic you are?"

"No," I breathed. "Kiss me."

His body tensed under my arms, but he didn't let it show on his face as he dipped down and tried to plant another tender peck on my forehead. I pulled away at the last second, shaking my head.

"No. Not like that."

His eyes snapped to mine as he tilted his chin slightly. I took a half step back, resting my hands on his hips, before lifting my sunglasses back into my hair.

Reaching up with one hand, he took my chin between his thumb and forefinger and lifted before meeting my lips to his.

A thousand fireworks exploded behind my eyes as I closed them, leaning into him. He wrapped his other arm around my back, resting it on the opposite hip as he pulled me into him, chest to chest. His hand slid from my chin to behind my neck, cradling the back of my head.

His shoulders hunched as he kissed me harder. I grabbed his shirt and held on for dear life, never wanting to let go of him again.

The two of us stayed like that, locked in each other for an indefinite amount of time. I couldn't fathom ever pulling away, but eventually Reid did, his lips leaving mine cold and deserted.

"Thank you," he whispered, his forehead resting on mine for a beat as he took a deep breath. "Thank you for asking. I've been wanting to do that for weeks."

I blinked, trying to come back down to reality and decipher what he just said. "Weeks?" I croaked, my voice not yet returning.

Reid reached up with both hands and cupped my face, his thumbs brushing over my cheeks as he stared at me and nodded. "Yeah."

His dark eyes sparkled as one side of his mouth twinged into a small smile. "Since the moment I almost swung at you with that baseball bat, all I've wanted to do is wrap you up and kiss you until I had no breath left in my body."

My legs shook. My entire body had melted like a bowl full of jelly after. "This whole time?"

"This whole time, Mars."

"But... you kissed me yesterday. By the pool?"

"That... that was a brief lapse of control."

"What?"

"I couldn't *not* kiss you then. You were right there, and I just... I'm not explaining this well."

Reid slid his hands down my neck, brushing over the necklace I had yet to take off, and down my arms until he reached my hands. He squeezed them, then let go, turning and pointing to a bench not too far away.

He slipped one arm around my waist. I leaned my head onto his shoulder as we made the few steps over to the bench.

We sat side by side at first, until Reid moved over a few inches, his knee touching mine. The second it did, I flinched, and my leg started bouncing.

I didn't know what he was going to say. Whatever it was, it would change everything. Nothing from this moment on would be the same as it was the past few weeks.

I licked my lips, waiting to see what he would do. How he was going to explain what he just said. I replayed it in my mind, focusing on the part where he said he wanted to kiss me until he was breathless.

Which was *exactly* how I felt. Were we on the same page again? Did he really feel the same way about me?

Had he this entire time? While I was hanging out with Declan? While he flirted with the girls on the beach?

Had we literally wasted this *whole* time?

Reid cleared his throat, his fingers dancing along the back of my hand, fidgeting. "I haven't been entirely honest with you, Mars."

37

Haunted Horizions

THE FIREWORKS BEHIND my eyes from his kiss slowly turned to ash, raining down over everything around me.

I tried to swallow, but my throat had closed up. My entire body tensed and my vision went into some sort of weird tunnel-y thing, where I couldn't see anything except Reid's gray shirt in front of me.

This was it. This was when he told me that while he used to love me, we shouldn't be together. No matter what happened right now, or back at his pool, it wouldn't work. It wouldn't last.

It was last summer, all over again. The two of us, standing in his driveway, my hands in his as he told me he wanted to break up.

He said I should find someone on the island who could be here all the time for me. I told him we could make distance work.

He said I deserved better. I told him all I wanted was him.

He said he loved me. I told him I loved him.

He said goodbye. I said nothing.

My chest spasmed, my lungs pleading for the oxygen I didn't have.

Not while my entire world was imploding.

Reid took a deep breath, his chest rising, pushing his shirt up. "Let me rewind. Start at the beginning."

I didn't want him to. I wanted him to rip the bandage off and get it over with. The world around me spun, my vision clouding up by the second.

"You know my first summer here wasn't easy," he started, shifting just so slightly. I took that as a sign to move, to distance myself from him. But Reid didn't let go of my hand. He clasped onto it like a life preserver, like it was the only thing saving him from slipping under.

Except *I* was the one that needed the saving right now.

"You and the crew made things so much better for me here. But especially you, Mars. Always you. From the very start. But things at home weren't easy either. It was the same as here on the Cove, but the opposite."

"I know," I somehow breathed out.

I tucked my lips in, biting down to keep from sobbing. I didn't want to hear this. I didn't want this to be the moment he told me how much he had once loved me, that I would always be special to him, and then continue with the harsh reality. I needed to hear the truth, not the sugar coating.

"But this past year was worse. Mom and Dad were gone for business a lot more than usual. We moved out of the two-bedroom house I grew up in and to the other side of town. My friends... well, they weren't around as much either."

My breath hitched. I knew he had issues with his friends, but how he was talking right now... the way his voice dipped, becoming harder and harder to eke out the words...

"You were alone," I whispered.

He nodded, staring down at his hands over mine. He exhaled sharply and straightened his shoulders. "I mean, it wasn't a big deal."

That was a brush off. One to throw me off and pretend that what he was saying hadn't shaken him to his core, hadn't affected him in any way. It was meant to try to convince me that he was fine, when he clearly was anything but.

"I got by. I started running. I even took Noodle with me sometimes, but he was less than eager to keep pace and not stop every two houses or so." He glanced over at me with a sad smile, like he was trying to make *me* feel better.

But all he did was make me even more confused. Why was he talking about Noodle, running, and his friends? Wasn't this about the two of us? How far back did he need to go in his story in order for me to get the whole picture?

"Anyway... working out led me to a gym in town. The guys there were great—they always encouraged me, supported me, and they didn't... discriminate," he added, like he was trying to find the correct word.

"I'm glad." I genuinely was. Reid struggled to fit in here on the island and at home. It was rough for him, and if he finally found a group of guys that accepted him like we did here, then that made me happy, too.

Reid swallowed, looked at me, then darted his gaze away, as if what he was about to say next was too painful to look me in the eye for. I steeled myself, waiting for the ball to drop.

"The whole staying at home thing for the summer was a lie."

My stomach flipped.

"My parents bought it, but they were probably just excited, thinking I was hanging with the guys again."

I wanted to vomit.

"I planned on staying home alone. I knew the guys were going to the cabin without me the entire time. But once Mom said they were leaving for the month, I came up with a new plan. I had one thing on my mind."

My shoulders hunched, actively trying to keep my body in check on this bench.

But now Reid looked at me. I could barely see him with the way my vision had gone both hazy and starry at the same time.

"You. All I thought about was you. A plan to get you back, Marlowe. That was my intention from the second I booked my flight. I know I told you I just wanted to lay low, but that was after I saw... Well, yeah."

Declan. He changed his tune when he saw Declan.

My breakfast vowed to make a reappearance soon.

"I wanted it to be like last summer. When I surprised you. I had hoped... I had hoped that you didn't hate me."

Hate him? He broke my heart, but I had never hated him. The opposite, actually.

I had never stopped loving him.

"I tried asking Caleb and Livvy, and they didn't think you did, but they also said you guys didn't really bring me up in conversation, so they couldn't be sure."

"I didn't hate you," I said, barely above a whisper, not even certain if I said it out loud or just mouthed the words. I put most of my energy toward trying not to faint or vomit. Both were possibilities right now.

Reid shifted again, this time turning more toward me.

His fingers danced along my wrists until he held both hands in his, holding tightly.

"I was scared, Mars. Last summer. I was so scared of the future. Of leaving the island. Of being away from you. I thought I would fail. I thought you deserved better."

The mere mention of the words brought me back to that night in his driveway, the pain wracking through me all over again.

"I *thought*," he stressed, like wanted to emphasize that he knew he was wrong, "that you should have been with someone who lived here year round." He hung his head in defeat. "I couldn't have been more wrong. It was stupid."

He didn't have to clarify to know he was referring to Declan.

"I wanted you to have someone who could be here for you all the time. Who could make you happy and not just in the summer." He took a deep breath before continuing, still locking his eyes with mine. "Most of all, I was scared of how much I loved you, Mars. I spent all year trying to convince myself that I made the right decision, but all I could think about was you. I fell into a hole I couldn't get myself out of. Thinking of you was the only thing that kept me going, and deep down, I knew I had messed up. I screwed everything up. I hurt you, Mars, and that's what killed me."

I blinked, trying to orient myself while processing his words. "So you came back..."

He squeezed my hands. "For you. The only reason I came back was for you."

Seaside Serendipity

FELL SILENT AGAIN. What was I supposed to say to that? He had been one of my best friends for almost four summers now.

He had been my boyfriend, the guy I had been so insanely in love with.

He had broken my heart, shattering it to pieces and stomping on the shards.

Reid Bennett had joined the not-so-exclusive club of people I loved, who I assumed loved me back, but ended up leaving. That proved that I wasn't meant to be loved.

Reid stared at me like he was silently begging me to say something.

I blinked. The sun peeked out behind a cloud, making me squint. For another minute, I replayed his speech in my head. All of it. From the beginning, like he had wanted.

"Loved. You said loved. You said you were scared of how much I *loved* you. Past tense," I said, quoting his exact words. They were burned into my brain by now.

In a flash, he let go of my hand and flew them to my face, holding onto my cheeks as I let just one singular tear fall.

He ignored it and lifted my chin slightly to make sure I was staring him directly in the eyes.

"Loved. Love. Will always love. Put it in whatever tense you want, and it will mean the same thing. I love you, Marlowe Mitchell. Past, present, and future. You are my Mars. My entire universe, galaxy, and solar system. And I will love you until the day the sun dips over the horizon and becomes extinguished for the last time. I know I can't expect you to still love me, but—"

I didn't let him finish. I couldn't. Because I knew what he was going to say, and I needed to show him how wrong he was.

I grabbed onto his wrists and smashed my lips into his.

I kissed him like I had been dreaming of doing again for so long.

I kissed him enough to make up for the past year of kisses we missed out on.

I kissed him like he was the only boy I had ever loved. The only one who understood me at my core. The only one who could take away my worries and stress and calm me from a panic attack.

I kissed him like he was my forever.

And he kissed me back, telling me without words how much he loved me. How deeply he felt about me. How sorry he was.

He slid one hand away from my cheek, to the back of my neck, his thumb brushing over my pulse point and sending electric sparks all the way to my toes. His other hand stayed put, more so pulling me toward him, attempting to get me closer.

With one last kiss, he leaned his forehead on mine, his lips brushing mine as he took a shaky breath. "When I said I waited weeks for you to ask? I meant it. I didn't know where I stood, but from the second I saw you in the kitchen, wearing that towel, I wanted to kiss you just. Like. This. I was just waiting for you to ask."

I sighed. "We wasted so much time. Let's make up for it now?"

"As much as I'd like to continue, I think we have an audience."

My eyes popped open, the sunlight streaming directly into them. All of time and space had become a distant memory, leaving me woozy and unaware of my surroundings.

Once reality came crashing back in, I launched myself away from Reid, remembering we were on a bench outside the lighthouse.

A public bench.

A *very* public bench.

With three girls standing ten feet away, their arms fallen to their sides, their jaws dropped. A tiny one with bright red heart sunglasses. Another with dark brown hair swept to the side in a braid, her hand shielding the sun from her eyes as she stared. And the last, with bright blonde hair like her brother, a little smirk on her face.

Emma held a tray of drinks in her hand, dangerously close to tipping over and dumping the liquid all over the ground. Norah held a to-go bag from the cafe, and Livvy had her arms haphazardly wrapped around a blanket.

"Um..." Reid started, trying to get everyone's attention back.

"So... that happened," Emma said after snapping out of it. She gestured to us with the hand holding the tray before realizing what she was doing. She dropped the bag on her other arm in order to steady the drinks. I suppressed a laugh at her expense.

"What are you two crazy kids up to here at the lighthouse?" Livvy asked, her head cocked like she knew there was some big secret going on. And the secret wasn't Reid and I.

I pursed my lips, not sure how to answer. I pulled my sunglasses down to cover as much of my face as possible.

"Is this where you went after you both ran out of the cafe like you had just robbed the place?" Emma stated, finally putting the drinks on the ground.

I nodded. Reid coughed, shifting his legs slightly so his knee brushed against mine.

"Coming to make out in a park full of tourists? Not your usual style, Bennett," Norah added with a raised eyebrow.

Reid just shrugged. I knew he wouldn't give anything about the scavenger hunt away unless I told him to, but we were treading in dangerous waters. There was no way the girls really believed that we came here just to make out. We weren't fans of PDA like that and they knew it.

"It's the new and improved Mareid. Relowe? Yeah, I think Relowe is the better ship name. Relowe two point oh likes to make out in public parks," Livvy said as she shimmied and waggled her eyebrows. She let go of the blanket and shook it out, letting it float to the ground. "You guys want to join us?"

Reid tapped me on the knee before reaching up and running a hand through his hair. "Nah. We... we've got to go. But hey, come on over later. Tell the guys."

Emma stared at him suspiciously, but he ignored her.

"My parents are coming back in a few days and we

haven't even had a party or anything while they were gone. What kind of teenagers are we?" he said casually, like he was trying to change the subject without it being too obvious.

"What kind of *Baysider* teenager, you mean," Emma teased, giving him a smirk. He shot her a faux-glare.

"I'll shoot Liam a message. I'm sure he's out with Caleb right now, since we both are guarding later this afternoon. But we'll be off right as sundown hits, and can come then?" Livvy jumped in, interrupting the silent conversation Emma and Reid seemed to be having.

I had yet to say a single word. I had no idea what words to even say. The conversation happened around me just fine, without any sort of input from me.

That, plus all I wanted to do was dig a hole and curl up inside, never to see the light of day again. While kissing Reid had been amazing, the embarrassment of being caught almost outweighed it.

Reid agreed with Livvy and told them to all bring their suits so we could swim. It would be a Baysider pool party, without the cringy Baysiders.

My face was still on fire, and even though no one mentioned it, they definitely all saw. I just waved as Reid stood and took my hand, leading me away from our friends. I had no doubt all three of them had their gaze set on our hands, but they kept their mouths shut.

"Where are we going?" I asked as soon as we were far enough away from the group I couldn't feel their gaze on my back. "We walked here, remember?"

Reid just nodded. "I know. We have a clue to work on, though. Let's go wander through town—maybe it'll spark something."

A walk definitely wouldn't spark anything for me. I had enough sparks shooting around my body at the moment that I could self-combust at any second.

Cove Comforts

I F SOMEONE TOLD me I was floating down the street instead of walking, I would have believed them. It felt like I was floating, anyway, with only Reid's hand in mine keeping me on the ground.

Actually, I had both hands around Reid's, holding on to him like I was afraid he was going to disappear.

After his confession by the lighthouse, my mind was all over the place. I had no idea what to do about what he said. It went in the complete opposite direction from what I thought, and that left me a jumbled mess.

A jumbled mess back together with the guy I loved.

For however long it lasted.

I pushed that thought to the back of my mind. I didn't need to be thinking about it right now. I was happy for the first time this summer, and I wanted to keep that feeling going for as long as I could.

Except this clue business nagged at me. The lighthouse had been a bust when I had been *so* sure it was the right answer. Every time I felt like I was close to cracking a clue, the real answer evaded me.

This time, though, Reid had thought the same thing. So we were both wrong. As dumb as that was, it brought a little smile to my face. Even someone as smart as Reid didn't get this one.

We headed down Main Street, dodging tourists who were too busy looking at maps or wrangling kids to look where they were going. Doing the duck and weave had become an expert level sport for those of us that lived here year round.

As we made it to the main stretch, I caught a glimpse of a girl with dark hair across the street.

"Who's that?" Reid asked, guiding me around a light pole.

"Chloe. She works at the country club, in the catering department, so I see her at the mansion occasionally."

Reid frowned, staring across the street, but not at Chloe. His interest seemed to be in the boy next to her, someone that looked familiar, but I couldn't place the name of.

But he didn't keep my attention long. My gaze shifted, looking at a vintage car.

"Hey! Mrs. Ruth is at the shop. We should swing by and say hi."

Reid jerked his head toward me, then nodded. We continued down the sidewalk another few yards, before we crossed.

The second Reid took a step off the curb, though, I froze. Without my momentum, Reid stumbled back, tripping over his feet before he righted himself.

"What's going on?" he asked, his voice a little shaky.

My hand was equally shaky as I lifted it to point at the sign across the street. I stared at it, unblinking, while

Reid turned in what seemed like slow motion to see what I pointed at.

"What? What is it—oh. *Oh.* Oh! You think?" He whispered the last part, his mouth falling open as he fixated his eyes on the sign.

Without diverting my gaze from the lighthouse on the Cove Candy Shop sign, I whipped my phone out from my bag and opened it to the clue. "At the end, it says what you crave—"

Reid cut me off. "And how many times a day do you crave Sea Salt Caramel Pearls? You're always wanting them. Specifically from Cove Candy."

My eyes lit with happiness. I nodded, and Reid grabbed my hand again. We crossed the street together, a little spring in my step, and Reid practically beaming.

Once we got to the front windows, almost to the door, I stopped, looking up again.

"Where could the envelope be, though?" The sign above us had a lighthouse the same as town one, with the beam of light pointing to the Cove Candy name, pieces of candy replacing the o and the a in each word.

The lighthouse. The beam of light. The craving. It all made sense, but there was more to it. Just like the clue had been in the dollhouse, this wasn't going to be as easy as it seemed.

Reid pointed through the front window. "There's a lighthouse display of candy inside. We can check there first."

With no other option, we entered the shop. The moment we entered, the bell jingled over our heads, alerting Sam.

"Marlowe! Glad to see you. Mom is in the back harassing Elliott over their taffy pulling skills. Want to go relieve them from the beratement for a few moments?"

I laughed. If anything, Mrs. Ruth was relentless when it came to making the candy her way. She always said, if it worked for fifty years already, why not fifty more?

Honestly, I didn't see a problem with that. Why mess with that kind of success? Sure, new sweets could always be added, but messing with her signature recipes seemed silly. Especially when they were so good already.

"Go. I'll mosey around, but won't look for anything until you get back," Reid whispered.

I pushed through the half door, finding Mrs. Ruth perched on her stool, her eagle eyes trained on the sweating employee. I wasn't sure if they were sweating because it was warm by the ovens or because Mrs. Ruth was letting them have it.

I waited until she was done with her current tirade before announcing my presence.

"Hi, Mrs. Ruth! Nice to see you today!" I called, a little louder than usual because of the noise from the convection oven fans.

"Yes, yes, nice for today. But what about lately? You haven't been around. Where have you been? You're not at home. I looked," she snapped without taking her eyes off of the taffy being stretched on the hook.

I grimaced. "I've been house sitting over on Bayside for a while. But don't worry, I'll be back soon," I said. My heart gave a lurch as the words left my mouth. "I have extra shifts at the cafe coming up too, so I'll make sure to grab you some of your favorites."

The lack of remembering that I had been in the candy shop and had stopped by her house with food just four days ago worried me. I made a mental note to mention it to Sam on the way out.

She waved her hand toward me. "Always grabbing favorites, always coming during nap times. Maybe one of these days you'll look at a clock and come while I'm awake."

I pursed my lips to keep from laughing. I loved her cantankerous attitude, especially when directed at me. Mainly because I knew she didn't intend it to be unkind. And because it reminded me of Grandmum. They both were stubborn and blunt, but that was how they showed their love.

"Maybe I'm just sparing you the heartbreak that comes with the devastating loss when I beat you at gin, Mrs. Ruth. Have you recovered from the last time?" It had been well over a month, which meant we were due for another game soon. Sometimes Saul, her next-door neighbor, joined us. I usually beat them both.

Mrs. Ruth huffed, but it finally got her attention on me instead of the taffy puller. I grinned at her and raised an eyebrow.

"Lucky draws, that's all it is."

"Is that so? Is that what you call winning six times in a row? Lucky draws?"

She glared at me. "If you think I won't tell your grandmother how you're chastising an old woman, you're wrong, little M and M."

That got me to laugh out loud, as well as her use of the nickname she gave me as a toddler. Marlowe Mitchell—aka M and M, like the candy.

"Grandmum would commend me for standing up to you, Mrs. Ruth. And you know the next time the two of you had your little 'book club,' she would tell you the same."

Grandmum, Mrs. Ruth, and a few other older Gennies had been having a book club ever since Grandmum moved to the neighborhood. In the last few decades, it had turned more into drinking whiskey and gossiping about the town than reading. But Grandmum left the house with a book in her hand every time. To keep up pretenses, I supposed.

"Bring me croissants next week and I'll show you what a real game of gin is, dear. Now go on with you. I need this child to learn how to put their muscles into this taffy pulling."

I grinned. "You're on. See you next week." I shot a look of apology over at the employee who stood with their hands on their hips, out of breath for a moment while the taffy slowly descended toward the ground hanging over the hook.

My mind switched gears quickly as I passed through the half door, remembering exactly why I had come into the store. I saw Reid's head over the top of the far shelves, and my heart started pounding.

The lighthouse. The clue. It had to be here somewhere.

I practically skipped over to him, but came to a full stop when I rounded the shelving unit and saw the person in front of him.

Grace.

Island Encounters

MY EYES WENT wide as I caught sight of her. The bright purple crop top and black shorts accentuated her flawless dark skin. Her long, black hair was up in a messy ponytail, like she had just come straight from the beach.

But it was her hands that I focused on. The way her fingers wrapped around each other, but her thumbs tapped together to a beat no one else could hear.

Grace was nervous.

With so much that happened since the seagull incident, I had all but forgotten about Grace. What she did and said that night hit me like a ton of bricks then, but with Reid... and the clues... and everything else, I had pushed her out of my mind.

Or maybe I did it on purpose. Maybe I wasn't yet ready to put the past few years of betrayal behind me just because she apologized.

Though she did more than apologize. At least, Sean did with his warnings to the Baysiders. And if I knew Grace the way I used to, then she had most likely been behind that proclamation.

What really got me was seeing Reid and Grace talk so openly. They were chatting like old friends, not two people in separate parts of my life that I wasn't sure I wanted intertwining.

As if she sensed me, Grace turned. Her face blanched, and she hesitated. She was waiting for me to say something, since she left the ball in my court.

But I didn't know what to say. I desperately wanted to know what she and Reid were talking about. A selfish part of me wondered if it was about me, since that was the one thing they had in common. But it also seemed somewhat unlikely. What would they even discuss?

I took the last few steps toward the two of them. Reid tossed a glance my way and frowned. I shook my head slightly. He looked over at Grace, back to me, then bowed his head a bit before backing up and going around the shelves to another part of the store, giving Grace and me some space.

"I never thanked you. For what you did that night. What you and Sean did. And to Sean for... well, just thanks." I cut myself off, knowing my tendency to ramble on if I didn't.

Grace shrugged, like it had been no big deal. But it had been. It made a very loud statement, not only to me, but to the rest of the Baysiders who sided with Declan. Her gaze darted down to the necklace resting on my chest before coming back to meet mine. "We don't hang out with those guys anymore."

Those guys. Declan and his friends. The ones at the pool party, where Grace tried to make me feel like an outsider.

And then, a few weeks later, she saw what happened to me and rescued me. What changed in that time?

"You know, there's a whole group of Baysiders that don't act like Declan. They're actually pretty nice."

I knew that. Not every Baysider was a stuck-up snob like Storms. Just like not every Crescent kid was as intolerable as Isla Covington, who thought just because she had the last name, that she was in charge and everyone else was below her.

Eleanor Covington had been the exact opposite. She had been selfless to the people of Covington Cove, not acting as if she owned the place.

"There's a whole group of Gennies that are nice too," I shot back, giving her a pointed look.

She knew that. She had been a part of it all of her life until she found Sean.

"I know. And I would like to apologize to them too," she started, catching my eye and showing me her sincerity. The frown on her face seemed wrong. She had always been smiling, always laughing when we had been friends. But then again, it had been easier for both of us to smile and laugh when we didn't have any other worries in the world.

"...just like I was doing with Reid right now," she finished. I had zoned out for a moment and missed what she said in between.

What was she doing with Reid? Had she been apologizing to him? I whirled around, finding Reid on the other side of the shelves, listening in to our conversation a little. With his height, he loomed over the shelves by a good foot and a half. He didn't even look ashamed as he nodded his head once, then mouthed 'give her a chance.'

I turned back to Grace. She wanted to reconcile. Even though she hadn't been the greatest in the past few years, was I the kind of person to stand in the way of someone wanting to make things right?

No. I was the forgiving type, sometimes too forgiving. But Grace had been my best friend since we were toddlers. Just because she chose the wrong group of people to hang out with didn't take away all those years.

She looked up at me. I still didn't know what to say, but she talked first anyway. "Maybe we could hit up Gennie's soon and talk? Sandwich and chips on me."

I paused. Talking couldn't hurt. Especially if the talking was anything like this conversation or the one we had in her car in Reid's driveway.

Besides... this entire scenario was new. It was rare. People in my life didn't usually drop me, leave me, abandon me, and then come back.

Mom and Dad never did.

The first person to prove to me that I *was* loveable, that I was capable of being loved the same way I loved them, was Reid.

He had come back. He came back specifically for me.

If I could forgive him, if I could let him back into my heart again, then why couldn't I do the same for Grace?

It was different from what I was used to. The betrayal from Mom and Dad didn't set in for a few years. I grew up. Then Grace left. Reid left. Even Declan had worked his way onto the ever-growing list.

I just never thought people were capable of being taken off my lists.

"Okay. Next week?" I mumbled. I really wanted to solve the rest of this scavenger hunt before dealing with a best friend reunion. With so many things going on in my life at the moment, I needed to start compartmentalizing.

I had Reid in one list in my mind. That list had so many entries, many of them scratched off, rewritten, and so many question marks I couldn't even count.

The hunt was another list, still waiting to be dealt with.

Grace had to be on a third list, tucked away until I was ready to check things off.

She nodded. "That'd be great. I'll, uh, text you?"

I hadn't had a text from her in over a year. It was a good thing I never changed my number. But I nodded in confirmation.

A hesitant smile grew. "Awesome. Well, I just saw you guys crossing the street earlier, so I thought I'd catch you. That was the only reason I came in here. So... see you later?"

She waved to Reid on her way out, the bell over her head jingling.

Reid appeared behind me, resting one hand on my hip, his mouth close to my ear. "Finally. Let's get looking."

Scenic Secrets

OUR FIRST STOP was the lighthouse display. The almost seven-foot-tall unit, with the shelves inside the lighthouse, was a replica of the Covington Cove Harbor one.

Except it was better by housing bins of saltwater taffy, licorice ropes, and other candy. The regular lighthouse didn't have anything exciting like that.

Reid and I started moving bins around, checking to see if there was an envelope under or behind any of them. I didn't think I would have to go as far as digging through each bin, since Sam changed out the candy often.

We both came up empty. It had been the most obvious idea, but we were still missing something.

"Here's my newest thought," I said to Reid as we both stood staring at the display. "If they left it in plain sight, wouldn't someone have noticed by now? Wouldn't someone have grabbed it or even turned it in?"

He chewed on his cheek and nodded. "Maybe it's with Sam or Mrs. Ruth?"

I shook my head, pulling on one of my curls. "I was just back there. She didn't say anything to me about an envelope, and she's not one to keep secrets."

Not wanting to seem overly suspicious, I grabbed a bag of Pearls and headed for the counter.

"Everything alright? You kids were standing there for a while and Grace left without so much as a word or her favorite Raspberry Rose Delights," Sam said as he rang me up.

I shrugged. "We're good." I didn't know what else to say, so I just kept quiet. I took my bag and waved goodbye, joining Reid by the front doors.

Once outside in the bright sun again, we moved over to allow a family to enter the store.

Reid shoved his hands in his pockets and rocked back on his heels. He stared down the street, his lips twisted in thought.

I glanced to my left, finding a bench. I went to sit, but right before my butt hit wrought iron, I jumped up with a gasp.

Reid whirled around. "What? What is it? Are you okay?" He rushed to my side, laying a hand on my arm, his worry crossing his features.

Once again, instead of answering, I just pointed, like I had with the Cove Candy sign.

Reid's gaze followed my outstretched hand in line to the lighthouse statue, resting on the sidewalk at the edge of the Cove Candy property. Neither of us had noticed it yet. Part of that was because it had been there my entire life; by now it just blended into the background.

"We're smart people, right?" Reid whispered. We both stood frozen in place.

"Well, I know you are. I like to think I am occasionally," I whispered back as we both still stared.

As if on cue, we turned to each other and smiled.

"After you," Reid said, gesturing me forward with his arm. His other hand rested on the small of my back as we walked toward the decorative lighthouse statue.

The concrete statue was painted in the same colors as the Cove Harbor one, but chips in the paint revealed it hadn't always been that way. At only about four feet high and two feet across, it was significantly smaller than the inside shelving unit, but massively heavier.

I circled around, looking for an envelope to be taped somewhere. Then, I crouched down, hoping to see something blended in with the white paint, like camouflage.

Suddenly, the whole thing moved, making me jump. I fell onto my butt and looked up, finding Reid tilting the statue back, a devilish grin on his face.

I scrambled to my hands and knees, then tipped my head upside down to look beneath.

And there it was. Taped to the bottom of the lighthouse was an envelope with my name.

I shrieked, grabbed it, then jumped to my feet and launched myself onto Reid.

He caught me easily, his strong arms winding around my torso, holding on tightly. The feeling of him embracing me, plus the excitement of finding the next envelope, had me practically jumping out of my skin.

"Want to open it?" he whispered in my ear, sending chills down my spine. All I wanted to do was turn my head and kiss him, I was so happy.

As if he could read my mind, he planted a kiss right behind my ear. My body shook in a full on shiver.

Reid put me down gently and we sat on the bench. Before I tore into the envelope, I dug into the forgotten bag of caramels and popped one in my mouth, chewing contemplatively. I handed the bag to Reid, who also took some before settling it on the bench between us.

"That was a tough one," I mentioned, considering how much time we spent on figuring it out. When you lived in a small island beach town, having a clue about a lighthouse was about as vague as it could get.

"I mean, once you figured out it was a lighthouse, it left us with a one in, oh, I don't know," Reid pretended to count on his fingers, "six hundred chance of finding it."

I laughed, still clutching the envelope in my hands. "That's the truth. I wonder how many more clues there are. Like, how long is this supposed to last? I'm not sure if my anxiety can handle much more."

Reid shrugged and knocked his shoulder into mine. "Only one way to find out."

Nodding, I tore open the envelope, only to find...

Nothing.

Well, not exactly nothing. But it definitely wasn't a clue like it had been with the others. There was only a single sliver of paper with one line on it.

Your _last_ *clue will come soon.*

"Um, excuse me?" I whispered to myself, turning the paper over to see if I was missing something. After coming up empty-handed, I handed it to Reid and dug into the envelope. I tore it all the way open, still not finding a single shred of anything else.

"That's... anti-climatic," Reid mumbled, handing the paper to me. I tucked it into my bag and frowned.

"No kidding. After that search, there should have been, like, step-by-step instructions straight to the prize." I leaned back on the bench, feeling rather defeated. So far, every clue had stressed me out, but this? Now I had to just sit back and wait for something to come to me? With absolutely no time frame given?

I'd need a good therapist after this hunt was over. My anxiety was going through the roof.

"Also, the fact that it says last makes me nervous," I sighed. I folded and unfolded the envelope over and over again.

"Why?"

I shrugged. "I don't know. Just knowing that it's almost over? Wondering if I'll be able to figure it out? Being that close to some sort of unknown prize?"

"The unknown," Reid echoed. "You're scared of the unknown."

I quirked my brow and looked at him out of the corner of my eye. "Yup."

He leaned back and raised an arm behind me. I shifted, resting my head on his shoulder as he dropped his arm over mine. Immediately, his thumb started creating swirl patterns on my bicep. Soothing, calming circles.

"The unknown is scary. But think of it this way—whatever the prize is, will be a benefit to your life. Having it be unknown means that even if you're not elated with it, it changes nothing about your current life. It can only be a positive thing if you want it to be. If not, at least we had some fun hunting down clues."

I sat with his words for a minute. He, of course, was right. It wasn't like house sitting for the Bennetts, where

Mrs. Bennett told me the compensation from the start, so when I thought about losing it, it hit hard.

This prize could make a huge difference in my life, or it could not affect it at all. It was a bonus, and having it be unknown meant that even if I was disappointed with it, it changed nothing.

"What should we do now?" Reid asked.

I pursed my lips. "We have no clue to solve, so that only leaves one thing."

"What's that?"

I sat forward and smiled at him over my shoulder. "Get ready for that party you promised the crew."

Treasures Untold

AFTER WE BACKTRACKED to the cafe for Reid's car, leaving my bike to come back for later, we stopped by the store and grabbed some food and drinks. Even though it was going to be a low-key party, we still needed some things. Neither of us had been good about stocking the fridge or pantry over the last few weeks, mainly living on takeout or food I brought back from work.

Reid went to take the dogs on a beach walk while I sat at the edge of the pool blowing up inflatable rafts and inner tubes. As I did, a thought came over me. While this technically was a Baysider party, it was nothing like the one I went to earlier this month with Declan.

There would be no buffet. No DJ. Not a million people milling around.

It would be just us. My best friends.

It already was way better.

I had just finished blowing up the last tube when Reid and the dogs returned. He took them off their leashes once they passed through the fence, letting them run around the grass to get the sand off their paws.

When he reached me, he wound an arm around my waist and pulled me into his shirtless chest. I still hadn't gotten used to the new view, but I didn't hate it.

I looked up, and the second I did, Reid dipped down to kiss me, planting a soft, brushing kiss over my lips.

I rolled my eyes. "We're never going to finish setting up if you keep doing that."

He gave me another peck. "I don't care."

"Well, *I* do," I chastised, while taking a small step back, not meaning it even in the slightest. Our friends wouldn't care if we didn't set anything up.

I swatted at his chest, my hand instantly stopped by his hard pecs. I stepped back and scanned him from top to bottom, not ashamed of doing so.

"Someone likes what she sees," Reid said. He wound a leash around my back and pulled me into him again, where he traded the leash for his arms, picking me up and twirling me around.

We danced dangerously close to the edge of the pool.

"Don't you dare," I threatened, knowing exactly what he was thinking.

"Oh, I dare. I *so* dare," he answered with a wicked grin.

I gripped his arms as tight as I could. If I was going in, he would go with me.

Thankfully, we didn't get a chance. A second later, the door banged open, a blur raced past, and within half a second, a giant splash came out of the pool, soaking the two of us.

"Liam! You're such an idiot!" Livvy's voice rang out from my left.

Liam surfaced as Reid put me down. I scurried a few feet away, leaving Reid to take the brunt of Liam shaking his shaggy blond hair like a dog, drenching Reid again.

"Oh, it's on!" Reid exclaimed. He pushed his dark ringlets away from his forehead and took a flying leap into the pool, tucking his legs under his arms mid-air and landing in a perfect cannonball.

Unfortunately, I hadn't backed away enough to miss that splash. I attempted to gather my curls in a bun, but they were already knotty and unruly. I gave up and looked over my shoulder at the girls.

Norah, Emma, Livvy, and I all seemed to be on the same page. I didn't even have to count before they dropped their stuff and all four of us rushed toward the pool together, jumping in around the guys, and creating the biggest splash yet.

I kicked off the bottom of the pool and surfaced face first to let my hair fall behind me and not in my face. As soon as I did, Reid was there.

He grabbed my jawline and ducked his head, kissing me hard. Instinctively, and so I didn't drown, my legs wrapped around his waist as he moved one hand to my back, holding me up. All while not letting go and not stopping kissing me.

His lips traveled, placing soft kissing across my cheek and down my jaw, eliciting a round of oohs coming from our friends around us.

I blushed hard, biting my lip and wrinkling my nose.

"Hey! Guys, what the heck? You're already in without me?"

Collectively, we all turned toward the house, finding Caleb weighed down with a cooler in his hands, a bag of stuff hanging over one arm, a few towels over his shoulders, and a floatie around his neck. The exaggerated frown on his face only made us laugh harder.

Reid cupped his hands over his mouth like a megaphone. "Show us what you got!"

It took a minute for Caleb to untangle himself from all his stuff, but once he did, he took a few giant steps and launched himself into the deep end, twisting in some sort of sideways somersault motion mid-air.

It wasn't quite the cannonball splash, but we all clapped appropriately when he came up.

We played a few games of chicken, floated and chatted, then the boys decided they wanted a dive contest off the diving board. The girls were the judges, so we sat on the edge, in the shallow end to avoid more splashes, and held up fingers with our scores.

After about eight rounds of that, the boys were wiped and everyone was starving. The sun had already set, leaving the floodlights in the backyard to brighten up the pool area.

I walked behind the main table on the patio and started putting the food out for everyone. Reid came to join me, grabbing the drinks and making sure there was still ice in the cooler Caleb brought.

"Hey, do you—" but the ringing of his phone on the table behind us interrupted him. He reached over and glanced at the screen, his brows furrowed. "I'll be right back."

I frowned, but let him go, attending to the other guys whose stomachs needed to be filled instead.

Once the boys had their food, the girls wandered over and we filled our plates, taking them back to the lounge chairs. Reid still hadn't returned.

"So..." Emma started, popping a chip into her mouth and biting down with a loud crunch. She stared at me as if she expected me to understand where her mind was.

I didn't.

She rolled her eyes and sighed. "What's up with you and lover boy? Are you two official now? I mean, the way you were sucking face earlier says if you aren't, then we're about to throw hands." She gestured to Livvy and Norah, who nodded in agreement.

"Yeah, I mean, you two sure look just as adorable as you did last year. But if he's playing with you, obviously we take sides," Norah added, her lips snarling in jest at the end.

I laughed. "It's fine. He's not playing me. I mean, I don't think he is."

"That's not his style," Livvy agreed. "Besides, anyone who knows him knows he's head over heels in love with you. Always has been. That boy gave you his whole heart a long time ago and won't ever ask for it back."

Emma pushed Livvy's arm. "When did you become such a hopeless romantic?"

Livvy sneered at Emma, and gestured toward me. "Um, hello. Have you seen these two? They're like the perfect second chance love story. Their relationship last year was absolute couple goals, and the tragic breakup was just one to move their plot forward. They had to mature. They had to grow. They had to—"

"Okay, okay, I'm right here, you know," I interrupted, waving a hand in her face. "But sure. We matured. We grew. Yadda yadda yadda. Our story continues, it seems. Whatever you want to say."

"As long as you're happy, Marlowe," Norah chimed in. "That's what matters."

"But if he breaks your heart again, my fist meets his face this time. Mean it. Love you. Mean that too," Caleb yelled from the table a few feet away. Liam held up his sandwich, as if agreeing with Caleb, but his mouth was too full to verbally agree.

I sighed, shaking my head in disbelief. My friends were great, but I didn't need them to go punching people in my defense.

"Marlowe?" Livvy asked a minute later, after we all had fallen silent while eating. "Are you scared about what's going to happen at the end of the summer?"

I frowned. I had pushed that thought to the back of my mind, not wanting to even consider it. It did scare me a little. Last summer the possibility of breaking up because of distance hadn't been on my mind at all. Which was what made the break up even harder—for me, it came out of nowhere. I didn't see it coming.

After a minute of pondering, I answered with the most confidence I could summon. "No. We'll figure it out."

As I said the words, I tried to commit them to memory. We would figure it out. I wouldn't be blindsided this time. The two of us would talk about it when we got closer to the end of the summer.

Until then, we would enjoy moments like this. Time with our friends. Being together on the island in the summertime. All the things we used to do, but this time, being more cautious about the future.

It didn't mean I wasn't slightly terrified, though.

The sound of the door opening across the patio took my attention away from my friends and food. I glanced over, finding Reid in the doorway.

An uneasy expression had settled on his face, two little worry lines appearing between his eyes.

But as soon as he caught my eye, he plastered a smile on and waved. He jerked his thumb over to the table of food, silently telling me he was going to fill up before coming over.

I couldn't stop thinking about that troubled expression, though.

Who had he been on the phone with?

43

Whispering Waves

SHOOK OFF MY initial concern and tried to enjoy the rest of the evening. Reid didn't say anything about it, so it couldn't have been anything too horrible. It wasn't my place to pry. If he wanted me to know, he would tell me.

After we ate, Liam suggested a trip down to the beach to see who would win in some beach games. Usually he and Caleb dominated, but now that Reid had been working out and running on the beach every morning, I had a feeling he was about to shake things up.

And I was right. Reid tore up the beach, winning both the sprint and the handstand contest. He chose me to be his partner in the wheelbarrow race, but I face planted in the first few steps, so we lost.

After that, we saw too many other Baysiders down the beach, having a party of their own. A few of them looked like they were making their way toward us, so we called it quits and went back to Reid's pool instead.

"Caleb. Truth or dare," Liam said as we all floated in the water. He and Livvy were laying on some rafts, staring up at the dark sky. Norah and Emma sat on the side, swinging their feet in the water methodically.

Reid and I shared an inner tube, both of us draping our arms over the side and resting our heads on it.

"Dude. Since when have I ever turned down a dare?" Caleb answered. He had two pool noodles under his legs and two under his shoulders, keeping him afloat in a sort of half seated, half laying manner.

Liam rolled off his raft and treaded water toward Caleb, whispering in his ear when he reached him.

Caleb had a wicked grin on his face when Liam finished. He folded in half and disappeared under the water.

He surfaced right in front of Emma. He grabbed onto her legs, and she squealed in shock, but he didn't pull her in. Instead, he pulled them apart, placed his hands on either side of her body on the ground, and lifted himself out.

Then he planted a kiss on her lips, really going for it for a second before Emma finally came to and shoved him off.

"Ugh, *as if*," she cried, using the back of her hand to wipe her face. "Honestly Caleb, you said you'd never do that again."

"Liam! You jerk!" Livvy screeched at her brother before slicing her hand in the water and splashing Liam in the face.

I raised my brows and looked at Norah. We had a quick silent conversation, both of us remembering how Caleb asked Emma out a few years ago and she turned him down. Then, on a dare, he kissed her, hoping it would help change her mind.

It didn't. She thought his antics were funny and didn't hold it against him, but she told him not to pull such a stunt again.

But Caleb wasn't someone who listened well. He shrugged and said, "Had to check. Thought you might have the hots for me now that I'm older, wiser, and more hotter."

The wink he added at the end made the rest of us laugh, but Emma just kicked her feet and splashed Caleb until he ducked under the water.

A little while later, Reid and I gathered up the trash and leftover food while everyone else packed up their stuff. They designated Caleb as the mule once again, sending him to and from their cars.

Reid leaned over my shoulder as I put lids on the fruit bowls. "Hey," he quietly whispered, causing shivers to run through me. Every time he was that close, his lips brushing my ear, made me quiver.

"Oh, just kiss her already!" Emma shouted from across the patio.

"If you say so," Reid yelled back.

I gasped as he wound an arm around my waist and spun me to face him, my back pinned against the table, my chest against his.

He put two hands on my hips, holding me down as he crashed his lips onto mine. It took me by such surprise that I didn't even have time to put my own hands anywhere. Reid reached up with one hand and cupped my cheek, while tilting his head slightly to the side. I grabbed onto his wrist and lifted onto my tiptoes to kiss him even harder.

The group started cheering, someone throwing out a wolf whistle. I had yet to close my eyes and enjoy it before I saw Reid lift a hand into the air and fist pump while still kissing me.

I planted both hands on his chest and gave him a little shove. "Oh my God, will you *stop*," I said, trying to sound convincing, but the massive blush on my cheeks had to give me away. "Go home, all of you."

"Hey, I live here!" Reid shot back, grinning and waggling his brows at me.

Everyone else left a minute later, leaving Reid and me alone finally. I fed the dogs a late dinner, which they weren't happy about, while he gathered up all the towels outside.

"I'm going to take a quick shower and get the chlorine out of my hair," I said as soon as he returned from the laundry room.

Before I could make it even a step, his arms wrapped around my shoulders, burying my face into his chest. He pushed my hair away and planted a kiss on my temple. "I know you're disappointed about the last clue, but I want to remind you how amazing you've been through this whole thing. Your dedication to solving each clue. Your tenacity. I know this summer hasn't quite gone according to plan so far, but you've adapted. You've dealt with it. Eleanor would be so proud of the way you've handled everything. I am too. And you should be proud of yourself as well."

I. Ate. It. Up.

He always knew exactly what to say at exactly the right time. Once the group left, the clue, or lack of clue, had popped into my mind again. It must have done the same for him.

"Thanks," I whispered, hugging him tight. We stood there for a moment, wrapped in each other, his heartbeat under my ear.

I didn't spend too long in the shower, wanting to hang out with Reid instead, knowing I only had another day or so left in the house. So I gave my hair a quick wash and some conditioner, scrubbing my body fast while it set.

After, I threw on a pair of old sweatpants and a giant Covington Cove High t-shirt from a few years ago. I took my microfiber hair towel with me, blotting at my curls while looking around for my phone.

I found it on the bed, next to Marshmallow's paw.

"And who have you been calling, ma'am? Your doggie boyfriend?" I asked, sitting down and finding a message waiting. "Hope you didn't read this, you snoop."

I gave her a little scratch behind her ear, then swiped the phone open.

UNKNOWN: Where past and present intertwine, in his arms, your heart aligns.

I stopped scratching Marshmallow as I read the clue over again. My hand flew to my neck, clutching the charms.

The last few had been so much more vague. They had so many options as to what it could be. And even when I figured it out, it still had a meaning within a meaning, like the dollhouse inside the playroom.

But this... this one I didn't need any help with.

This one I figured out all on my own, and faster than any other clue.

This one only had one option.

I knew *exactly* where this one led. I just didn't know what to do about it.

I scrunched my hair a few more times, getting as much water as I could out of it before padding down the hall.

The light on the opposite side of the living room guided me toward my destination. I made my way to the library as quietly as possible.

My mind jumped back to that first night, finding Reid in the library after the masquerade. How my heart practically leaped out of my chest.

Seeing him in person before the masquerade showed me just how much I missed him.

Knowing he waited up for me, even though he had a long day, a long flight, and absolutely did not have to do so... made me realize how much I still loved him.

And, in hindsight, how much he still loved me.

Tonight was the same. I found him sitting in the same chair, his pajama t-shirt wet at the back of his shoulders, his hair damp on his forehead.

Except this time, he was leaning forward with his elbows on his legs, tapping his knuckles over his knees.

"It's you," I said. Or, at least, I thought I said. No sound had actually come out of my mouth, so I cleared my throat and tried again.

That got Reid's attention. He stared at me, his gaze intense.

"It's you."

Instead of answering, Reid just continued to stare. He raised an eyebrow, like he wanted me to continue talking. To explain.

I had to give him my reasoning, I realized. I didn't know why, but I did anyway.

"Past and present intertwine. Our past. Our present. Both of them with us being together." I sucked in a deep breath, holding it for a minute before continuing. "In his arms, your heart aligns. There's no one else's arms I'd rather be in than yours, Reid."

One side of his mouth quirked, lifting in a slight grin. But it didn't reach his eyes.

He stood and crossed the library over to me, and that's when I noticed it.

An envelope in his hands.

With my name on it.

44

Covington's Continuum

"WHAT'S THAT?" I asked, not bothering to reach for the envelope just yet.

My brain needed time to process a whole long list of things.

First, having the last clue lead to Reid. He was waiting for me. He held the envelope with my name on it. A clue. Or... maybe not a clue? The one from the lighthouse said my last clue would come soon, and wasn't that what the text message was?

So if the message was the last clue, then what was Reid holding? And why did he have it?

It was also suspicious that I figured it out so quickly. Whoever sent it wanted me to know right away. There was a timeline for this clue, especially since Reid was waiting for me, like he knew I would be coming as fast as I did.

Second, the fact that I would be leaving the Bennett house in another day, therefore basically leaving Reid.

Lastly, Reid himself. Us. Our relationship. That was an entirely new list on *its* own, one I couldn't dive into yet, *be*cause what?

"Mars..." he said softly. I looked up at him, realizing my gaze had been on his hand for the past few minutes as my brain went haywire. "Open it."

He held the envelope out to me. I lifted my shaky hand and took it, but otherwise didn't move.

"It's you?" I said, this time as more of a question than a statement. The last clue led to him, but... was it always him? "You were behind all of this?"

Panic began to rise, bubbling in my stomach, my heart fluttering as my mind spiraled.

His brows furrowed, a little wrinkle forming between them, and he frowned, like he was confused. But after a second, his eyes widened with realization.

"No! Oh my God, Marlowe, no! I promise, I had nothing to do with all of this. Someone called earlier, during the party. Told me there would be something at the door soon and to make sure you got it, but not to give it to you until you came to me. It was all very... secretive? Odd? I didn't really get it, but then sure enough, an envelope was at the door with my name on it. This," he gestured to the one in my hand now, "was inside of it. The person on the phone said you would get your clue tonight, so I figured if you didn't get it while at the party, it would be now."

He shook his head like he was also trying to figure it all out. Like none of it made sense to him, but he did the best he could with what he was given.

Honestly, I got it. I had no idea what to do with these clues either. I didn't know what they meant, where they led, or why I was given them in the first place.

I flinched when a hand landed on my arm. Reid cupped his hand under my elbow and led me to the chair in the corner, sitting in the one next to me, leaning forward so we weren't that far apart.

"I'm pretty sure you should open it tonight, Mars. It seems like something that needs immediate attention."

I nodded, still unable to process everything going on. Sliding my finger under the flap, I plucked out the piece of paper and immediately recognized the handwriting.

All the other clues had been typed. All but this one.

This note was in Eleanor Covington's handwriting. Everyone on the island could recognize it, if they looked around hard enough. The Covington Cove Country Club signage was in her handwriting. Charlotte's Haven Beach's sign was as well, as she was the one to name it decades ago.

Eleanor Covington was wound into the soul of this island.

The way she capitalized all of her R's, no matter if it was cursive or print, was a telltale sign. Also the way she never dotted an I, but sometimes double crossed her t's, like she did once and forgot, so she went back over the line again. She printed her b's, never the correct cursive, and there was a slight slant to all her letters.

Most of all, it looked like it was a font made on a computer. The writing was so perfectly written, it almost didn't look like handwriting at all, except for those few human aspects.

"Eleanor wrote this. She actually wrote this for me," I whispered, still not even reading the words, just staring at the writing.

"How incredibly special, Mars," Reid said just as quietly. "You really meant something to her."

As much as that comment should have made me insanely happy, it actually did the opposite. My heart sank to the floor and a wave of sadness washed over me.

"I never knew. I mean, I enjoyed her company too, and we always had good conversations while at the mansion, but I never knew I meant *this* much to her."

I thought back to the day at the cafe, when I found out she had died. How incredibly gutted I had been. How sad.

Eleanor was just as special to me as I was to her. I just didn't realize it while it was happening.

"Marlowe... read it," Reid said, nudging my knee with the back of his hand.

It took a moment for my eyes to adjust again, having zoned out for a while.

"In order to claim your prize, you need to find the connection. Figure out what all your clues have in common. Then, come tell me."

I gasped, tears welling up.

"Come tell me? How... that doesn't even make... oh goodness. She was supposed to be alive for this, Reid. For all of it—she was supposed to be alive."

Reid scrunched his face. "Maybe. Maybe not. Maybe her death was the catalyst. Maybe it triggered into starting because of her death."

That... that made a lot of sense, too. Which was why I kept Reid around—he was able to talk sense into me and understand situations I tended to spiral into.

"So, what do you think your clues have in common?" he asked a minute later.

I frowned. "Well, there was the playroom. The lifeguard tower. The candy store. And... you," I paused, staring up at him. "What are the similarities between all of those?"

He just held my gaze, waiting for me to say more instead of interjecting. This time, I wished he *would* chime in.

"I have no idea, Reid. The only thing I can think of is how Eleanor wants me to tell her. Which means... I probably need to end up at the mansion."

Or her gravesite, I thought. She was buried in the Covington family cemetery, within the Covington estate's property at the south-east corner of the island. Every Covington had the right to be buried there, regardless if they lived on or off the island.

"Tonight?" Reid questioned, a hint of worry in his tone.

I shook my head. "No, not tonight. Not until I can figure out what all the clues have in common. Which... might be a while."

Having to find a location of a clue was one thing. Finding the connection between those locations? Seemed near impossible.

"Think it can wait a few days? There's only two more days until my parents come back..."

Reid took the paper and envelope from my hands and laid them on the table next to us. Then he slipped my hand into his and gave it a gentle pull. I stood, and he drew me toward him.

He leaned against the back of the plush armchair and settled me on his lap. His fingers played with the charms on my necklace. "Whatever this prize is, it'll be good for you, Marlowe. I can feel it. I won't say your life is about to change, because that would be cliche. Eleanor wouldn't do something this big without it having some sort of meaning behind it. She chose *you*, Mars. *You're* the special one. Whatever she planned will be amazing. Because it's for you."

He reached up and slid his palm over my cheek, wrapping his hand around my jaw and brushing the side of my face with his thumb. "Eleanor saw what we all see in you, Mars. An incredible, extraordinary, wonderful person who we love deeply.

And with that, he pulled me down, meeting my lips with his, and kissing me until I was left breathless.

45

Heights of Reflection

I N THE END, we had one full day left. And we spent it by not leaving the house at all. We swam, watched some movies, ordered take out, and otherwise never stepped into the outside world.

We were wrapped up in each other yesterday, snuggling on the couch, when Reid got the text from his mom, saying the plane was due to land mid-day the next day. They would have a driver take them from the airport to the island, but it was still earlier than either of us thought it would be.

So this morning, I packed up all my stuff and headed out to Reid's car. Emma had taken my bike from the cafe and dropped it off at my house the day before, so that would be there when I got back.

She said Grandmum gave her one of her patented death glares when she wheeled the bike up the drive and leaned it against the garage wall, which made me laugh.

I had barely spoken to Grandmum the entire time I was at the Bennett's. She only called when she needed to relay information about working at the mansion. Otherwise, she left me alone.

Had she missed me? Or was she enjoying the quiet house she had without me there? I texted her early this morning to tell her I was coming back, but she only answered with a message about how she would be at the mansion today, and added a date for later this summer she needed me on schedule.

She also told me she fed Mr. Munchkin already today.

Just as I bent down to give Noodle and Fluff one last pet, she sent one more message saying there was a fresh pineapple on the counter, which made me smile. She hated pineapple, but I loved it, so I took it as a sign she did miss me.

Reid grabbed my backpack, laughing when I told him how I had strapped it across my back to ride my bike halfway across town to his house the first day. He was also quite impressed I hadn't fallen, to which I shot him a glare, not wanting to relive the whole Crash experience.

When we got to my house, we both sat in the car, a heaviness falling upon us. It seemed like this was the summer of deep thoughts in cars on driveways.

"This is fine, right?" I whispered, staring down at my hands. I hadn't noticed, but during the drive, I must have picked at my cuticles, as there were multiple pulled off and hanging there. Gross.

Reid reached over and took my hand in his. "Of course. It'll be just like last year."

That didn't comfort me the way he probably meant it to. It drove a stake through my heart, thinking of how elated I had been last summer. All the way until the day Reid left the island.

The day he left me.

The day he joined the never ending list of people who abandoned me without a second thought, going on to bigger and better things with their lives. That didn't include me.

But I had already vowed not to let that be us this summer. We would talk. Communicate. There would be no blindsiding this year, no unexpected plot twists.

"Reid, when summer ends—"

He squeezed my hand, stopping me. "No. I'm not scared anymore, Mars. No matter what happens at the end of the summer, no matter where in this country I am, I'll still love you. We'll make it work, I promise. We'll power through."

I wanted to believe him. I *did* believe him. In my head, it would all work out just fine. So why was my heart not accepting it the same way?

I leaned over and kissed his cheek. "I'll talk to you later."

"We'll grab some ice cream after dinner?" he asked.

Making plans made things easier. But the goodbye that came after didn't.

He hopped out and grabbed my bag from the trunk, walking me all the way up to the door. I asked if he wanted to come in, but he said he had to get home and tidy up a bit before his parents arrived.

I stared at him as he set the bag on the front step. He lifted his eyes to mine and smiled. A full, real Reid smile. Then, he kissed me. It was a soft, slow kiss, his hand steady on my hip. He rolled away, planting another kiss on my cheek before breathing a soft goodbye.

I watched until he got in the car and backed out of the driveway.

There was something different about this goodbye. It felt... odd. Specific. Real.

Like heartbreak all over again.

With a sigh, I picked up the bag and unlocked the front door, shutting it behind me.

Everything looked exactly the same as it did a month ago. Not that I was expecting Grandmum to remodel the entire house during that time, but to me, it *felt* different. So I expected it to look different.

I stopped at the coffee table, glancing at a few envelopes that had come in the mail for me. One was junk. The others were college brochures and informational packets I had requested through the guidance counselor's office at school a few months ago.

Not wanting to deal with all of that right now, I shuffled my way to the back of the house to unpack. I needed to do a load of laundry, but also wanted to get re-acclimated as soon as possible. As I passed the couch, I started making a mental list of things, in the specific order in which they needed to get done. The first being laundry, as I could get other things done while the wash was going. Then, I could—

I froze a foot away from my room. The door was closed, which was my first clue that something was off. Grandmum hated having the doors closed for anything other than bedtime. She said it cut people off from the world.

So having it completely closed made me nervous. Had she shut it the whole time I was gone? Was she shutting *me* out of the world while I wasn't here?

That thought was sobering. It didn't sit well, but then again, I never really knew what was going to Grandmum's mind most of the time.

I shifted my bag so I could turn the knob and head inside my room.

But I didn't make it further than the doorway.

While the rest of the house remained untouched, the same couldn't be said for my bedroom. My jaw dropped in awe, my eyes wide as I took in my new surroundings.

The furniture was the same and in the same places. But that was about it.

Pictures in cute frames littered the dresser top, my small desk, the windowsill, and my nightstand.

Pictures of my parents when they were young. Pictures of me with Emma, Norah, and the group. There was even a picture of Reid and me, from last summer, on the beach.

Some of them had come from the box in my closet. But the rest... ones with Grandmum, with Mom and Dad holding me as a baby... those must have come from Grandmum herself.

I paused at my dresser, running a hand over a frame of me and Mrs. Ruth, standing outside of Cove Candy a few years ago. I forgot that one existed, but it was really cute.

It was the last one that caught my eye that got to me. Tears welled up in my eyes when I saw a small, dark walnut frame positioned horizontally at the back of my dresser. It was tucked behind a picture of me and Livvy on paddleboards at Charlotte's Haven Beach two summers ago.

It was of Eleanor Covington... and me, as a toddler. I couldn't have been more than three years old, meaning Mom and Dad had still been around.

Eleanor stooped over slightly, her stark white hair tucked behind her ears as she held my hand. My tiny hand wrapped around just two of her fingers. My golden curls were wild, looking like I had just wrestled a barrel of monkeys, and I had on a pair of pink corduroy overalls with flowers on them. Eleanor pointed to one of them, but I was looking up at her, a big grin on my face, my eyes shining.

This picture really brought together how much Eleanor kept *me* close. Always seeking me out when I was in the mansion. Always stopping by the cafe for an extra blueberry muffin.

I sighed, then turned around, away from the pictures to find a brand new bedspread and a painting of Charlotte's Haven Beach on the wall above it.

I knew that picture. It had hung in the mansion for years, before they took it down recently. I assumed it went to storage, but now it was here... in my bedroom. I leaned in close, my fingers trailing over the acrylic paint until I found the signature in the corner—RC.

Rebecca Covington. Eleanor's niece. She lived on the estate too, with her cousin Pearl. Except now, I presumed they would move into the mansion, as the most senior Covington's on the island.

I left my bag on the floor and headed back out to the kitchen, needing some water. Just as I opened the fridge, the front door creaked open and Grandmum made her way inside.

We stared at each other for a moment. I didn't know what to say. She hadn't called. She hadn't sent messages.

But this was an obvious display that she missed me.

"Don't just stand there with the fridge open, girl, you're letting the cold air out," she snapped before putting her purse on the dining table and sitting down to take off her work shoes.

I quickly shut the fridge door and quietly joined her at the table, still unable to say a word. I wanted to tell her thank you a million times over, but it didn't seem like it would be enough.

"I called your parents," she said a moment later.

I blinked, sure I heard her wrong. "What?" My heart came to a screeching halt at what she said next.

"I chastised them for missing your birthday once again. This little game of theirs has gone on too long now. They're full-grown adults, but you wouldn't know that with the way they act. Heck, you act more responsibly than they ever did. They'll be flying back later in the summer to visit."

My jaw practically became unhinged by the way it dropped at that admittance.

First, Grandmum hadn't forgotten my birthday. Well, maybe she had, and realized it later. But it seemed like she ripped Mom and Dad a new one for missing it. And whatever she said to them, to get them to come back? After all these years? It had to have been serious.

Every list I had ever made about my parents flashed in my mind. The whole list-making thing started because of my parents. Shortly after they left, when I realized they weren't coming back, I started making lists of things I could do to get them to return. To come back to me.

At first, it was ways I could be better. How I could behave correctly for Grandmum, so she would tell them what a good girl I was, and they would want me again.

Then, it became lists of changes I could make in order for them to want to return. How I could save up money and buy a new house for all of us to live in. Even though I was only six or seven years old, it seemed logical at the time.

I stopped making lists about my parents around the age of ten. Five years was a long time for them not to care. Five full years of them being gone made reality set in. But by then, my list making ways had become a habit.

The one thing that had never been on any of those lists?

Have Grandmum call and just *tell* them to come back. After all this time, that was all it took?

And that brought another thought to the forefront of my mind.

They were coming back. After all these years.

"I... I haven't seen them since I was five, Grandmum," I whispered. They hadn't even called in the last few years. They knew nothing about me, about my life. Just like I knew nothing about them. "What am I supposed to do? To say?"

"You let me take care of that," she said sternly. But the look she gave me didn't match her tone. The look in her eye was more of confidence. Of protectiveness.

I couldn't stop myself.

I launched myself forward and gave her a hug.

Secrets Unveiled

THE NEXT FEW days were rather boring compared to the rest of the summer so far. I spent a lot of time in my newly updated room, laying in my bed with my feet propped up on the wall, staring at the beach painting.

Usually while talking to Reid on the phone or over Face-Time. Once, he even sat with me, and we both stared at the painting, contemplating life and its meaning.

It felt weird not being able to pop down the hall and find Reid sitting in the library reading a book. Or seeing the coffee pot already on with a mug waiting for me.

He always thought of the little things, the tiny details no one else would see.

During the day, we tried to hang out, but between my work schedule and Reid's parents wanting him to do things with them, it became more difficult.

Even though nothing was really all that out of the or-dinary, except our locations, something still felt... not the same. Different. I couldn't put my finger on it, but there was a slight change in how we were together.

It had been almost a week since I got the clue from Reid at his house. Well, more like five days, but it felt like an entire year. I still hadn't come up with an answer as to what all the clues had in common, and I was getting worried there was something I was missing by not doing it quickly.

So, this morning, while eating a boring breakfast of oatmeal and blueberries because we ran out of avocados *and* bread, I made a decision.

I was going to go to the mansion and try to figure it out there. Maybe being around the space Eleanor occupied for close to a century would help me solve whatever it was she wanted me to think of.

Quite possibly, I would come up with nothing. But it was the only thought I had, so I needed to follow it.

I asked Reid to join me, as he had been such a help in all the other clues. Eleanor said I could tell someone I trusted implicitly. I learned my lesson the hard way with Declan, but Reid proved himself time and time again.

Right after I finished my breakfast, which was more like a brunch considering the time, Reid pulled into the driveway. Grandmum was out at her book club, so I didn't need to explain where we were going or why.

Not that I thought she would mind. Grandmum loved and respected Eleanor just as much as I did. They had some sort of odd connection that was based on a mutual respect for each other that I never really understood.

Neither of us talked on the way to the mansion. The air in the car was thick, the anticipation killer. We both knew what could possibly be on the other side of today—a prize.

It didn't matter what it was; knowing that it came from Eleanor specifically made me already love it.

We parked in visitor parking so we could go in through the front door. I didn't have any excuses today. I just wanted to wander the mansion and hoped they were going to allow that.

The same girl as last time manned the hostess desk when we walked in.

"Caterina," I said as we made our way over to sign in. "How are you?"

She looked up at us with a bored expression. "Thanks for visiting the Covington Mansion. Tours are at—"

Her eyes widened as she took in Reid and I. She hopped to her feet, dusting off invisible lint from her uniform jacket. "Marlowe Mitchell," she said in awe.

I glanced over at Reid. "Um, yes? That's me."

She nodded curtly and straightened her sleeves. "Please, come with me."

She took off across the foyer, expecting us to follow. So we did.

"What's going on?" I whispered to Reid out of the side of my mouth. Caterina didn't look back, just kept breezing through doors and hallways. We came to the entrance of a wing I had never actually been in before.

Eleanor's private residence wing.

As we passed through, two older women turned a corner. I recognized them immediately—Rebecca and Pearl Covington. They walked by and gave us small, polite smiles.

I waved, not knowing if they also knew who I was. They didn't appear around town as frequently as Eleanor had, especially with Pearl needing a cane to walk now.

We turned down one more hall until Caterina came to a stop in front of a rather unremarkable wooden door. Everything else in the mansion was ornate, but this was a door like I had at home. Just plain, stained a light oak color to match, but that was it. She took a key out of her pocket and unlocked it, opening it just enough for Reid and I to slip through.

"Enjoy," she said, closing the door after us.

Soft sconces lined the walls, illuminating a few staggered rows of plush, reclining armchairs, and a large, floor to ceiling, wall to wall screen.

"A movie room?" Reid questioned, walking forward through the chairs. There were five in each row, three rows in total. We sat in the middle of the middle row, dead center.

As soon as we did, the lights dimmed, and the projector behind us came to life.

With Eleanor's face filling the screen.

I gasped, one hand flying to my face. Reid grabbed my other hand and slipped an arm around my shoulder, pulling me in close. The arm rests were up, so we could snuggle in tight together.

"Marlowe. My sweet, sunshiney Marlowe. You've finished the hunt I left for you. I'm so proud of you for figuring everything out. I knew you could do it. I hope this time has brought you more smiles than frustrations, even though I know the clues had to be hard. But with your tenacity, your determination, I expected nothing but the best from you, sweet girl."

"See? I remember saying the same thing," Reid whispered into my ear. I shushed him, wanting to hear every word Eleanor said.

"There's one last thing before you can claim your prize,"

she said, her eyes soft, as if she were looking directly at me instead of a video camera. "Every clue was put in a specific place for a specific reason. Your last task was to figure out the connection between all the places. Have you done that?"

I shook my head. Never in a million years did I think having to tell Eleanor the connection literally meant *tell Eleanor*. Directly to her face. On a floor to ceiling screen. "I didn't. Not yet. I was hoping for some inspiration from being here."

"I hope you thought long and hard about the connection. There's a special reason I chose each of them."

The video paused. I whirled around toward the projector, but found no one. But someone had to be watching, hearing what I said in order to pause the video. Was it Caterina? Someone else? Was it whoever had been in charge of putting the clues in their locations?

Sitting back in the chair, I exhaled a deep breath and closed my eyes.

I thought about Eleanor. The mansion. The connection between her and the playroom. The lifeguard chair. The candy store. Reid.

Eleanor. Reid. Lifeguards—Livvy. Candy store—talking to Mrs. Ruth.

Eleanor. Reid. Livvy. Mrs. Ruth.

My mind flashed to the picture frames Grandmum put in my room.

Grandmum. Eleanor. Reid. Livvy. Mrs. Ruth.

The pictures were all of people who loved me. My friends. Mrs. Ruth. Grandmum. Reid.

I had spent so much of my life convinced that I was unlovable. Knowing that when people said they loved me, they ended up leaving. All my life, I thought I wasn't good enough to be loved because of what my parents did when I was little. Because of Grace ditching me for Sean. Because of Reid breaking my heart, even though he had told me he loved me.

Time and time again, life showed me that as much as people liked me, I was unable to be *loved*. I kept that close to heart, latching on to anyone who showed me the slightest bit of attention, hoping it would lead to a different outcome. It rarely did.

Except for recently. For Grace. For Reid. They came back. They still loved me.

Grace. Eleanor. Reid. Mrs. Ruth. Grandmum. Livvy and my friends.

There was a connection between all of those, but there was a bigger connection between all of Eleanor's clues.

The clues led to people who loved me *regardless* of anything else.

Mrs. Ruth, who always looked forward to our chats, who kept me in line, reminding me to bring her food. Who always left a key outside so I could let myself into her house, to vent, to whine, to cry, to get advice. She was like a second grandmother and she treated me like I was family to her, too.

Eleanor... of course there was Eleanor. The playroom that she only let me use. The special bond we shared within the walls of this mansion. They way she felt like a grandmother of sorts to me as well, having known me since I was a baby.

Livvy. Emma. Norah. Liam. Caleb. All of them always being there for me, having my back when things went wrong. Lifting me up when I needed it. Staying by my side when Reid left last summer. Even Caleb saying he would punch Reid in the face for me if he broke my heart again, in a show of love for me.

And Reid. The boy who said he loved me and never stopped, even after he got scared. Who went to bat for me when I needed him to, but supported me when he knew I could do it. There was a difference between Reid saying he loved me, then leaving, and my parents doing the same.

They cut me out of their lives like I didn't matter.

Reid had never stopped thinking about me. Never stopped loving me, just like I had never stopped loving him. Even when he didn't have to, he still stood up for me, protected me, stayed with me.

And even though Grandmum hadn't been a clue, I knew she had to be a part of this. Her standoffish nature wasn't a direct hit against me; it was her personality trait, not a measure of love. She wouldn't have taken me in and raised me after my parents left if she didn't love me. She wouldn't have decorated my room if she didn't love and miss me.

Plus, there had to be a way she got that Rebecca Covington painting.

"It's people who love me," I whispered, my voice hoarse with emotion. I cleared my throat, trying again. I had no idea who I was speaking to, so I looked directly at Eleanor's smiling face and said, "It's people who love me. That's the connection."

Reid squeezed my shoulders and placed a kiss on my temple, but stayed silent.

The video started.

"You are *loved,* Marlowe Mitchell. You've been dealt some harsh cards in your short life, but the best advice I can give is to leave those behind. Deal a new deck. Focus on what cards are still in your hands versus those you put down. Find the ones that love you and hold on to them tightly."

I gripped Reid's hand tightly, just like Eleanor said, with tears in my eyes threatening to spill over any second. It was like when I watched her original video—I couldn't get through without crying. Except this time, it wasn't only because I loved and missed her.

It was because she reminded me of all the good in my life. I spent too long focusing on those that left and not the ones who were still here, giving me their unconditional love.

"That is your prize, Marlowe," Eleanor continued. "Knowing you are loved and having those that love you surround you every single day. I have loved you since the moment you were born. You always brought sunshine into my life, every time we crossed paths. My life was better for having you in it, and I thank you for that. Goodbye my sweet sunshine Marlowe."

The screen went dark, Eleanor's face disappearing.

"No," I cried. I wanted her to come back. I wanted to watch it again. To replay it over and over, searing it into my soul.

We sat in silence for a few more minutes as I digested everything Eleanor had said. Then Reid stood, extending his hand down to help me up. We headed to the door.

"You figured it out, my love. Everything Eleanor wanted you to learn with this scavenger hunt. And what a prize to receive."

I looked over my shoulder and smiled at him, warmth spreading through my body.

As we got to the door, I went to reach for the handle, but Reid stopped me.

"Marlowe," he said in a hushed tone. He pointed to a table a few feet away, one I hadn't noticed when we came in.

On the table was another envelope with my name on it. It was bigger and wider than the ones that held clues, but it definitely said Marlowe Mitchell on the front.

I opened it and took out the contents. A second later, my head became woozy, and I felt like I was going to faint.

Reid wrapped an arm around my waist, supporting me. "What's wrong? Are you okay? Do you need to sit?"

I nodded, but didn't make any motion to move. I just showed him what was in the envelope.

A check.

Made out to me.

For ten thousand dollars.

In the notes section, it said, "The prize isn't always the prize."

"That's what the original text to me said. The prize isn't always the prize."

"But this is a dang good prize," Reid added.

I nodded. "It is. But opening my eyes to know those who love me are all around is one heck of a good prize, too."

Hearts Reclaimed

A WEEK AFTER I almost passed out in Eleanor's private residence wing, I was back on my bike, the wind in my hair.

This time, my belt bag was safely secure around my chest and I vowed not to look at my phone. The last thing I needed was another crash.

I had my swimsuit on under my tank and jean shorts. When I got to Reid's I bypassed the front door and went to the side gate, letting myself in and finding Reid by the pool.

We didn't get in right away, instead opting to hang out on the lounge chairs.

"What's up with you, my love? You've been quiet lately. Still processing the check?" Reid asked after we had been sitting for a bit.

That wasn't it. On the way back from the mansion, we swung by the bank and asked to see a manager. I already had an account, but we figured with such a large deposit, privacy was best.

The manager didn't even blink when I handed him the check. It was almost like he expected it, which didn't make sense, but we didn't question it. He got it all set up, and we were on our way shortly after.

The conversation with Grandmum took way longer than the bank had. She wasn't angry, which I had feared. When I offered her a lump sum, for taking care of me and all, she almost got offended. She told me to keep my money and do something with my life, something better than my parents had done. To which she had then added the date they were coming—the last week before school started.

The same week Reid would be going home.

"No... actually I had a random thought earlier and haven't been able to get it out of my mind."

"What's that?" Reid asked, rolling onto his side, and propping his head up on his hand.

"I was thinking about this summer, about how crazy everything's been, and one thing keeps popping up. I know neither of us wants to talk about it, but... Declan."

Reid's face immediately hardened. His onyx eyes stormed over.

"What do you know about him?" I asked quickly. I needed the answer, but also wanted to get out of this conversation quickly.

He sighed and flopped back onto his back, lacing his fingers together and placing them behind his head.

"I know you said it didn't matter but—"

"Last summer, on my last day here, I was on the beach behind the house, just hanging out with Noodle. There was a boat out on the water, some Baysiders messing around.

They were jumping off the boat, doing all sorts of stupid stuff. Then, someone pushed another person off. There was a scream, but then the boat took off."

I held my breath, unable to even blink as he spoke.

"The only people I got a good look at were Declan and Smitty. The next day, word got out that Gabrielle had a broken leg. And they just left her there in the water."

"Left her? And she—"

Reid shook his head. "No, another boat grabbed her a minute later. But I knew it was Declan. When I saw him, here in the kitchen the day I came back, with you... well, I had to know what happened to him."

That explained the text. And the phone call I thought had been his parents.

"When I found out he got away with it, that no one suspected him, I knew I had him. So when he messed with you, I used it as leverage. He knows I know because I shot him a text a few days before. A picture of him on the boat and Gabrielle in the water, right after he pushed her."

My jaw dropped. Reid *blackmailed* Declan?

"But don't you think turning him in would be the right thing? He shouldn't have gotten away with it."

"His parents paid Gabrielle's medical bills. But they kept it all hushed up to protect Declan. If word got out, though..."

"Declan's rep would be trashed. The whole family would be," I concluded for him. "Wow. That is not at all what I thought you'd say."

"I'm not the only person who knows Declan isn't who he pretends to be, but—" His phone went off, interrupting him. It dinged a few times in a row, like someone sent out a few texts one after another. He picked it up off the table and looked.

"We have to go," he said quickly. "Let's finish this conversation when we get back."

"Back from where?" I asked, but he just grabbed my hand and dragged me through the house and to the garage. We hopped into his car, but he didn't speak as we pulled out and headed toward town.

We ended up at Gennie's, which made everything even weirder.

"What is going on?" I questioned as we climbed the wooden steps up to the front patio and doors inside.

"Surprise!" The word echoed off the ceiling as we crossed through the doorway, the noise startling me. I stumbled back, but Reid's hand was on my waist, keeping me in place.

Except he also stumbled a foot, like he was also surprised.

"What in the *world*?" Reid said as our eyes adjusted to the sight in front of us.

We glanced around and I immediately saw the handmade sign over the table. "Happy staying here, Reid?" I turned the exclamation point into a question. Turning to Reid, I put my hands on my hips and stared. "What does this mean?"

His shocked face gave me no answers. His lips flapped open and closed like a fish out of water, but no words came out.

Emma skipped over first, hugging Reid, then me. "I heard the news this morning. So I decided, why wait until the end of the summer to do this? Makes more sense to do it now, right?"

My jaw dropped. "Excuse me?"

Then, finally, Reid turned toward me, his cheeks

beginning to turn a bit pink. He raised a hand and pulled on his ear while he said, "My parents told me last night. I was going to tell you today, I promise. Literally while we were at the pool. But then I got this text from Caleb that said 911, and I figured we had to run over and see what was wrong."

I blinked once. Twice. Three times. Nothing he said was still adding up.

"Told you what?"

"After my parents told me, Caleb came over to hang. He, um, must have spread the word before I could tell him not to." Reid shuffled his feet, not looking at me.

"Told you *what*, Reid?" I demanded again. My fingers clasped around my necklace, holding on to it like it would give me the answers I needed. "Talk to me like I'm dumb, please. Spell it out."

Reid and Emma laughed. He pulled me in against his chest and hugged me. "First of all, you're not dumb. Your brain just isn't processing yet." With that, he held me out at arm's length so he could stare me in the eyes. "I'm not leaving, Mars."

"You're not leaving," I echoed, still in shock. "Not leaving where?"

I couldn't get my hopes up. I didn't want to believe what my heart was saying. I needed to hear it straight from him.

"I'm moving to Covington Cove full time. Starting right now. Mom, Dad, and I all talked yesterday afternoon. It's something they have been thinking about for a while, but didn't want to do unless I was on board. Since they're away on business a lot anyway, shifting locations for them wouldn't be that hard. They said I might as well be with the friends I have here..."

"Be with..."

He dipped his chin and planted a soft kiss on my lips, like that would solve everything. It did, but I still wanted to hear him say it. "You, Marlowe. Be with *you*. Like I told you before, where you are, I am. There is no me on this island without you. We don't have to worry about summer ending. Because I'm not leaving. I'm not leaving you, I'm not leaving them," he gestured to the group staring and smiling at us, "and I'm not leaving the Cove. Be prepared to be sick of me, my love, because I'm staying. For good."

AFTER THE PARTY finally died down and we were all sitting around the table, I fessed up. It was time to tell everyone about the scavenger hunt Eleanor sent me on.

"I have something to tell you. A secret I've been keeping. Well, we've been keeping," I said, nodding toward Reid.

His eyes widened and his brows lifted, but he stayed quiet.

"This has to do with the whole Declan thing at the cafe, doesn't it?" Emma asked, leaning forward with her elbows on the table. "Man, I've been wondering what that was all about, but just chalked it up to Declan being a stupid obnoxious Baysider who thinks he can get whatever he wants, whenever he wants it."

I shook my head, curls flying everywhere. "No. Well, yes. Yes, but no. Will you just listen?"

She sat back and mimed zipping her lips shut.

"Emma knows how devastated I was to hear that Eleanor Covington died. You all know that I was kind of close to her, especially any time I went to the mansion." They all nodded. Even if they didn't know our relationship exactly, they understood. "Well, shortly after she died, I got a text. Then a video message. From Eleanor."

"From beyond the grave?" Caleb asked, his face in shock. Liam swatted the back of his head.

"No, not from beyond the grave. It was pre-recorded, you doofus. Anyway," I continued, "it all led to a series of clues. Sending me to locations around the island I had to figure out to get the next clue. A scavenger hunt, of sorts. Reid helped me, and in the end, Reid became a clue himself."

The looks of confusion made me dive a little deeper into the story. I told them all about the first clue, about Livvy's guard chair, and all the way to the mansion, when I had to make the connection.

Norah wiped a tear away after I mentioned the last video. "That's amazing, Marlowe. I'm so glad she did that for you."

I grinned. "Yeah. And finding out the people who love me was great. But so was the check with my name on it." I leaned in close and whispered, "For ten grand."

Before anyone could yelp or scream or shout, I put my finger to my lips. "No talking! I want that part to be a secret, okay?"

"I'll say I really, truly didn't hear the last part, but I did overhear the first," a voice from behind me said.

I whirled around. Reid jumped to his feet and reached out for me. But I brushed him away when I saw Sandra Connor, a reporter for the Cove Times.

Everyone knew Sandra. She grew up on the island, went to college for journalism, and returned to work for the Times when it was about to shut down. She ran it almost as a one woman show, and her reports were fair and entertaining. It wasn't a massive newspaper, but she said she loved the island too much to leave, so she combined her two passions.

Almost every business kept an ad in her paper and most year-round residents bought subscriptions to keep it afloat. That was how small island life worked.

"Overheard what?" I questioned, not wanting to give anything away.

"The scavenger hunt. With your permission, I would love to do a story on it. People would go crazy over it, especially because the will is still being held back. The town wants to know why, and this might help the curiosity."

I had no idea if the hunt had anything to do with the will, so I shrugged. "I get final say on what's released?"

Sandra smiled sweetly. "Of course. You know I don't print anything the interviewee doesn't want printed. I'm not a monster."

"Then I'm in."

A New Tide

**Local girl sent on scavenger hunt
by the late Eleanor Covington.**

The shock on Marlowe Mitchell's, 17, face when she opened a text from an unknown number earlier this summer would be the same as anyone's. Especially if that text had a video attachment from the late Eleanor Covington. Little did Marlowe know, it was the start of a scavenger hunt of sorts that would eventually lead her all around the island.

Marlowe quickly learned...

WORD SPREAD ALL across the island fast after Sandra's article came out five days later. She and I sat down for a formal interview the day after Reid's staying here party, and she sent me the final file to review before she published it.

It had barely been out a full twenty-four hours, but I had turned into a town celebrity instantly. Even though no one knew what the prizes were, because I kept those out of the article, it still seemed like everyone was interested for their own reasons.

Seeing my face staring back at me from the paper on the dining table took some getting used to. So did the stares and the questions everyone had that I couldn't, or wouldn't, answer.

I was just about ready to leave to meet Reid and the group at the beach when my phone buzzed. It rang a lot lately, so I kept it on silent to save my sanity. And Grandmum's.

> **UNKNOWN:** A scavenger hunt from Eleanor? Where did your first clue lead?

I stared at the screen. It wasn't an unusual question. I didn't say the locations in the article on purpose. I just said each place had a special meaning and a specific reason behind it. And it was spread out in various locations.

> **UNKNOWN:** Sorry, this seems a bit stalker-ish. I promise, I'm not some crazy person. I just need to know where the first location was.

I frowned. It really wouldn't hurt to tell. No one could go up there on their own anyway, as it was within the mansion. And a closed off location.

I decided to be vague at first. I had no idea who this person was, or why they wanted to know. While I believed the best in people and hoped they had no bad intentions, I couldn't be too sure.

ME: The Covington Mansion.

UNKNOWN: Specifically?

ME: Charlotte's playroom.

Stating the playroom would turn most people off, considering they weren't allowed inside. I didn't mention the dollhouse, though. That part didn't need to be shared, especially with someone who hadn't even told me who they were yet.

UNKNOWN: Well, that's interesting…

ME: Why? Who is this, by the way? Why do you need to know where the clue was?

UNKNOWN: Because that's not where mine was.

Want more Reid and Marlowe?
Grab a bonus scene now!
https://www.authordaniellekeil.com/bonusscenes

Did you love *Reclaimed Hearts*?
I'd love to hear!
Drop a review for me on Amazon and GoodReads
to let me know your thoughts!

ALSO BY DANIELLE KEIL

Looking for another story with forced proximity? Check out *Protect Me Not*, an enemies to lovers romance with a fairytale retelling twist.

At Fairview-Teller High, light mixes with dark. Good with evil. And heroes with villains. But there's a reason the students call it Fairy Tale High. They'll get their happily ever after, even if they have to fight for it.

Popular girl Jessa is caught off guard when the school bad boy—the guy she hates—moves into her house temporarily.

Not knowing how her friends, or the rest of the school, will react, she keeps her new housemate a secret.

Though Jessa loathes Adam for humiliating her at school last year, the more they're around each other, the more her hatred starts to wane.

And when Adam kisses her?
She doesn't hate it—or him.
But it does ruin *everything*.

Read *Protect Me Not* on
Amazon and KindleUnlimited today!

ACKNOWLEDGEMENTS

EEPS!!

Writing a new book is always scary. Writing a new book in a brand new series is even scarier. Writing a new book in a new series after taking a break from writing due to burnout is downright terrifying.

I hope you liked Reclaimed Hearts! Covington Cove has become like a second home to me already. I would move there in a heartbeat! The rest of the series is going to take you on some more twists and turns thanks to Eleanor and her scavenger hunts!

Without the following people, none of this new world would exist, and for that, I thank:

Shain and Andrea for always being there for me, no matter what. Even on my bad days. My annoying days. My obnoxious, ridiculous, silly days. And every day in between.

My EVAN group—without you guys, this world *literally* wouldn't exist. Thanks for helping me throw spaghetti until something stuck. Thanks for our chats. Thanks for reminding me its okay if I'm not completely sane, because we're all in this together.

Stephanie for *literally* bringing this world to life with the most amazing covers (yes, coverS...just wait). For not wanting to throw me over the cliff when I tell you I wanted a map, a family tree, illustrations, and more. For always indulging in every ridiculous task I throw at you and yet still tell me I'm not the most annoying creature on the planet.

Amanda D and Megan— you've stuck with me this far, I'm never letting you go now. Thank you for always allowing me to throw the most random questions at you. For beta reading RH and giving me all the feedback necessary to make this the best book possible.

Amanda and Robynne, for also beta reading RH and giving the best possible feedback. I'm so thankful for you taking on such a rough draft and helping me turn it into something better!

And to everyone who helped promote, shared, spread the word, read the ARC's, left early reviews, and all the things that allow me to continue doing this job—THANK. YOU. You and every single reader are the only reason I can continue writing and I am deeply grateful for that. You have my eternal appreciation.

ABOUT THE AUTHOR

DANIELLE KEIL grew up in the Chicagoland area. A recent transplant, she is enjoying the Mississippi life, especially the pool in her backyard.

Danielle has been happily married for over 10 years, and has two young children, a daughter and a son, who are exact replicas of her and her husband.

Danielle's love language is gifts, her Ennegram is 9w1, and she loves everything purple.

The way to her heart is through coffee, chocolate, and tacos (extra guac).

Want to hang out?

Find her on Facebook, Instagram, and TikTok!
Or join the Dandelion family on Facebook!
www.facebook.com/groups/daniellesdandelions

Learn more at:
www.authordaniellekeil.com

www.ingramcontent.com/pod-product-compliance
Lightning Source LLC
Chambersburg PA
CBHW051131130726
47988CB00005B/1798